Other books by Gemma Halliday:

The High Heels Series:
SPYING IN HIGH HEELS
KILLER IN HIGH HEELS
UNDERCOVER IN HIGH HEELS
ALIBI IN HIGH HEELS
MAYHEM IN HIGH HEELS

GEMMA HALLIDAY

Scandal Sheet

Making it.

NEW YORK CITY

MAKING IT®

November 2009

Published by

Dorchester Publishing Co., Inc.
200 Madison Avenue
New York, NY 10016

ISBN 10: 0-505-52805-3
ISBN 13: 978-0-505-52805-6
E-ISBN: 978-1-4285-0767-8

The name "Making It" and its logo are trademarks of Dorchester Publishing Co., Inc.

Printed in the United States of America.

10 9 8 7 6 5 4 3 2 1

Visit us online at www.dorchesterpub.com.

*For Ruthanne, Grampa, and all
of my amazingly supportive family.
(Though I'd like to note that all Aunt Sues in this work
are purely fictional and bear no resemblance to any other
Aunt Sues I may know.)*

ACKNOWLEDGMENTS

I want to send a huge thank you out to my fabulous critique partner, Eden Bradley, who tirelessly reads every single thing I ever write, and never forgets to put encouraging smilies at all the funny parts.

Thanks to the Crit Wits for their continued support and inspiration. If I ever had a thought of giving up, I'm sure they'd beat it out of me.

I want to thank the Romance Divas for giving me a place to celebrate every victory, whine about every bad day, and gossip about everything in between.

And last but never least, a huge thank you to my extraordinarily talented editor, Leah Hultenschmidt, without whom this book would not be. She's a good friend, a great editor, and a kindred spirit who understands the inescapable draw of TMZ (to which I am now completely addicted).

Scandal Sheet

Chapter One

TEEN SENSATION ON MORAL VACATION

LAST NIGHT THE *INFORMER* CAUGHT EVERYONE'S FAVORITE TEEN ACTRESS, JENNIFER WOOD, AT THE HOLLYWOOD MARTINI ROOM WITH A MEMBER OF A BOY BAND IN ONE HAND AND MARY JANE IN THE OTHER—

"Shit!"

"Tina!"

I swiveled in my chair to face my boss, Felix Dunn, standing in the doorway to his office, hands on hips.

"What?"

"Swear Pig."

I pursed my lips. "That doesn't count."

"I just heard you say 'shit.'"

"It was computer related. Everyone knows computer-related swearing doesn't count."

He narrowed his eyes. Clearly my argument wasn't cutting it.

"It's your own fault, you know," I protested, changing tactics. I'd been typing up a juicy tidbit about *the* It teen actress, who'd been caught with a joint in her hand at last night's after-party, when my backspace button stuck, taking out one very cleverly worded line, even if

I did say so myself. "I mean, how many centuries old are these things anyway?" I went on. "Would it kill you to buy some new hardware once in a while?"

He shook his head. "Swear Pig, Bender," he repeated, then disappeared back into his office.

"Shit."

"I heard that!"

I stuck my tongue out at his door and dropped two quarters into the purple piggy bank on my desk. Somehow our newly appointed editor in chief was under the impression that yours truly swore too much. I have no fucking idea where he got that impression. But he'd set up the Swear Pig as a way to break my bad habit. Personally, I was fine with my bad habit. It's not like I was shooting heroin or anything.

Which brought me back to my story.

I swiveled around, pushing my glasses back up onto my nose, and put my fingers to the keyboard, re-creating my perfect line.

IT MAY BE ONE JOINT TODAY FOR OUR FAVORITE FAIR-HAIRED TEENYBOPPER, BUT WITH THE WAY HER LIFE IS SPIRALING OUT OF CONTROL, CAN COCAINE, METH, OR EVEN HEROIN BE FAR BEHIND? HOW MANY BLONDES DOES IT TAKE TO SPELL "REHAB?"

I sat back in my chair, surveying my work. Okay, so it was a little mean. And the truth was Wood claimed someone had thrust the "stinky cigarette" into her hand just before the paparazzi flashbulbs went off, after which she'd promptly thrown it out. But, seriously, she played a perky cheerleader in a tween cable show. This was tabloid gold.

I hit "send," letting my daily gossip column zip through the *L.A. Informer*'s network to Felix's inbox, then gave my knuckles a satisfying crack.

I glanced at the clock. Quitting time. And somewhere there was a big beefy burrito dinner with my name on it. I grabbed my Strawberry Shortcake lunchbox that doubled as my purse and made for the exit.

Unfortunately, not before Eagle Eyes Dunn could catch me.

"Bender?"

I thought a dirty word and turned around to find him leaning against his office doorframe. "Did you want something, chief?"

"You finish up that Wood piece yet?" he asked.

"Just emailed it to you." I loved it when I was one step ahead of the boss.

"What about Pines?"

"Pines?"

Edward Pines was the director who'd recently been arrested when police found a stack of pornography under the seat of his car during a routine traffic stop. Not that naked bodies were a novelty in Hollywood, but these particular magazines had included photos of thirteen-year-old boys in the buff. I don't care how much his last action pic grossed, that guy was total Hollywood roadkill now.

"What about him?" I asked.

"Being arraigned today. It's your story, right?"

Damned straight. My headline the morning after Pine's arrest had read: PINES PINES AFTER PINT-

SIZED PRETEENS. What can I say? I have a thing for alliteration.

But as much as I was relishing the story, I wasn't thrilled with the timing.

"He's being arraigned *now*?" My stomach growled. "It's dinnertime."

"The news waits for no one, love. Cam's meeting you at the courthouse," he said, ducking back into his office.

So much for my burrito. "Shit."

"Bender . . ."

"I know, I know." I reached into Strawberry Shortcake, pulled out another quarter, and dropped it into the ceramic pig on my way out.

At this rate, I'd be broke by Christmas.

The Beverly Hills courthouse was located on Burton, just a block south of Santa Monica. An unimpressive building, it had a sixties glass-and-concrete esthetic going on that made me think of a Doris Day movie. Totally outdated, totally utilitarian, totally at odds with the rows of Jags and Beemers in the parking lot.

I slipped my Honda Rebel into a space near the entrance. Yep, that's right, I ride a motorcycle. A bitchin' hot pink motorcycle. With yellow flames. I'll admit, it was no Harley, but for a gal my size, five foot three on a good day, it fit just right. And with L.A. gas prices shooting through the roof, it was the only way I could afford my rent and my regular Swear Pig deposits.

I pulled off my helmet, locked it to the handlebars with a metal chain, and shook out my hair. Luckily when your hair is as stick straight as mine, helmet head isn't much of a problem. I gave it a good fluff and felt the shag cut fall back into place. Currently it was auburn with deep purple highlights. Though I've been through so many shades in my lifetime, I'm not even really sure what my natural color is anymore.

I grabbed Strawberry Shortcake and made my way inside, the cool air-conditioning a sharp contrast to the heat outside. Even in fall, the temp in So. Cal never goes much below seventy, and this week we seemed to be hitting Indian summer in spades. After sending my purse through the conveyor belt and stepping through a pair of metal detectors, I made my way up to the second floor where Pines was scheduled to be arraigned.

A towering blonde in jeans and sneakers, holding a big, black Nikon, leaned against the drinking fountain outside the room.

"Hey, Tina," she said, raising a hand in greeting.

"I see Felix gave you late shift, too, huh?" I said, gesturing to her camera.

She nodded. "Caught me in the middle of the dinner rush at Mr. Chow. And Britney had reservations today, too."

Cameron Dakota was the *Informer*'s only full-time photographer. Most of the time Felix found it cheaper to pay freelancers by the picture, but Cameron had a knack for not only capturing celebs with their pants down (literally, if she was lucky) but also providing clear, quality shots that kept readers coming back time and time again to the *Informer*'s pages. And, oddly enough, she actually seemed to enjoy being stuck on Brit watch. Personally, if I had to follow Hollywood half-wits to Starbucks every day, I'd shoot myself.

Lucky for me, I only had to cover them in court.

"Pines in there yet?" I asked, gesturing to the large oak doors.

Cam shook her head, long blonde hair whipping at her cheeks. "He's up next. Right now he's in the room next door with his lawyers. No cameras allowed in the courtroom, so I'm waiting for a walk-of-shame shot." She gave me a wink.

"Go get 'em, tiger."

I pushed through the doors and slipped into the back of the courtroom.

Contrary to the world of *L.A. Law*, there was nothing glamorous, sexy, or exciting about sitting in L.A. County Court. The rooms were squat, square boxes filled with metal-framed tables, hard wooden chairs, and depressingly beige walls. Think DMV décor. Only worse. Since this was only an arraignment, no jury was present, just a bunch of people sitting in the gallery, family members who'd likely be putting up bail for the various guys in orange jumpsuits being paraded through the room. Currently up was a guy with earrings the size of nickels stuck in his ears, apparently pleading no contest to a drug possession charge.

Yawn.

I shifted in my seat, pulling my digital recorder from my back pocket as they let Mr. Meth out the side, telling a skinny brunette with tattoos that she could post his fifty-thousand dollar bail downstairs.

But I sat up straighter as the side door opened and the next defendant shuffled in.

Edward Pines was in his fifties, though he looked about seventy-five today. Apparently jail did not agree with the man. Dark circles ringed his eyes, his jowly features softer and flabbier than the last photo Cam had snapped for our front page. He walked with his head down, as if already playing contrite despite the absence of jurors. Beside him stood his attorney—tall, pressed suit, pasty complexion. I didn't recognize him, but that wasn't surprising. High-profile pedophiles didn't make legal careers.

"Mr. Pines, you've been charged with possession of child pornography," the judge boomed from his bench. "How do you plead?"

The pasty attorney took his cue. "The defendant pleads not guilty, Your Honor."

I raised an eyebrow. Pines had been caught red-handed by the police. I wondered just how his attorney planned to tap dance out of that.

"Very well. Prosecution on bail?" The judge turned to the pencil-thin district attorney, who, with the exception of his slight height, could have been a carbon copy of the pasty defense attorney. Didn't any of these guys ever see the sun?

"Your Honor, the People request bail be set at ten million dollars."

"Sonofa—" I sucked in a breath and heard a round of gasps ripple through the courtroom at the exorbitant amount.

Pines might have been a public figure and a creep, but it wasn't like he'd killed anyone. Even murder charges rarely topped a million in bail. I leaned forward in my seat. This was about to get juicy—I could feel it.

"Your Honor, that's outrageous," the defense attorney argued. His cheeks actually showed some color now. "My client is an upstanding member of society, highly regarded by his peers. He has deep ties to the community, and, quite frankly, I feel the D.A.'s bail request is ludicrously out of proportion to the crime at hand."

The judge raised his bushy eyebrows. "You think child pornography isn't a big deal, counselor?"

"Of course it is, Your Honor," he quickly backpedaled. "But the D.A.'s request is . . . severe," he finished, this time choosing his words more carefully.

Severe. Good way of putting it. I made a mental note to use that word in my copy.

"Mr. Atwood?" the judge asked, addressing the D.A.

"Your Honor, the defendant has considerable means, dual citizenship in the U.S. and Canada. He is a flight risk. And," he said, shooting Pines a withering look, "considering the defendant is a director with access to all manner of photographic equipment, we feel it is our duty to protect the children of the community by requesting ten million in bail."

"That's insane, Your Honor," defense argued. "My client is being persecuted by the D.A. because of his fame."

"I've heard enough," the judge said, holding up his hands.

The entire courtroom, myself included, went silent, holding our collective breath as the judge chewed the inside of his cheek, his gaze going from one attorney to the other. No doubt wondering just how this would play out in the press.

Finally he seemed to come to some conclusion.

"Mr. Pines, if you think celebrity is an excuse for immoral behavior, you'll be sorely disappointed in my courtroom. Bail is set at ten million dollars."

I let out a low whistle as the judge banged his gavel.

The D.A. gave a triumphant lift of his chin, almost exactly proportionate to the slump in Pines's shoulders as the bailiff accompanied him out of the room.

I slipped my recorder back in my pocket. An interesting development indeed. Whether Pines actually had ten mil in change for bail or not, I had no idea. But a Hollywood director stuck in jail for days? This was almost as good as Paris Watch '08. What do you want to bet he'd be claiming mental anguish in under a week?

I mentally rubbed my hands together with glee as I slipped back out the door to find Cam waiting for me. After all, one pedophile director's mental anguish meant front-page coverage for yours truly.

God, I loved Hollywood.

Chapter Two

After the arraignment, Cam and I hit the Del Taco on Santa Monica. I got my steaming hot burrito, ordering a second to go just in case, and Cam did a taco salad before we parted ways—her to camp out on Sunset for the evening club crowd and me to home.

Which, for me, was South Pasadena, a sleepy little suburb wedged between Glendale and the San Gabriel Valley. Wide streets, palms on every corner, and strip malls with Trader Joe's and Pier One at all the intersections. Pretty typical American every-suburb, except for the fact that Nicole Richie lived just over the freeway.

I pulled my Rebel off the 2, roaring to a stop at the front entrance to the Palm Grove community, and cut the motor. I hopped off the bike, walking it silently through the wrought-iron gates into the complex. The residents didn't exactly appreciate the sound of my twin engines as much as I did. Mostly because they were all eighty. Yep, I lived in a retirement community.

When my great-uncle Sal finally cashed in his chips, Aunt Sue traded in her four-bedroom in Long Beach for a cute little condo in Palm Grove. Lucky for me, that was right about the time the lease had expired on my apartment across town, and I'd needed a place to hang my hat for a few weeks.

That was three years ago.

Turns out Aunt Sue isn't as sharp as she used to be. And having a person who doesn't forget to turn off the oven and knows that socks don't go in the freezer has come in handy. Which suits me fine. You can't beat the fixed-income rent on the place, my neighbors are always quiet, and I have the entire pool to myself as soon as *Jeopardy!* comes on.

I wheeled my bike down Sanctuary Drive to Paradise Lane before turning onto my street, Oasis Terrace. I know, someone was a creative genius when it came to street names in this development. Aunt Sue and I lived in a little two-bedroom number, third on the left. White siding, blue shutters, low-maintenance square lawn. Exactly like the other thirty-two units in the complex, except that ours had a pink flamingo out front.

"That you, Tina?" A woman in a pink housecoat and fuzzy slippers shuffled onto the porch of the house next door, fifty years of a pack-a-day habit grinding her voice into a gravelly baritone.

"'Evening, Mrs. Carmichael," I said, waving.

She put her hands on her bony hips and narrowed a pair of eyes beneath her cap of white curls. Though her eyes were always kind of narrow. Mrs. Carmichael had had one too many face-lifts in her fifties, and her seventies weren't being kind to her. "I can always tell it's you," she said, clacking her dentures. "That motorbike of yours is so noisy."

"It's off," I said. "See?" I paused, putting my ear to the bike. "No sound."

"Hmm." She clicked her upper teeth again. "Well, it's still noisy. Can't hardly hear Pat Sajak over the thing." Mrs. Carmichael was the only person in the complex who didn't wear a hearing aid, a fact that had not only earned her the title of Neighborhood Watch Captain, but also tickled her vanity to no end. Mrs. Carmichael never turned her TV volume up past three.

"Sorry. I'll try to be quieter."

"And tell your aunt to turn down her music," she shouted after me. "It's been blasting all day!"

I waved in agreement as I tucked my bike around the corner of the house and let myself in.

Aunt Sue was waiting for me at the kitchen table, wearing a powder blue polyester track suit. Her snow-white hair was curled into tight ringlets against her scalp, and her watery blue eyes shone behind a pair of thick, wire-rimmed glasses. A plate full of steaming brown stuff sat in front of her.

"Hi, peanut, how was your day?" she asked.

"Fab. Mrs. Carmichael said you should turn down your music." I crossed to an old eighties boom box playing Frank Sinatra. At top volume. Unlike Mrs. Carmichael, Aunt Sue had industrial-strength hearing aids. Which would have worked wonders if she ever wore them.

"Hattie Carmichael is on old fuddy duddy," Aunt Sue protested.

"Amen. What's that?" I gestured to her dinner.

"Meatloaf."

I sniffed. It smelled like meatloaf. But it looked like dog crap. "It looks a little, um, runny."

Aunt Sue glanced down at her plate as if seeing it for the first time. "Well, now, it does a bit, doesn't it?"

"What did you put in it?" I crossed the galley kitchen to make sure the oven was, indeed, off.

She pursed her lips, pronounced wrinkles forming between her thin wisps of eyebrows. "Same things I always do." She paused. "I think. It's hard to remember. Maybe I forgot the bread crumbs." She shrugged.

I pulled my "just in case" burrito out of my bag and set it on a plate for her.

"What's this?" she asked, her eyes shining like I'd placed a Christmas present in front of her.

"Beefy bean and cheese."

"Hot sauce?"

I dropped a couple packets of Del Scorcho on the table next to her.

"You are the best niece I ever had," Aunt Sue said, digging in.

"I'm your only niece." I grabbed her plate of runny meatloaf and gave it a proper burial in the garbage disposal.

"That's beside the point."

"Thanks. You're my favorite, too." I dropped a kiss on the top of her head.

"Mmm," she said, making little yummy sounds. "Why is it that the worse a food is for you, the better it tastes?"

"Burritos aren't that bad," I countered.

"Come on now, all that fast-food stuff is terrible. Full of preservatives and cholesterol. That stuff will kill you. Clogs your arteries, you know. Millie Sanders said her cousin ate that McDonald's stuff every morning, and he dropped dead of a heart attack just last week. He was only seventy-three!"

"Well, then it looks like I've got a few good years of drive-thrus ahead of me before I have to start worrying about it." I gave her a wink.

"Got any more hot sauce?" Aunt Sue asked around a huge bite.

I dropped a couple more packets on the table.

"You eat already?" she asked.

I nodded.

Her shoulders sagged. "Darn. Because I made meatloaf."

I bit my lip. "I know, Aunt Sue."

"Oh." She paused a moment, as if her brain was struggling really hard to make those connections. Finally she shrugged. "Well, maybe I'll make lasagna tomorrow."

I put the pan of meatloaf mush in the sink. "Well, I've been warned."

Aunt Sue gave me a playful swat on the arm as I brushed past, stopping to deposit another quick kiss on her little old forehead, before scooting off to my room.

Once there, I kicked off my shoes, sat cross-legged on my patchwork bedspread, and booted up my laptop, going through my nightly ritual of checking various email accounts, Twitter posts, and celebrity watcher blogs for any hot leads to pad tomorrow's column. Thanks to a carefully cultivated network of informants, I had eyes all over Hollywood.

A couple baby-bump sightings on Melrose, a fender bender in Malibu involving a judge from *American Idol*, and one from a guy who worked at Dunkin' Donuts in Santa Monica who swore a certain bulimic actress was in buying glazed old-fashioneds like they were going out of style.

Envisioning tomorrow's headline, GOLDEN GLOBE WINNER GORGES ON GLAZED GOODIES, I opened a Word doc and started snarking away.

I was halfway through tomorrow's masterpiece when an instant message popped up in the corner of my screen. From ManInBlack72.

A quick jump of adrenaline hit my stomach, and I bit my lip to keep the corner of my mouth from curving into a smile.

Like most of Hollywood, I have my own dirty little secret: an online crush.

When Felix took over as managing editor, he was appalled by the paper's lack of "digital exploitation," as he put it. Personally, I figure a paper should be on paper, but Felix was more of a computer whiz than I, and his first steps were to put everything online—an interactive *Informer* webpage, daily tweets, blogs, and Facebook and MySpace accounts for all the staff.

ManInBlack72 first contacted me through my new MySpace account this past summer. He was a friend of a friend of a friend . . . Well, you know the drill. How does anyone know anyone online, but suddenly you've got five hundred friends, right? And one of them was him. He put a pic of that cartoon robot, Bender, from *Futurama* in my comments section. You know, for Tina *Bender*. Ha, ha. Pretty cheesy. And I told him so. Surprisingly, he had a sense of humor about it and sent me a cartoon with a wedge of Swiss cheese in it the next week. Pretty soon comments turned into private messages, which turned into emails, which turned into giving out our IM handles.

Which turned into me suppressing a smile as I clicked the "accept message" button.

Hey, Bender.

I quickly typed back. *Hey.*

How was your day, babe?

If anyone else had called me "babe," I would have given him a thorough lecture on the history of the feminist movement. But ManInBlack was the only one, aside from Aunt Sue, who ever asked about my day. And considering Aunt Sue didn't remember what I'd told her two seconds later . . . it was nice someone asked.

Good. Got my column in on time.

Look at you being all prompt.

I grinned at the compliment.

Anything juicy to share? he asked.

Sorry, pal, you'll just have to read the papers like everyone else.

You're a cruel woman, Bender.

I know.

Good thing you're so damned cute.

My stomach did a funny little shimmy. Even though I knew he was full of it. I never posted photos of myself online. The fewer people who knew what I looked like, the easier it was to do my job. The only avatar pic I had up on my MySpace page was of me morphed into a Simpson's cartoon character that I'd gotten during the movie promo. Not really an exact likeness.

But, instead of calling him out as a blatant liar, I responded with, *I try.*

Hmm . . . that was where you were supposed to mention how hot I am.

Like a tamale, I joked back. Even though I had no idea what he looked like, either. The only photos on his page were of Johnny Cash, Darth Vadar, and the Will

Smith/Tommy Lee Jones duo. You know, all men in black.

So, how was your day, hot stuff? I asked.

Ahn. But it's getting better.

Rough day at the office?

I had no idea what Black did. He'd joked a few times that he could tell me, but then he'd have to kill me. Not that I minded. It added to the mystique that he had some unmentionable job. In my mind, he was kind of like Batman—too modest to tell me he was a billionaire by day and a superhero by night. So I never pushed the issue. It would have totally killed the fantasy to know he pumped gas for a living.

I've had better, he typed back. *How about you cheer me up?*

Hmm . . . You like knock-knock jokes?

Not exactly what I had in mind . . . but let's hear it, Bender.

Okay . . . Knock, knock.

Who's there?

Boo.

Boo who?

Don't cry, tomorrow will be better.

There was a pause. I wasn't sure if it meant he was laughing or groaning.

Cute.

I let out a breath. Cute was good. I'd take cute.

Thanks.

Hey . . . look outside.

For one irrational moment, my stomach clenched on that burrito as I whipped my head to the window, half expecting Black to be standing outside on the lawn. Instead, as I pulled the gauzy white curtains back, I saw the tail end of the sun's descent onto the horizon. Or, in my case, onto the roof of Hattie Carmichael's Cadillac in the driveway next door. But the glow of bright oranges and reds as the last rays of daylight fought through the thick Indian summer smog was brilliant. Like a surreal oil painting . . . or some kid's Creamsicle smearing across the sky.

Wow, I responded

Beautiful, huh?

Very.

Amazing how something as toxic as our smog layer can create a picture so gorgeous. There was a pause before more words appeared on my screen. *That's how you are.*

Hmmm . . . had he just called me toxic?

Me?

You're the brilliant sunset ending my smog-shitty day with a smile.

I felt a big goofy grin take over my face.

Thanks.

'Night, Bender. Be good.

'Night, Man in Black.

Then the little "online now" icon next to his name disappeared.

I looked at the little blinking cursor, the quiet screen bringing me back to reality.

Sad that the most intimate relationship I had was with a computer screen. I know in reality there was some guy on the other end, but, like I said, he probably pumped gas for a living and lived in his mother's basement.

Man in Black was a fantasy, nothing more. I knew that the image in my head was nothing like the real guy would be. In my mind he was six feet tall, dark hair, even darker eyes. A sort of crooked, imperfect, but oh-so-sexy smile, kind of like Elvis, lifting one side of his lip at a time. Maybe a scar. Something he'd gotten at his very dangerous and mysterious job.

I sighed, clicking shut the screen. Until tomorrow, fantasy man . . .

Instead, I turned on the TV, threw in an old *Seinfeld* DVD, and let the canned laughter fill the silence as I finished my column.

The next morning I woke up late, shoved myself into a pair of purple jeans, black Converse, and a black T-shirt with pink lettering that read, "If You Can Read This, You're Too Close." Then I hopped on my bike and pulled up to the *L.A. Informer*'s offices *almost* on time. The *Informer* was situated on Hollywood Boulevard, just bordering the trendy tourist part of town and the part where you don't walk alone at night without body armor. The building was a square, stuccoed, three-story thing that was at one time white, but now lay something closer to dingy beige. Built around the same time as the famed Hollywoodland sign, it might have been charming once, but that had been many years and many uncaring landlords ago. Sun-faded awning over the door, peeling paint near the windows, a rusty metal fire escape clinging to the side of the building as if its life depended on it. Trump Towers it was not.

I pushed through the doors and rode the elevator to the second floor, dropping Strawberry Shortcake on my desk with a clang.

"That you, Bender?" A head popped up from the neighboring cubicle. Balding, gray stubble along the chin, droopy, bloodshot eyes—Max Beacon, the oldest, most experienced, and generally the most hung-over member of the *Informer*'s staff. He covered obits and had his own, detailing how he'd died of liver failure, pre-written and tacked to the fabric-covered wall of his cubicle, right next to a poster of a bulldog saying, "This *is* my happy face."

"Hey, Max. What's new?"

"Remember that guy who played Bette Davis's son in that film about the traveling theater group?"

"Uh huh." I nodded. Even though I had no clue what movie he was talking about.

"Died today. Sixty-four. Heart failure."

"Bummer."

"Very. Hey, did you see the new applicant on your way in?"

I pushed my chair back, glancing toward Felix's glass-walled office in the far corner. Until this summer—when he'd moved up in the world to take over as editor—Felix had been the *Informer*'s star reporter. Ever since he'd become the boss man, Felix had been interviewing applicants to fill in his former position. So far none had passed his test.

I squinted at the latest victim sitting across the desk from him. Blonde, miniskirt, jugs out to here.

I did a low whistle. "She applying to be a reporter or go-go dancer?"

Max chuckled. "She's been in there for over an hour."

"Really?" I raised an eyebrow. "Well, I'm sure Felix wants to *thoroughly* go over all her professional *assets*."

Max chuckled. "Maybe he's checking her *experience*."

"Or he's outlining the *benefits* of working here."

Max snorted. Then tilted his head to the side, eyes clearly trying to get inside Ms. Jugs stretchy little top. "Tough being the boss, huh?"

"That's why they pay him the big bucks."

"How come you never wear little skirts like that, Bender?"

I shot him a look. "All right, enough ogling, old man. Back to work. Those people aren't getting any deader."

Max gave a watery-eyed last look at our new applicant, then disappeared back behind the partition.

I flipped on my monitor and, while I waited for my system to boot up, checked my voice mail for any salacious overnight news. Lucky me, I had two messages.

I keyed my pin into the *Informer*'s ancient message retrieval system and heard a male voice in answer.

"Hey, girl, I was at Basque last night and, baby, do I have a good story for you."

I grinned. One of my informants. A former sitcom star from the nineties who still held on to enough fame to get into all the right places, but whose bank account had nosedived right along with his ratings. He needed cash, I needed insider info—the relationship was a win-win.

I grabbed a pen and listened as the message continued.

"Guess whose dealer was there, talking about how he'd delivered a certain package to someone in rehab last night? . . . Blain Hall."

"No way!" I blurted. I did a little happy dance in my seat. Blain Hall was the front man for Dirty Dogs, an angsty rock band that had recently swept the Grammys. Unfortunately, it turned out Blain's raspy vocals and unending stage energy were due less to natural talent and more to cocaine. A totally eighties drug. A fact I'd pointed out in my column, citing that his choice of vice was almost as passé as his ballads of teen malaise.

Yeah, I probably wasn't going to be on Blain's Christmas card list this year.

I made a note to call back for all the gory details and erased the message, moving on to the next one.

At first, heavy breathing was the only sound to come through. I was about to discount it as a wrong number and delete, when the caller finally spoke up.

His voice was distorted and mixed with some sort of electronic equipment. It almost sounded like he was far away or talking in an echoing tunnel. Mechanical, deep, and eerily inhuman.

"I've had enough," the odd voice began. "Enough of your malicious lies. You delight in ruining people. Well, I've had it with your kind. Stop printing stories about me. If you don't . . ." The voice paused, heavy breaths puffing through the other end before he finished his threat. ". . . Tina Bender, you're dead."

Chapter Three

I froze, my hand clutching the receiver as the voice mail system beeped and asked me if I wanted to delete, save, or listen to the current message again. On instinct, I replayed it, straining for any sign of the caller's identity. Was it a friend punking me? Some irritated starlet out drinking with her friends? A couple of kids crank calling the local paper?

No clue. The voice was so distorted I couldn't even be sure it was male. It was deep, but that could easily have been manipulated by whatever machine he/she had used to make it sound like I was getting a threat from Stephen Hawking.

While the *Informer* had an entire file of nasty reader letters to the editor, some that even bordered on terrorist manifestoes, this was the first time I had personally received anything this weird. Granted, every now and then I got an irate call from someone's publicist, but generally Hollywood operated on the theory that there was no such thing as bad publicity. Celebs usually started worrying when they *stopped* showing up in our paper.

As soon as the message ended, I hit the save button and crossed the newsroom to Felix's office. I knocked softly on the door before pushing it open.

Felix looked up from the blonde, his gaze slowly shifting from her "girls" to me.

"Tina?" he asked.

"Sorry to interrupt," I started. Then took my first real look at the new interviewee. She was just as much the sorority girl up close as she was from across the room. Big blue eyes, gooey pink lip gloss, mouth in a permanent sexy pout. And a shirt that was at least a size too small. She looked like she was smuggling cantaloupes under her top.

And, I noticed as I gave her the up and down, she did the same thing back to me.

"Did you need something, Tina?" Felix asked.

"Uh, I need to speak with you."

"About?"

"Something's come up."

"What kind of something?" Felix prompted.

"A phone call," I hedged, not sure how much I wanted to say in front of Barbie.

"From?"

"I'm not sure."

"What did they say?"

I glanced at the blonde again. "Um . . . any chance we could discuss this in private?"

Felix shook his head. "Sorry, where are my manners? Allie, this is Tina Bender, our gossip columnist. Tina, Allie Quick. Our newest reporter."

I raised an eyebrow his way. Seriously? He'd hired the pair of tits?

"Nice to meet you," Allie said, extending a hand.

Reluctantly, I shook it. Her grip was firm, though my hand came away smelling like some sort of peachy lotion.

"Allie will be taking over as field reporter," Felix went on. "Covering my old beat."

"Fabulous." I swear I really tried to keep the sarcasm out of my voice. I gave Barbie a week before she realized this job involved actual work, not just cozying up to Christian Bale.

"What was this call you got?" Felix asked.

Obviously I was going to do this with an audience whether I wanted to or not. So, I told him about the weird caller and the mechanical voice and the threat on my life. Though even as I keyed my pin into the system a second time, replaying the message for the boss, I realize how silly the whole thing was. We were a tabloid. It would have been surprising if people *didn't* hate us. Ninety-nine percent chance it was just some idiot blowing off steam.

Unfortunately, Felix didn't bet odds.

"I don't like this," he said, replaying the message a second time. "When did this come in?"

"Last night. The time stamp says eleven thirty."

"Were you here last night?"

"No. At home."

"Alone?"

"My aunt was in the other room."

"Any idea what story this guy is referring to?"

I threw my hands up in the air. "Are you kidding? I've reamed dozens of celebs this week alone."

"Any of the articles nasty?"

I shot him a look.

"Right," he said. "Stupid question. You check the caller ID?"

"Restricted number."

"Maybe you can trace the call?" Allie piped up.

I nodded. Reluctantly. "Maybe," I hedged. Techno genius I was not. However, considering our editor in chief's pockets were tighter than Joan Rivers's last face-lift, our phone system was hardly state of the art. I made a mental note to look into it.

"In the meantime," Felix continued, "I don't feel good about you being out there alone today."

" 'Out there?' " I asked.

"Let's keep to the desk for now, okay, Bender?"

"Fabulous."

"Was that sarcasm?" he asked.

"Damned straight." And before he could say it, I added, "I know, I know. Swear Pig."

The first thing I did when I left Felix was visit Cece, our accounts receivable/human resources/office manager lady. As her title hinted, anything that didn't directly end up in the newspaper fell under her forty-something, sensible-shoe-wearing, über-organized territory. Her desk was in the corner near the elevator and constantly cluttered with beanie babies.

"Hey, Cece," I said, popping my head around her partition.

"Yes?" she asked, not even looking up from the spreadsheet she was typing.

"I need a favor. Last night, eleven thirty, a call came in. I need to know who made it."

Her forehead furrowed. "Well, I know our program keeps track of all outgoing calls." She paused, then sent me a wan smile as she added, "Felix likes to know who's using up our long-distance minutes."

"Of course."

"But, other than a time stamp, I don't think there's a way to record the incoming calls."

Drat. I chewed the inside of my cheeks, rapping my fingernails on the side of her partition. "What about the phone company? They must have a record, right?"

Cece nodded. "Most likely."

"Who's our provider?"

Cece opened a new window on her screen, then pulled a Post-it from her pink dispenser and wrote down their name and number. "L.A. Bell. But I don't really think they're going to give out that kind of information."

"Wanna bet?" I asked, giving her a wink as I took the Post-it back to my desk.

I immediately dialed the customer service number, going through the automated options until a mere fifteen minutes later I was connected to a real person.

"L.A. Bell, this is Jeff speaking, how may I help you?"

"Hi, Jeff. This is . . . Carol. Carol Brady. Listen, I have a problem."

"Well, I'm sorry to hear that, Miss Brady. What can I do for you?"

"I'm knocked up."

There was a slight pause on the other end. Then, "Oh. I . . . well . . . oh."

"That's right. With child, bun in the oven, in a family way, one condom short of a bikini body."

Again with the awkward pause. "Er, ma'am, I'm not really sure what I can—"

"Jeff, I'm gonna level with you," I said, plowing right over him. "When I saw that positive pregnancy test, I may have said a few things. Things I shouldn't have. Things about my boyfriend not being able to keep it in his pants long enough to roll a condom on. Things that, quite frankly, hurt my boyfriend Mike pretty bad. He left me, Jeff."

"Uh . . . I'm sorry to hear that, but Miss Brady, I don't really—"

"You got a dad, Jeff?"

"What?"

"A father. You have one, Jeff?"

"Um. Yeah."

"I bet he took you to baseball games, didn't he, Jeff?"

"Sure. I guess so."

"And taught you how to ride your bike. How to tie your shoes. I bet he even taught you how to wipe your own tushie, Jeff."

"Uh . . ."

"Here's the thing. My baby won't have that. Poor little Bobby's gonna grow up fatherless unless I can find Mike and apologize. That's where you come in."

"I do?" he squeaked.

"Look, last night Mike calls saying he's leaving L.A. for good. But the caller ID was blocked. I have no idea where he is. If I could find out where he was calling from, I might be able to stop him before he makes a terrible mistake."

He paused so long on the other end I thought maybe he'd hung up.

"Jeff? You still there?"

"I feel for your situation, ma'am, but we can't give out addresses of other clients."

"I don't even need his address. Just . . . can you tell me the name of the person who owns the number?"

"I'm not sure that's in keeping with our policy . . ."

"How about just the number? Can you at least give me that? Please, Jeff. Little Bobby deserves a real family." Even if my story was utter crap, the desperation in my voice was real. This was the best lead—scratch that, only lead—I had on Mystery Caller's identity.

I think maybe it was the "real family" bit that got him, as his voice dropped to just above a whisper, and he said, "When did the call take place?"

I did a mental "squeee!" and said, "Last night. Eleven thirty p.m. to this number."

I heard the sound of a keyboard clacking in the background. "I'm really not supposed to be doing this," Jeff repeated.

"You are doing me such a favor. In fact, I'm thinking Jeffery would make a fine middle name for Bobby, huh?"

"Okay, I've got one call logged, coming in at eleven thirty-two."

"That's it! And the number?"

Jeff took a deep breath, and I could almost feel him looking over both shoulders for hovering supervisors before he rattled off the digits.

"You are the best, Jeff!" I grabbed a pen and paper and wrote the number down. An L.A. area code, I noticed. When he was finished, I promised him that he'd be mentioned at little Bobby's bris and hung up the phone.

Immediately, I dialed the number. It rang on the other end. And again. Fifteen rings into it, I gave up.

Instead, I pulled up a reverse lookup directory on my computer and typed the number in.

Bingo.

The number came back as being owned by PW Enterprises.

I pulled up a Google screen and typed in the name. Not surprising, about a million hits came up, ranging from mortgage brokers to used car dealers. I bit my lip, narrowing the search to L.A. County. What do you know, only half a million hits this time. I mentally cracked my knuckles, going in deep for a serious web-crawling session.

Two hours and several dozen webpages later, I was bug-eyed, brain-dead, and no closer to identifying what PW was, let alone who there might not be my number one fan.

"You get the tip on Blain Hall?"

I looked up to find Cam hovering over my desk.

"The drugs in rehab?" I asked, struggling to focus as my eyes adjusted from squinting at the computer monitor.

She nodded. "Felix is sending me over to snap a few pics of Blain through the rehab windows to run next to your story. Got a headline yet?"

"DIRTY DOG TAKES REHAB AS SERIOUSLY AS CRITICS TAKE HIS SAPPY BALLADS."

Cam laughed, flipping her blonde ponytail over her shoulder and showing off a row of perfectly white teeth. I am about as heterosexual as a gal can get, but even I had to admit, Cam was hot. Volcanic. Rumor was she'd been a model or something in her teens. I had no idea if it was true, but I swear seeing her fresh face and never-seen-a-split-end gorgeous hair on a billboard would sell me on any product.

"Harsh headline, Tina."

"He deserves it."

"Aw, have a heart. You know, I kinda like those sappy ballads."

"Ugh. Seriously? They're like saccharine. And so trite. 'I'll love you 'til the end of time.' How many times have we heard that same line before?"

Cam shrugged. "I dunno. It's still kinda sweet. Besides, his voice . . ." She sighed. "It gives me shivers."

I rolled my eyes.

"You're going soft on me, Cam."

She just smiled. "What's PW Enterprises?" she asked, pointing to my screen.

"The home of some jerk with too much time on his hands."

She raised an eyebrow in my direction.

Quickly I filled her in on my morning and the friendly phone call I'd received last night.

"Wow," she said when I was done. "I had a drunk reality show contestant throw a punch at my camera once, but never anything like this. You must have really pissed someone off."

"Or it's a stupid prank," I was quick to point out.

"Yeah, well, Felix doesn't think it's a prank."

I narrowed my eyes at her. "Why do you say that?"

"He just told me I'm supposed to take the new girl with me to the evidence hearing in the Pines trial this afternoon."

I spun around in my chair. "Seriously? But that's my story!"

Cam shrugged. "Felix said you were off it. I guess now I know why."

I looked across the newsroom. The new girl was sitting at a vacant desk near the window. Where, coincidentally, her double D's were directly in our editor's line of vision. She was staring intently at a computer screen, her little ski jump nose scrunched up.

No doubt trying to figure out how to spell "google."

"Don't worry," Cam said, laying a hand on my shoulder. "I'm sure he's just trying to get her feet wet."

"Yeah, well, I hope she drowns," I responded, jumping up from my chair and stalking toward Felix's office.

Our editor in chief was deep in conversation with some other guy, but I didn't care. I didn't even stop to knock before pushing my way through the glass doors.

"That was my story!" I yelled.

Felix looked up, his brows forming a concerned V over his eyes. "What story?"

"Don't 'what story' me," I said, advancing on him. "Pines. Cam said you gave it to the new chick."

"Allie. Her name is Allie."

"My. Story."

Felix sighed, crossing his arms over his chest. "You received a death threat this morning, Bender. It would be completely irresponsible of me to send you out in the field."

I threw my hands up in the air. "It was a prank call! Probably a couple of teenagers."

"Probably," he said, jumping on the word.

"This is so unfair. This is so fuc—"

"Bender . . ." he warned.

"So *flipping* unfair. That is my godda—*goldarned*

story. I've been *freaking* reporting on that *sonofagoat* Pines since the beginning, and you give it to a hot pair of *cantaloupes* because some little *snotweasel* of a kid pranks me?"

I think I heard the other man chuckle, but I tuned him out, my entire pissed-off being focused on Felix.

"I have a responsibility for your safety, Bender."

"It's a courthouse. I'll be perfectly safe!"

"Yes, you will."

I opened my mouth to argue, when I realized he'd agreed with me. I shut it with a click.

"Right. Thank you."

"You'll be perfectly safe because I've hired you a bodyguard."

I blinked. Feeling my face go hot until I'd swear there was cartoon steam pouring out my ears. "A what?"

"Tina, meet Calvin Dean." He gestured to the other guy.

I turned, giving the man my full attention now. He was tall, almost a head taller than Felix. Broad in the shoulders, slim in the waist. I could tell by the way his T-shirt fit over his biceps that he spent a fair amount of time at the gym. His hair was dark, just curling over his ears, and he had a neatly trimmed goatee that gave him a slightly devilish look. And I could swear his dark eyes were laughing at me.

Which did nothing to lighten my mood.

"You got me a rent-a-goon?" I asked, turning back to Felix.

"Play nice, Bender," Felix warned. "Think of him like your insurance plan."

"Hi." The bodyguard stuck his hand out.

I looked at it.

"Nice to meet you, Tina."

I stuck my hands on my hips. And turned back to Felix.

"I don't need a bodyguard. It was one phone call. I can take care of myself."

"It was a death threat. Made from a blocked number by someone who disguised their voice. These were not some drunk kids. Whoever did this thought it through, took their time, and made sure not to get caught."

I bit my lip. While I was pretty sure this was still just a prank, Felix had a point. And the fact that someone had put so much thought into trying to scare me took the wind out of my sails a bit.

"Look, Tina," Felix said, advancing on me, "yes, it's possible this is just some idle threat. But it's possible it's not, and I, for one, can't take that chance. I don't know if you know this, but I once worked a story where an actress was receiving threatening letters. She ignored them. Two dead bodies followed. I know this may seem a little overprotective to you, but I can't take the chance of that happening to you."

I felt my irritation subsiding a little, the genuine worry in his voice touching me. "I appreciate your concern," I said, meaning it.

He shrugged. "Of course I'm concerned. Half our advertising comes in because of your column."

And just like that the irritation was back. "Gee, love you, too," I said, sarcasm dripping from my voice.

Felix elected to ignore me. "So," he continued, "you have two choices. Desk duty or . . ." He trailed off, gesturing to the rent-a-goon.

I took a deep breath, thinking about three dollars worth of nasty words.

"Fine," I finally spat out. "But I get Pines back."

Felix bit the inside of his cheek, contemplating the negotiations for a moment. "You can share."

"With Barbie?"

"Allie."

"Whatever."

"Allie works with you on this. End of discussion."

I crossed my arms over my chest and stared him down.

He crossed his arms over his chest and returned the look.

Neither of us gave an inch.

Unfortunately, it was his name on the door, so I knew who was ultimately going to win.

"Fine," I repeated. Then I turned on my sneakers and stomped out, well aware that I probably looked like a truculent three-year-old.

I plopped myself back down at my desk with a huff.

And realized the goon was right behind me.

"Please tell me you're not going to hover all day," I told him. "Seriously, I think I'm safe at my desk."

He took the hint, moving to an empty desk a couple feet away. But he didn't take his eyes off me.

"You're creeping me out. Quit staring at me."

I looked up to find him grinning. And not just with his eyes this time. One corner of his lips tugged upward in something that I could only describe as a smirk.

"What?" I asked.

He shrugged and shook his head. "Nothing."

"Look, pal—"

"Cal. You can call me Cal."

"Fine. *Cal.* This was not my idea."

"Clearly."

"I don't need a bodyguard."

"So I heard."

"Felix is totally overreacting."

"Probably."

"This was just a prank."

"Could be."

"You always this agreeable?"

"No."

I narrowed my eyes at him. His eyes? Still laughing at me. Big, hearty chuckles.

"Well, if you have to be my shadow, just . . . don't talk to me. Okay?"

He nodded. "Done."

"Good."

I turned back to my computer screen.

This was going to be a very long day.

Chapter Four

Cal spent the rest of the morning silently staring at me while I spent the rest of it silently shooting daggers at Barbie's back. I tried to concentrate on proofing the column I'd written last night, but for some reason, my heart just wasn't in it. I guess death threats did that to me.

Since the PW thing wasn't leading anywhere, I found myself instead replaying the message again, listening for any background noise that might give me a clue as to where this mystery-caller slash threat-maker slash ruining-my-life-guy was calling from. Nada. It was like he'd called from a padded cell.

Well, if I couldn't hear anything in the background, I'd start with what I could hear—his voice.

I played it a third time, the mechanical cadence crawling up my spine. Something about its cold, inhuman tone gave me the creeps far worse than the menacing words. The caller had gone through a lot of trouble to disguise his voice. Why? Because I'd recognize it? If so, that left two options—either someone I knew was playing a prank or it was someone famous, someone whose voice had boomed at me from the big screen countless times.

Which didn't narrow things down a whole lot.

Time to try another tactic.

I pulled up a search engine and typed in "voice disguise." I followed the top link to a site with a list of different voice-altering programs. I hit the first one, which took me to a page called AlterAudio. For a small fee, the website promised you could change your voice from male to female, high pitched to low pitched, robotic, echo, and any other number of effects. "Create your online persona!" it touted.

I could only imagine the practical applications. How many losers were sitting at home in their underwear, chatting in Cary Grant's voice to some unsuspecting woman?

Then again, she probably didn't sound like Marilyn Monroe either. How did anyone ever hook up before the age of cyber lies?

I hit the "buy it now" button, cringing just a little as I charged it to the *Informer*'s expense account. I waited while my computer recognized their software and began loading the application on to my hard drive. Five minutes later I was hooking my pocket recorder to my computer and speaking into the end.

"Tina's gonna catch a creep," I said. I turned on my speakers and pressed the button to play it back.

"Tina's gonna catch a creep," my own voice told me.

Cal shot me an odd look.

I just waved back.

I adjusted the buttons to up the bass, lower the treble, and create a male voice. I hit play.

"Tina's gonna catch a creep," some guy said.

I blinked, the cadence and intonation exactly the same as mine, but in a completely different tone. Weird.

Max popped his head up over the partition, his watery eyes going my way again.

"Just testing out some new software," I explained.

He shook his head. "You know, I remember when reporting was going out in the field with a notebook and a stubby pencil."

"Welcome to the digital age, my friend."

He shook his head again, muttering, "You kids and your machines," before he disappeared behind the fabric partition.

Seeing how easy it was to change from female to male, I clicked another button, putting the website to the test. Mechanical voice. After fiddling with a few buttons, I crossed my fingers and hit the play button.

A robotic Tina came on, informing me I was gonna catch a creep. Unfortunately, it sounded nothing like the creep who had called me last night. Mechanical, yes. A match, no.

Undaunted, I went back to the page with the list of programs. Five others were listed. I hit the second one, instantly transported to their webpage and began downloading their package.

An hour later I'd gone through three more sites, two months of allowable expenses, and was just about to give up on this wild goose chase. Honestly, my mystery caller could have used any number of software programs. I was totally grasping here.

But, since I had nothing else to go on but grasping, I cued my audio file up one more time and put website number four, Audio Cloak, into use, once again transforming my own voice. I hit play.

A shiver went up my spine as my mystery caller said that Tina was going to catch a creep.

Audio Cloak sounded exactly like the message I'd gotten. No doubt about it, this was the one that my caller had used.

I was just about to email the webmaster and ask if anyone from PW Enterprises had used their site last night, when a sandwich dropped into the middle of my desk.

I looked up to find Cal standing over me.

"What's that?"

"Peace offering. Salami on sourdough."

"I hate salami." I was totally lying. Salami was my favorite. I'd eat it every day if I wasn't afraid of perpetual salami breath.

"You sure? You look hungry."

I was. Starving. I poked at the white wrapper. "Where did you get it?"

He nodded his head toward the window. "Had the deli across the street deliver."

I looked over to the spot he'd occupied all morning. A footlong, a bag of chips, and two sodas sat on the desk.

"Coke?" I asked, gesturing to one of the cups.

He nodded.

Caffeine and hoagies. I tried to resist . . . but I was only human.

"Hand it over," I said, gesturing to the cup as I unwrapped my sandwich.

I thought I saw the ghost of a smile twitching his lips again.

"Don't do that," I said, taking a bite of my sandwich. My taste buds sighed in appreciation. Just the right blend of spicy meat, tangy mustard, and soft, pillowy sourdough. I wasn't a particularly religious person, but I was pretty sure this was what heaven tasted like.

"Do what?" He handed me the soda.

"You're laughing at me."

"No, I'm not."

I nodded, feeling my bangs bob up and down as I took a sip. "You are. You've been silently laughing at me ever since you got here. You think I'm being childish."

He leaned his butt against the side of my desk, giving me a long, assessing stare. He crossed his arms over his chest, his muscles flexing. I had to admit, they were impressive muscles.

I tried not to look as unnerved as I felt.

Finally he nodded.

"Okay, yes. I think you are being childish."

"I knew it."

"I know this arrangement wasn't your idea, but I think you should take this threat seriously."

"You're right. People get killed through the telephone all the time."

"You have a real sarcastic streak to you, you know it?"

"It's one of my better traits."

"I'm serious, Tina. This isn't the kind of thing you should take lightly."

I opened my mouth to protest, but he held up a hand to stop me.

"Look, I know you think you can take care of yourself, that you don't need anyone's help, you're a strong, independent woman, yada, yada, yada. I've heard it a million times."

My turn to cross my arms over my chest. "Gee, I'm

sorry. I didn't realize we were back in the nineteenth century."

"I'd be giving the same lecture if you were a man."

"Yeah, I see guys getting dissed for being 'strong independent men' all the time."

"You know what I mean."

I opened my Strawberry Shortcake purse and pulled out a five.

"Actually, *Cal*," I said, spitting out his name like it was dirtying my mouth, "I don't need your help. Because I'm not in any danger. In case you haven't noticed, we are not in a Schwarzenegger movie, there are no bad guys gunning for me, and I write about celebrity hookups, not political scandals and government corruption." I shoved the five at him. "And I can buy my own lunch."

He took the five, turning it over in his hands.

Finally he tucked it into his pocket and silently moved back to his desk, unwrapping his own sandwich.

I sat back down and took another bite of salami. But some of the heaven had been argued out of it.

"What's Audio Cloak?"

I swiveled in my seat to find Allie reading over my shoulder.

Instinctively, I closed the window on my screen.

"Nothing."

"You think that's what he used to disguise his voice?" Cam asked, coming up behind her.

"You mean the caller?" Allie asked, her blue eyes wide.

Reluctantly, I nodded.

"How does it work?" she asked.

Man, she was a pushy little thing.

"It's . . . complicated." Which wasn't entirely true, but considering it was Barbie I was talking to, reciting her ABC's was probably complicated.

"Do you think that guy from PW used it?" Cam asked.

Allie turned to her. "What's PW?"

I vaguely felt Cal perking up in the corner, but I ignored it, instead shooting Cam a silent "Shut up, shut up, shut up!" look. While I might have to share an office with Neanderthal Man, he didn't need to know every detail of my personal business.

But Cam was either playing blonde or not receiving vibes today. "It's the name of the company she traced the call to. PW Enterprises."

"How did you find that out?" Allie asked.

"I'm a reporter, remember?" I answered. I think I showed great restraint for not adding, "One hired for more than her great rack."

"So, you know who did it then?"

"Well . . . almost. I know where the call was made from, but not who made it. Yet," I added, trying to save face.

"Hmm." She pursed her lips together, a furrow forming between her perfectly plucked brows.

I knew I was going to regret asking, but . . . "What?"

"Well, the caller did say to stop printing stories about him."

"So?"

"So, I'd think the easiest way to generate a list of suspects would be to make a list of people you've written about."

I snorted. "Look, I know you're new here, but some of us have published quite a few articles. I write a *daily* column. The list would be a mile long."

Allie blinked at me, and I wasn't sure just how many of my subtle insults had made it through her thick blonde skull.

"He said stor*ies*. Plural," she pointed out. "You could narrow it down to the people you've written multiple columns about lately."

I hated to admit, the Barbie had a point. While plenty of celebs had mentions in my column, there were only a handful I'd given more than one mention to in the last few weeks. Hollywood's attention span was about as long as an ADD-affected two-year-old's.

"Right," I said. "I was going to do that next." I cleared my throat. "So, did you actually want something, or were you just coming over to chat?"

Barbie blinked at me. "Oh. Yeah. Um, Felix said we should go to the courthouse together. Pines's evidence trial is starting in half an hour."

I looked down at my watch. "I'm on it." I grabbed my purse, notebook, and a ballpoint.

I felt rather than saw Cal rise from his desk, following a pace behind as I made for the elevator.

"Who's he?" Cam whispered as I hit the "down" button.

"No one."

Cam gave him a slow appraisal, her eyes resting on the fit of his T-shirt across his broad chest. "He doesn't look like no one."

"He's my insurance."

She gave me a look but, thankfully, didn't push it.

Once we hit the parking lot, we all dispersed to our respective vehicles. Cam's a Jeep Wrangler with mud caked into the tires. Allie skipped to one of those new little VW bugs. Powder blue. Figures. Even her car was adorable.

I unlocked my helmet and threw a leg over my bike.

"No."

I turned to find Cal at my side, shaking his head.

"Excuse me?"

"I can't let you ride that."

"Hold up—you can't *let* me?"

"You're completely exposed. Not to mention how easily someone could stage an accident on something that flimsy."

"My bike is not flimsy."

"It's the smallest bike I've ever seen. What's it made of, plastic?"

I clenched my teeth. "I'm petite. I need a petite bike."

"Not today you don't."

"Look, you—"

"No, look *you*," he countered, taking a step forward. Suddenly his jaw clenched, his eyes going intent. His entire demeanor shifted into something hard and dangerous. I felt my breath back up in my throat, realizing just how good at his job he must be. "I was hired to keep you safe. Which I intend to do, whether you cooperate or not. You want to go to the courthouse? Fine. We do it my way."

He gestured to his left, where a huge black Hummer sat at the curb. And not one of those new SUV-sized ones. This was an original tank.

"Seriously?" I asked. "A Hummer?"

"It's safe."

"It's a tank. It probably guzzles more fuel than some small countries."

He raised one dark eyebrow ever so slightly. "We could always go back inside?"

I looked across the parking lot at Allie, applying lip gloss as she pulled her Bug out into traffic. I clenched my teeth together. And swung my leg back over the bike, locking my helmet on to the handlebars again.

"Fine. But, you know what they say about big cars, right?" I asked as Cal opened his passenger side door for me.

"What's that?"

"They're compensating for something. The bigger the car, the smaller their . . ." I let my gaze fall to the crotch of his jeans. Then back up to give a long, meaningful look at the behemoth of a car he drove.

But instead of growling at me, the laughter returned to Rent-A-Goon's eyes.

"Oh, yeah? And what do they say about girls who drive hot pink Hondas?"

"I don't know," I said. "I've never met anyone ballsy enough to tell me."

The corner of his mouth quirked up. "Somehow, I believe that, Bender."

Next to the sentencing, the Pines evidence trial was a downright snoozer. Cops had found the kiddie porn in Pines's backseat, partially shoved under an old copy of *Variety*. The "partially" was the sticky word that had granted Pines's defense attorneys a hearing. Just how much had been exposed? Enough that the police had seen it was young boys, or just a naked person? Did they have probable cause for investigating the car?

I had to hand it to Pines's lawyer—the guy had a way of asking the same question so many different ways that the arresting officer began to doubt his own story. As the afternoon dragged on, he went from, "Yes, sir," to, "I really can't recall now." I feared just how fuzzy his memory might get by the time the actual trial started.

In the end, the magazines were allowed into evidence. Not really a shocker. We all knew there was no way Pines was getting off that easily.

As soon as the gavel fell, I stood and stretched my legs. Four hours on a hard, wooden chair had caused my right foot to fall asleep. I stomped on it as I made my way from the courtroom with the rest of the news hounds.

"That was so freaking cool!"

I turned to find Allie at my side, eyes shining. Throughout the entire boring proceeding, she'd been scribbling in a pink floral notebook like a demon.

"Cool? We're lucky we didn't go into a coma."

"But the way they got down to every little detail. Didn't you find that fascinating?"

Was she for real?

"Sure. Fascinating. Like paint drying."

We pushed our way outside, blinking back the assaulting sunshine. I squinted and noticed Cal's Hummer right away. He was semilegally parked at the curb, leaning against the passenger side, his eyes covered in dark sunglasses that reflected the glass courthouse building back at me in blinding clarity. He looked like a hitman. Or The Rock. Either way, the pedestrians on the sidewalk were giving him a wide berth.

Allie pulled a pair of designer sunglasses from her bag and slid them onto her nose, turning to me. "So, Felix told me this was originally your story."

"It *is* my story," I agreed, emphasizing the present tense.

"Right. And I don't want to step on your toes or anything."

"Thank you." I think that was the first smart thing she'd said.

"So, when I type up our notes tonight, I'll put your name first on the byline, 'kay?"

I felt my eyes narrow. "What do you mean *you're* typing up *our* notes?"

"You know, the ones we took during the hearing just now?"

"That was a no-brainer. Evidence in. I didn't take any notes."

She cocked her head to one side, her blonde hair cascading over her right shoulder like a shampoo commercial. "Huh. Well, then I guess I'll be typing up *my* notes. See you tomorrow, Bender."

For a second, I swore a glimmer of triumph sparked her eyes, and I suddenly found myself wondering if maybe the blonde wasn't as dumb as I'd originally thought.

Before I could protest, she'd turned on her kitten heels and was sashaying to her tiny little bug.

I clenched my jaw. So help me, if I wasn't being watched by a dozen security cameras right now . . .

"Ready to go?"

I turned to find Cal behind me, hands in his pockets.

"More than ready."

Because I had a sinking feeling that if I didn't get my version of the hearing in to Felix tonight, there was a strong chance Blondie might conveniently forget my name on that byline.

By the time Cal dropped me back off at my bike and insisted on following me home, it was dark and I was starving. Luckily, Aunt Sue had actually remembered the lasagna recipe. Unluckily, she'd forgotten to take it out of the oven. I pushed through the front door and into a thick cloud of marinara-flavored smoke. Coughing, I staggered through the kitchen, removed the offending casserole—which resembled a charred brick now—and opened up all the windows.

"Peanut, that you?" Aunt Sue called from the living room. I could hear the strains of *The Price Is Right* on the Game Show Network in the background.

"It's me. How long has this lasagna been in the oven?"

"I put it in just after *Deal or No Deal*."

Five hours. No wonder the place reeked.

"I think we might be having takeout tonight," I shot back.

"Oh, let's have Chinese," Aunt Sue agreed happily, shuffling into the kitchen. "Or maybe Indian. You know how I love curry."

"I do know." I used a spatula to try to wedge the noodle brick out of the pan. No luck.

"Oh, or Italian! That's my favorite."

"I know."

"I make a mean lasagna," Aunt Sue said, a faraway look in her eyes.

I sighed. "I know."

I gave up on the spatula and stuck the whole thing in the trash. I'd buy a new pan tomorrow.

"What's that awful smell?"

I turned to find Hattie Carmichael standing in the front doorway, wrinkling her nose.

"We had a little cooking mishap," I said, pulling the number for the Peking Palace off the refrigerator and dialing the phone.

"I made lasagna," Aunt Sue said.

"Ugh, it smells like you overcooked it," Mrs. Carmichael said.

"Ya think?" I mumbled, listening to the phone ring on the other end.

"Anyway, I came over because there's this strange car parked across the street. I just don't know who it belongs to, so I was about to call the police."

Aunt Sue and I looked out the window simultaneously.

To find Cal's Hummer parked at the curb.

Great.

"He's with me," I reluctantly admitted.

Both Aunt Sue and Mrs. Carmichael's eyebrows rose in unison.

"Oh? A new beau?" Mrs. C. asked.

"No, not a beau."

"A friend?" Aunt Sue supplied.

"Sorta."

"Well, why's he just sitting there? Why doesn't he come in?" Mrs. C. asked.

"He's shy," I shot back, willing the guys at the Peking Palace to pick up so I could avoid any further interrogation. Mrs. Carmichael was not only the head of the neighborhood watch, she was also the biggest gossip in the entire Palm Grove development. I know, hypocritical in the extreme, but I wasn't a fan of gossip when it revolved around me.

Or my need for a bodyguard.

"Well, maybe I should just go talk to him," Hattie said, clacking her dentures as she eyed the Hummer.

"No!"

"Hello, Peking Palace?" the phone said in my ear.

"Uh, hold on," I told the receiver. Then turned to my neighbor. "Look, he's really shy, and he won't be there very long. Just please leave him alone, okay? Really, he's harmless, nothing to worry about."

"I don't know. He looks dangerous. Like he's in a gang or something."

"He's not in a gang."

"Hello? You want to order?" the phone asked.

"Yes, just a minute," I told the guy.

"You sure he's not in a gang? I've seen those trucks on MTV. They look like gang trucks."

"I promise he's not in a gang. Cross my heart."

"If you say so." Though the little frown between Mrs. Carmichael's squinty eyes didn't look entirely convinced. "But I'm taking down his license plate number. You can never be too careful!"

"Great. Wonderful. Fab."

"And, make sure you air this place out. You know, maybe you should set a timer next time."

"Yep, thanks for the tip," I mumbled, not even attempting sincerity as I ushered her out the door and locked it after her.

I put the phone back up to my ear. "Hi, sorry about that."

My only answer was a dial tone.

I thunked my head back against the front door, then hit redial. Ten rings in, I gave up and ordered pizza.

Two hours and a large pepperoni later, the place was beginning to lose its eau de marinara, Aunt Sue was safely tucked in for the night with an Agatha Christie novel, I was putting the finishing touches on my version of the Pines hearing . . . and Cal was still parked at the curb.

I peeked through my bedroom curtains at his car. Jesus, what was he going to do, sleep in that thing? As weird as receiving a death threat felt, the idea of someone watching over me twenty-four seven felt even weirder. I squinted through the dark, trying to get a good look in his driver's side window. A pair of big black ovals stared back at me.

Was he using binoculars?

I jumped back from the bedroom window, pulling the curtains tight, suddenly having enormous sympathy for goldfish.

Trying to ignore my babysitter, I propped my computer on my lap and read over my latest shot at Pines.

PEDOPHILE PINES WILL HAVE TO SHOW HIS PORN:

IN AN EXPECTED MOVE, THE JUDGE IN THE PINES CHILD PORNOGRAPHY CASE SAID THE HIGHWAY PATROL'S SEARCH OF THE DIRECTOR'S CAR WAS, IN FACT, LEGAL. ALL EVIDENCE SEIZED IN THAT SEARCH WILL BE SEEN BY A JURY, INCLUDING THE INFAMOUS KIDDIE MAGS. MY ADVICE TO PINES: IF THE BOY IS UNDERAGE, YOU MUST NOT TURN THE PAGE!

Feeling pretty pleased with myself, I signed the article, with my name first on the byline, thank you very much. Then I hit send, instantly transporting my copy to the *Informer*'s offices.

I stood up, stretching my back. After the day I'd had, my muscles were full of more knots than a knitting circle. I tilted my head from side to side, working the kinks out of my neck. What I needed was a long, hard swim, followed by a long hot shower. I glanced toward the window. Unfortunately, unless I wanted an audience, the swim, at least, was going to have to wait.

Instead I opened my email, scanning for tomorrow's headlines. I was just delighting in one about a certain rising female country singer who'd been spotted cozying up to a certain lesbian DJ at a nightclub, when an IM window popped up in the corner of my screen. ManInBlack72.

I immediately hit accept and waited for his message to appear.

Hey, Bender.

Hey, Black.

How was your day, gorgeous?

I groaned out loud. *Don't ask.*

That great, huh?

Sucked big fat donkey balls.

You have such a way with words.

I'm glad somebody appreciated it.

What happened? Black prompted.

I paused a moment. Did I really want to spill my guts over the internet to some guy who most likely was typing with Cheeto-stained fingers and watching *Star Trek* in the background?

On the other hand . . . I looked up, listening to the silence of the empty room. Who else did I have?

My fingers jumped across the keyboard.

Because of some stupid prank call, my boss gave my story to a new girl and hired some rent-a-thug to follow me around.

Rent-a-thug?

Bodyguard. An annoying one.

There was a pause. Then, *Want me to take him out?*

I grinned. That was the nicest thing anyone had said to me all day. *Would you?*

Consider it done, babe.

Thanks.

Another pause. Then the words, *You okay?* appeared on my screen.

I took a deep breath. *Yeah.*

Good. Hey . . . Knock knock.

I grinned. *Who's there?*

Willis.

Willis who?

Willis corny joke make you smile?

I snorted out loud.

Funny.

I try. Same time tomorrow?

Wouldn't miss it.

'Night, babe.

'Night, Black.

He signed off, and the screen went dark, bringing with it the vaguely lonely feeling that always hit me when his "online now" icon disappeared. Which was ridiculous, because, as I reminded myself, he was just a name on a screen. A fantasy. Black wasn't any more real than Pamela Anderson's boobs.

I shook off the feeling and returned to my inbox.

While I'd been chatting with Black, a new message had popped in. It had come in through the *Informer* website, the subject line, "Breaking News."

Immediately, I opened it, leaning closer to the screen.

The note read:

"Breaking News—one stubborn reporter doesn't listen to warnings. Now, she's got a target on her back. Sleep well, Tina Bender. Because tonight may be your last."

Chapter Five

"That's it, I'm calling the police."

"No!" I wailed, lunging at Felix before he could reach his phone.

"Tina, this is serious. This is not some adolescent prankster."

"It was an email. No one got hurt."

"Yet." He gave me a pointed look.

I glanced at the open laptop on Felix's desk. After a sleepless night littered with visions of faceless men threatening me in mechanical voices, I'd reluctantly shown the email to Felix as soon as I'd got into the offices that morning.

He hadn't been any more thrilled about it than I had. And, I had to admit, he was right about one thing. This was looking less and less like some random prankster. In fact, I was beginning to think this really was someone with a grudge against me.

On the other hand, no way was I going to let Felix bring in the cops over this. "You can't call the police. What will my informants say?"

"Informants?" Cal piped up from the corner. He'd insisted on following me to work in his I'm-clearly-over-compensating-for-something mobile and had been my shadow ever since. Though, to be honest, I didn't mind quite so much today.

"Yes, informants," I repeated. "Look, no one's going to trust me with their dirt if it comes out I've been talking to cops. Who wants that kind of scrutiny? Most of these people are ratting on their friends."

"Nice group you hang out with," Cal mumbled.

I shot him a look.

"Alright, that's enough." Felix held up his hands. "Look, I know you don't like this, Tina. And I know you're scared—"

"I am not scared!" Which might have been more convincing if my voice hadn't raised two octaves. I cleared my throat. "I'm not scared, I'm pissed off," I clarified. "Really fu—"

"Swear Pig," Felix reminded.

I clenched my jaw. "Really *freaking* pissed off."

Felix shook his head. "Tina, this isn't something I can take lightly. What if something were to happen to you? I'd never be able to forgive myself."

"Nothing is going to happen to me. I have rent-a—" I stopped myself just in time. "I have Cal."

"Which is great," Felix agreed, "but it's just a temporary solution. Look, whatever this guy's beef is, he's clearly not letting go of it. What's next? Do we wait until he's actually followed through with a threat?"

I bit my lip. Yeah, that idea didn't appeal to me too much either.

"Look, give me three days."

"Three days?" Felix asked.

"Three days to track this guy down myself. If I can't, then you can turn it over to the police."

He narrowed his eyes.

"Think about it, Felix," I said, grasping to strengthen my case. "Cops crawling all over the place, confiscating our notes and archives. That's not going to look too good for the paper. Won't be good for sales."

Felix cocked his head to the side, contemplating this. "And just how do you propose to find this guy in three days?"

"I don't know. I'm a reporter, I'll think of something."

"You're a gossip columnist. That's a far cry from Bob Woodward. When was the last time you actually *investigated* anything?"

I snapped my mouth shut, narrowing my eyes at him. Mostly because I couldn't remember. While I'd done a pretty successful stint at my school paper in college, since then I'd been perfectly happy to leave the hard-hitting stories to other reporters. My talent was spinning. Give me any nugget of news, and I could turn it into a dishy, dirty, salacious bit of snark that cut the famed and fabulous down to the level of average Jane Reader.

Clearly, I hadn't investigated many death threats. But that didn't mean I was giving in.

"Three days," I repeated. "That's all I'm asking. Come on, I think you owe me that."

"Owe you?" Felix spat out the words, crossing his arms over his chest in a much scrawnier version of Cal's stance.

"Yes. For saddling me with Barbie."

"Allie."

"Whatever. Look, you know how long it's taken me to make the kind of contacts I have. They don't grow on trees. The best thing for all of us is to keep this thing quiet. Please. Three days."

Felix looked from me to Cal. Finally he sighed and shook his head. By the way all the fight drained out of his shoulders, I could tell before he even spoke that I'd won.

"Alright."

"Thank you!" Despite myself, I threw my arms around his neck.

"But if Cal feels there's even the slightest hint of danger to you, or anyone else on my staff, all bets are off."

"Aye, aye, captain," I said, giving him a mock salute as I backpedaled out the door.

As soon as I sat back down at my desk, I booted up my computer and opened my archives folder.

I could do this. So what if my reporter skills were a little rusty? I had skills. Mad skills. I would find this creep. And I knew just where to start looking.

The unlucky celebrities I'd written about.

I pulled up my columns from the past month. Monday through Thursday I put out a short daily, with a longer, detailed version on Fridays. Five days a week times four weeks, and I had twenty articles to work with.

Going on Allie's assumption that our Mystery Caller had multiple mentions, I scanned through the columns, making note of any name that appeared more than once.

"Who did you write about yesterday?"

I jumped in my seat and spun around to find Cal reading over my shoulder.

"Jesus, you scared me."

"A little jumpy?"

"No, death threats make me feel perfectly secure, thanks," I said. Then I swiveled back to my screen, taking a deep breath to rein in my heart rate.

Unfortunately, Cal didn't take my sarcasm as a hint, instead leaning his butt against my desk and making himself comfortable. "The email said you hadn't taken his warning. Which means that he didn't like something you printed between the time he called and last night," Cal persisted.

"I was getting to that," I said.

I pulled up the file containing yesterday's column and checked it against my list. Four names came up.

Cal pulled out a notebook and pen and wrote them down.

Katie Briggs, an actress whose volatile love life had single-handedly paid my rent last summer.

Jennifer Wood, the teen idol who unwittingly ended up holding the doobie.

Blain Hall, rehab-bound rocker.

And, of course, Edward Pines, pedophile director.

"Any of these characters stand out? Any have a history of erratic behavior?" Cal asked, his pen hovering.

I snorted. "They're celebrities. Everything they do is erratic."

"Who's this girl?" Cal stabbed his finger at Katie's name.

"Katie Briggs," I said.

He shrugged. "Should I know her?"

I blinked at him. "Seriously? Katie Briggs?"

"You keep repeating her name like that will help. Look, I don't know who she is. Wanna clue me in?"

"Daughter of David Briggs, only the most powerful

producer in Hollywood. Won the Golden Globe last year for playing the plucky paraplegic Olympian? Dated George Clooney, Leo DiCaprio, *and* Orlando Bloom? Katie *Briggs*."

"Oh. *That* Katie Briggs," he said. Only this time it was his turn to be sarcastic.

"You really never heard of her?"

"I don't go to the movies much."

"And apparently you don't read my column either."

"Not until now," he said, gesturing to the screen. "So, you think Katie could be your mystery caller?"

"Anything's possible. Any one of them could. Though, I gotta say, the whole macho threat thing feels more like Blain's style." I paused. "Please tell me you know who Blain Hall is."

Cal nodded. "I listen to the radio. Okay, so any one of them could have done it. Let's start at the top and work our way down. This Katie chick, how can we get hold of her?"

"Well, most people," I started, opening up my address book, "would have to call her publicist and either wait for a comment or promise their firstborn for an interview between shoots."

"I have a feeling you're not most people."

"You're not as dumb as you look, Cal."

"Ouch."

Instantly, I regretted the comment. Okay, so it was awkward, annoying, and painfully limiting having a brawny babysitter following my every move. But he was just doing his job. To be fair, the situation wasn't Cal's fault any more than it was mine.

"I didn't mean it that way," I quickly said. "Sorry."

"Wow," he answered.

"'Wow'?"

"'Sorry.' I have a hunch that's not a word you utter very often. I'm feeling kinda special right now." He grinned. And his eyes were definitely laughing again.

I cleared my throat. "Anyway, back to Katie. It just so happens that I have a close, personal friend at her hairdresser's."

Cal raised an eyebrow. "Close *personal* friend?"

"Not that kind of personal. He's gay."

"Ah."

"And chatty."

"Let me guess, that's where you got all this dirt on Katie's love life?"

"Hey, people will tell their hairdressers just about anything. It's crazy."

He glanced at my own purple locks.

"*Some* people," I quickly added.

He nodded. "Uh huh. So, this hairdresser guy, he can get us access to Katie?"

I nodded. "No sweat. Her new movie comes out next month, and she's in the salon daily for touch-ups during promo. All I have to do is find out what time her appointment today is and—" I paused, narrowing my eyes at the hulk of man sitting on the edge of my desk. "Wait, what do you mean 'us'?"

"Us. From the German Gothic uns. Plural form of I. I'm sure you're familiar with the word."

"There is no plural 'I.'"

"There is now."

I gritted my teeth together. Though I had to be just a little impressed by anyone who could rattle off word origins like that. "This is exactly why I didn't want Felix calling the police. These people trust me. I start bringing the National Guard with me, and there goes my lifeline to Hollywood."

"I'm hardly the National Guard."

I looked down to where the butt of his gun peeked out from the waistband of his jeans. "You're carrying a .32. You don't exactly scream 'friendly.'"

He pulled the hem of his T-shirt down to cover it. But instead of arguing the point, his voice took on a firm tone. "Let me help you."

I stood, meeting him almost at eye level. Give or take a foot. I lifted my chin, crossed my arms over my chest.

"I don't need your help."

He gave me a slow, assessing stare. "No, I don't think you do. But," he added, "if you're smart, you'll take it anyway."

I took a deep breath, biting back the refusal on the tip of my tongue. Mostly because he had a point. The smart move here was to take the assistance of the guy with the gun. No doubt he had a lot more experience tracking down bad guys than I did. And the sooner I found this creep, the sooner my life could go back to normal. And the sooner I could dismiss my muscle-bound shadow.

"Okay," I finally said.

"Good." It irked me just a little that he didn't seem the least surprised at getting his way. "So, Katie Briggs?"

I nodded. "Katie Briggs."

We were in luck. My friend at the salon said Katie had an appointment on the books for ten that morning. The bad news? It was nine thirty-five. And we were across town. I told my friend to stall her at all costs, then grabbed Cal by the sleeve and made for his ozone-killing machine.

Exactly forty minutes later, we pulled to the curb in front of the opulent glass doors of Fernando's salon in Beverly Hills.

Fernando was a famed hairdresser to the stars, an incredibly tanned, incredibly flamboyant, and incredibly talented man who'd burst onto the Beverly Hills radar about five years ago. While he claimed some sort of Spanish nobility in his ancestry, his actual past was a little hazy. But as long as his extensions kept winning oohhs and ahhs on the red carpet, no one really cared.

I pushed through the doors and into the reception area, this month decorated in a medieval castle theme. Plush red sofas lined the windows, and a large crystal chandelier hung over an intricate parquet floor. Beyond reception, cut-and-color stations outfitted with huge gilded mirrors lined the room, while lengths of thick tapestries hung from the walls, depicting scenes of men out for the hunt, while maidens wearing shockingly little for the cold English countryside fawned over fair-haired boys. A reception desk complete with turrets took up one corner of the room, and behind it stood a slim, Hispanic guy wearing more eyeliner than I even owned. As soon as he spotted me, he skipped (yes, actually skipped) toward me.

"Tina, dahling, where have you been hiding yourself?" he called, descending upon me with air kisses.

"Hi, Marco." I returned his quick shoulder hug and stepped back. "Marco, this is Cal, my . . ." I trailed off, not really sure what to call him. Bodyguard seemed so melodramatic. And rent-a-goon just seemed rude.

But Marco didn't seem to notice, grabbing Cal's hand in both of his. "Well, hell-o, Cal." He pumped vigorously, holding on just a little too long as his eyes rested on Cal's biceps. "Always a *pleasure* to meet one of Tina's friends."

Oh, brother.

"So, is Katie here?" I asked, lowering my voice as my eyes scanned the salon.

Marco nodded. "Getting a touch-up. In the back."

I looked over his shoulder to a discreet station near the rear. A brunette with big pouty lips was scrutinizing her reflection in the mirror while the master Fernando spun around her with a straight razor like he was Edward Scissorhands.

"Perfect. You think you could distract Fernando for a sec so I can talk to her?"

Marco clucked his tongue. "Aye, girl. You're gonna get me in trouble."

"Pretty please, Marco?" I batted my eyelashes at him. "With Brad Pitt on top?"

Marco grinned. "You know I can't deny you, doll. Give me two shakes of a lamb's tail, and that A-lister is yours." He threw me a wink as he made his way through the buzzing hair dryers and pungent chemical rinses to Katie's chair.

"Is that guy for real?" Cal asked, watching him skip (yes, *skip*) through the salon.

"Shhh," I said, batting him on the arm. "Just let me do the talking."

I waited two beats, then followed Marco's path, my

shadow a step behind me. I caught up just in time to hear him say, "So sorry to interrupt, Fernando. But something has come up at the front. Can I steal you away for the teeny tiniest moment?"

"I'll be right back," I heard Fernando promise Katie, then watched out of the corner of my eye as the pair made their way to the front.

Luckily, the station next to Katie was vacant. I waited a three-Mississippi count, then grabbed a copy of *Cosmo* from a rack on the wall and sat down. Cal hovered just to my right, pretending to rearrange the brushes at the next station over. I gave him a look that clearly said, "stay out of sight!" then turned to the brunette fluffing her hair beside me.

"Hey, you're Katie, aren't you? Katie Briggs?" I asked.

She turned, a bored expression in her big blue eyes as if even she was tired of hearing that name.

"I'm . . . Jeannie," I lied, sticking a hand her way. "I'm a huge fan. I love, love, loved your last movie! That scene with the mother, right before she died after being stabbed by the circus clown hired by the mob—so realistic!"

A smile tickled her oversized lips. "Thanks." Then she turned back to the mirror.

Okay . . . so what now? I bit my lip. I couldn't very well come right out and ask her if she was the one threatening my life. I tapped my nail on the plastic edge of my chair.

"You know, I've read all about you," I said, vying with her reflection for her attention. "In the *Informer*."

Her expression puckered into what would have been

a frown had she not been a plastic surgery devotee. "The *Informer?*"

"That newspaper. Have you read it?" I asked.

She clenched her jaw, her lips drawing into a thin line. (Okay, considering she had about a gallon of collagen injected in her lower lip, maybe "thin" wasn't an accurate description. But it was at least *thinner.*)

"I've seen it," she spit out.

"Oh, you should totally pick up a copy. That Tina Bender, she's a hoot!"

She glared at me. "Hoot?"

"Oh sure," I said, forging full steam ahead. "The way she likened your love life to a string of bad Spanish soaps just yesterday. I swear, I spit out my latte at that one."

"Tabloid trash. They're all printing lies. Malicious lies."

Malicious. My ears perked up. That was exactly the term Mystery Caller had used, too.

"Wow. I wonder how she gets away with printing lies. I mean, don't you think someone should stop her?" I asked, carefully watching her reaction.

She swiveled in her seat, turning back to her own reflection. "Please. Like anyone really pays attention to what that kind of tabloid trash writes."

Ouch.

Vehemently, I shook my head. "Oh no, a ton of people read that column. Tina Bender is very popular."

I thought I felt Cal smirk to my right, but I ignored him.

"Ha!" Katie barked. "Someone should put that sad woman out of her misery."

Again, ouch. But . . . now we were getting somewhere.

"Where were you last night?"

"Excuse me?" she said, her eyes shooting to mine in the mirror again as she clenched her jaw.

"I mean, did you go to any big Hollywood parties last night?" I asked, backpedaling. "I am just so fascinated by the lifestyle of an award-winning actress such as yourself."

"Oh." Her frown evened out instantly. Apparently flattery, as with all of Hollywood, was the key with this chick. "I went to a charity event. Some thing in the Valley. My publicist said I had to be seen there." She turned to me. "But did that Bender girl print that? No!"

A-ha! So she did read my column. I felt a little lift of triumph.

"What about the evening before?" I persisted. The night the first call had come in. It would have been easy enough to send the email from a cell while at some fab party. But, for the phone call, Mystery Caller would have had to have access to a computer to run the voice-altering software. Not quite as inconspicuous a task.

"I was at home," she answered.

"With a new guy?" I couldn't help the gossip hound in me from asking.

"No. Alone." And by the way she pouted again, this time with a true hint of sadness on her swollen lips, I was inclined to believe her. For a fraction of an instant I wondered if maybe the life of a famous actress wasn't even lonelier than that of a gossip columnist.

Out of the corner of my eye, I saw Fernando break away from Marco's grasp, threading his way back through the salon to his waiting client. I chose my next question carefully.

"So, what do you do when you're home alone? Ever spend time online, maybe trying out new programs?" Like Audio Cloak?

She turned away, flipping her hair over one shoulder. "I don't own a computer."

I froze. Then blinked at her. "Wait—you don't own a computer? Seriously? Even African tribesmen own computers these days."

Again she did the would-be-frown pucker. "They're trappings of a digitized society. Modern technology is only serving to distance us from the reality of living. I prefer real human interaction. I'm an artist."

Okay, her plastic surgeon was an artist; Katie was just a movie star.

Unfortunately, she was a movie star who couldn't possibly be my mystery caller.

Stifling a wave of disappointment, I shoved the dog-eared *Cosmo* back in the rack and slid off my seat just as Fernando approached.

"Well, great to meet you. Can't wait for your next pic," I called as I walked away.

Though I'm not sure it even registered. Katie was once again enthralled with her own reflection as Fernando appeared to fluff her hair into Rapunzel-worthy waves.

Cal followed a beat behind me. "So much for our starlet," he mumbled.

"Well, one down, three to go," I shot back, making my way back toward Marco's Camelot desk.

"Sorry, doll," Marco said, shrugging his slim shoulders as I approached. "I held him off as long as I could."

"That's okay," I reassured him. "You did great."

"Oh, but I'll call you tomorrow. The Lohan's coming in for a cut and color, and you know there'll be dirt." Marco gave me a wink.

"That's my boy. Hey, check your inbox for payment later."

I gave him a wink as we exited the salon.

I felt Cal shaking his head beside me.

"What?" I asked.

"I just can't believe there are so many people willing to sell secrets to you. You ever think of working for the CIA?"

I grinned, soaking up the compliment. Even if it wasn't intended as one. "Thanks. But, you know, not all of them do it for money."

"Oh?"

"For some it's revenge. Some it's a feeling of importance. Others just like to see their quotes in print."

Cal gestured back at the salon as he beeped his Hummer open. "So, what's Marco's story? He squeal for cash?"

I laughed. "Marco? Heck no." I looked back at my flamboyant friend. "He's much easier than that. As long as I send him the weekly Clay Aiken update, Marco's a happy camper."

Chapter Six

"Alright, so who's next on our list?" Cal asked as he pulled into traffic.

"Jennifer Wood."

"Tell me about her."

Mental forehead smack. "You don't know who Jennifer Wood is?"

Cal shot me a look over the rim of his sunglasses. "Humor me."

"Fine. Jennifer Wood was a pint-sized singing sensation in her hometown, winning the local cable access reality show *Sheboygan's Got Talent* at the age of ten. At twelve she went national with her first recording contract, at fifteen her own TV show, which exploded onto the tween scene and has been going strong ever since. The girl's got her face plastered on anything and everything an eight-year-old girl could want."

"So, she's a kid actress?"

"Correction," I said. "She *plays* a kid actress. Her character, Pippi Mississippi, is thirteen. In real life, Jennifer just turned eighteen."

Cal raised an eyebrow my way. "They grow up so fast. So, what's she been mentioned in your column for?"

"The usual. Drinking. Drugs. Partying. Flashed her

boobs at the cameras two weeks ago as she was getting into her limo."

"May I never have a daughter. Alright, let's go talk to America's sweetheart."

"Great. But first," I said, glancing down at the clock on his dash, "lunch. I'm starving. Wanna hit a drive-thru?"

Cal gave me a sideways look. "You know, that fast-food stuff will kill you."

"So will global warming," I countered, giving his Hummer a pointed look. "Oh, look, there's an In-N-Out Burger!" I pointed to my favorite fast-food joint a block up on the right.

He made a sort of clucking sound in the back of his throat, but, thank God, pulled into the parking lot anyway. I ordered a double double with grilled onions, fries, and a shake. Cal ordered a grilled cheese with no mayo and water.

"What's with the girly food?" I asked around a big mouthwatering bite of burger. A little ketchup oozed onto my chin, and I grabbed a paper napkin.

"'Girly food'?" he asked. "Isn't that a little un-PC for a feminist like yourself?"

I shrugged. "I'm a fair-weather feminist."

"Hmm. I don't eat beef."

"Why not? It's yummy."

He shrugged. "I care about what I put in my body. Most meat is full of hormones, antibiotics, E. coli. Even trace amounts of fecal matter."

I looked down at my burger. "Fecal matter? As in . . ."

"Poop." He popped one of my fries in his mouth.

"You're kidding, right?"

He shook his head. "Nope. It's the way the animals are slaughtered. Generally their bowels are still full when they're killed. It's actually incredibly tricky to cut the colon and intestines away from the animal without spilling any of the contents. Cross contamination happens all the time."

I set my burger down, feeling that last bite stick in my throat. "That is sick."

"*That* is why I don't eat beef."

I picked up my shake, trying to wash down the possibly contaminated double double with strawberry goodness.

"So," Cal said, snaking another fry, "where can we find this party girl of yours?"

I tossed my burger into the trash bin to the right. "*Pippi Mississippi* shoots Monday through Friday. She'll be at Sunset Studios. The only tricky part," I added with a grin, "is getting on the lot."

"Why do I have the feeling you enjoy this sort of challenge?" Cal downed the rest of his water and tossed the cup into the trash.

I felt my grin widen. "Watch and learn, grasshopper." I slipped my cell out of my Strawberry Shortcake purse as we walked back to his car. Three rings later, Max's voice croaked on the other end.

"Beacon," he said by way of greeting.

"Hey, Max, it's me. Listen, I have a favor to ask. Any Hollywood old-timers depart this cruel world today?"

I heard Max shuffling papers. "Three. Why?"

"Got names?"

More shuffling. "Frank Jones, did animation with Disney, stroke. Elliot Shiff, ran camera on a couple Monroe flicks, pancreatic cancer. And . . ."

I held my breath.

". . . Betty Johnson, did makeup for Lucille Ball, lung cancer."

Bingo.

"Thanks, Max!" I called, quickly hanging up and dialing a new number as I hopped into Cal's Hummer. He gave me a sidelong glance but knew better than to ask.

I waited two rings before someone on the other end picked up.

"Front gate, David speaking."

I dropped into my lowest register and did my best to channel Mrs. Carmichael's smoker voice. "This is Betty Johnson in Studio Seven. I have my assistants coming in and I'd like their names on the list, please."

David paused, and I could hear him checking his computer. "Betty Johnson?"

"Makeup artist."

David did a few more clicks, checking out my story. I mentally crossed my fingers that news of Betty's demise hadn't hit the studios yet. Finally, the guard piped up in my ear again, "Your assistants' names, Ms. Johnson?"

"Tina Bender and Calvin Dean."

"They'll be on the list, just have them come to the south entrance."

"Thank you, David," I said, before snapping my phone shut with a click of satisfaction.

I looked up to find Cal shaking his head at me.

"What?"

"Do you ever tell the truth?"

"Once. In fourth grade. It was overrated."

"I'm serious. You're beginning to worry me," he said as he pulled into traffic.

"Yeah, like you're honest *all* the time."

"I try to be."

"Seriously? You never tell your girlfriend she looks hot in that unflattering dress?"

"I don't have a girlfriend."

"You never called in sick to work when you were really heading to the Lakers game?"

"Self-employed."

"Not once have you ever told your mother that her dried-out Sunday meatloaf was culinary perfection?"

"Don't eat beef, remember?"

I slouched in my seat, conceding defeat. "You're no fun."

Cal gave me a lopsided grin, his eyes taking on a devilish glint over the rim of his sunglasses. "Oh, trust me, I can be plenty of fun."

The way my cheeks suddenly filled with heat, I totally believed him. I'm sure there were stick-figure bimbos all over Hollywood who had swooned under that very same grin.

I quickly looked away, clearing my throat. "Well, when we get to the studio, just leave the talking to me, okay, Honest Abe?"

"You got it, boss."

Sunset Studios was like a miniature city plunked down in the middle of Hollywood and enclosed by a ten-foot-high brick wall. Outside the gates, panhandlers, men wearing five coats and pushing shopping carts and ladies of the evening (or in our case, afternoon . . . somehow even worse) stood at every corner. Inside, the place was so clean and wholesome looking, it fairly sparkled. Which was a sure sign 99 percent of it was fake.

Cement warehouse buildings squatted down one side of the studio, housing the soundstages of hit TV shows, while the other half of the lot was filled with building facades for movie locations. A New York street, complete with brownstones and subway stairs that led to nowhere. A dusty main street in the Old West, complete with hitching posts. A quaint, tree-lined suburban street where you expected the Beaver to pop his freckled little face out of a tree house at any second. And through it all a tram full of tourists being given the Sunset Studios tour snapped pictures of every lamppost, mailbox, and production assistant on a coffee run.

Beyond the side gate was a small parking lot where Cal and I traded our gas guzzler for a small white golf cart—the studio's main mode of transportation. Cal took the wheel and quickly navigated our way through the soundstages until we found one with a huge pink "Pippi Mississippi" sign tacked to the front. Cal parked behind a wardrobe trailer and led the way inside.

The interior of the warehouse was dark, and I took a moment to let my eyes adjust to the change. The place was a maze of ropes, cables, and electronic equipment, all leading to a series of strategically placed sets that looked like oversized dioramas. I spotted the hallway of Pippi's junior high, her prissy pink bedroom, and the video arcade where she and her girlfriend hung out after school, the latter a buzz of activity as grips positioned lights, sound guys adjusted mics, someone lifted a camera onto a moving track, and no less than three women in overalls fluffed, primped, and powdered the blonde in the center—Jennifer Wood.

Beside her stood her two co-stars: a redhead whose

name I couldn't remember, and a brunette I recognized as being in the backseat of Jennifer's limo with her when the infamous boob shot had been taken. Lani Cline, reportedly Jennifer's best friend.

"That her?" Cal asked, stabbing a finger toward Jennifer.

I nodded.

"We need her alone. Got any ideas?"

I shrugged. "Give me a minute."

"Back to one, everyone," shouted the director, an overweight guy with glasses and a nose that could rival Pinocchio's. The crew scurried off the stage like cats being doused with a hose. Jennifer walked to a spot on the floor marked with an "X" in blue electrical tape, her co-stars a step behind her.

"Speed."

A guy with a black clapboard stood in front of the camera, then dropped the little arm, marking the tape.

"And . . . rolling!" the director shouted.

A bell went off somewhere, and silence hit the set, all eyes on Jennifer.

"Chloe, I can't believe you told Ryan about my diary," she said to the brunette.

"I'm so sorry, Pippi! But I didn't know he'd read it to the whole school."

"Now no one will ask me to the spring dance. I might as well be—God, Lani, you're doing it again!"

"Cut!" the director yelled. He slipped off his canvas chair with a groan, slowly ambling up to his star. "Jennifer. Sweetie. What is it now?"

"Lani's totally standing in my light!" Jennifer said, pointing an accusing finger at the brunette.

"I am exactly where I'm supposed to be!" Lani shot back. "If you'd bothered to be at rehearsal, you'd know that."

"I don't need rehearsals to know that you're totally making a shadow on my face. You need to move back."

"Any farther behind you, and I'd be invisible to the camera!"

"Good, maybe then they wouldn't have to see that zit growing on your chin."

Lani gasped, her hands flying to her face.

"Geez, nice kid," Cal mumbled in my ear.

I waved him off, shushing him as the director yelled, "Makeup!"

One of the ladies in overalls immediately descended upon the brunette with a pot full of flesh-colored goo, as the girl ducked her head, her cheeks a bright pink.

"And can we get another light in here?" the director asked, pointing toward Jennifer. "Everyone else, take five," he said with a resigned wave of his hand. As he walked away I could hear him mumbling to himself, "Or ten, or twenty. Not that it matters, we're so far behind already . . ."

The crew scattered, and Jennifer happily sauntered off set.

I nudged Cal in the ribs. "I'm going in."

I did a quick jog over the camera tracks, watching Jennifer as she slipped out the side door. A minute later I followed, squinting in the sunshine, a harsh contrast to the darkened set. I spied Jennifer a few feet away, sipping an iced latte. Though where she got it from, I had no idea. There didn't seem to be anyone else around, let alone a Starbucks. The magic of being a teen-ebrity.

"Hey? Jennifer, right?" I asked, approaching the actress. I noticed Cal move off to my right, trying to blend into the scenery. Luckily, Jennifer didn't seem to notice, too engrossed in her creamy drink.

"Yep," she answered, slurping through her straw.

"How's the shooting going?"

Jennifer shot me a wary look. "Fine. Who are you again?"

"Samantha Stevens. I'm on that new Steven Bochco show, two doors down," I said, waving my hand in a very vague direction.

Luckily, Jennifer didn't seem to need specifics. "Oh. Right," she said, between sips. "Yeah, I heard that's a really cool show."

"Well, it's no *Pippi Mississippi*."

She shot me a wan smile. "Right, like the Emmys are gonna be calling me any day now."

"Hey, you won a Kid's Choice Award! That's awesome. Besides, you're wicked popular," I said, laying it on thick. "I see your name all over the place."

"All over kid's lunchboxes."

"No, just the other day I was reading about you in the *Informer*," I said, carefully gauging her reaction. "In Tina Bender's column."

Jennifer snorted. "That trash?"

'Kay, if people didn't stop dissing me this way, I was likely to get a complex.

"Not a fan of Tina's, huh?"

Jennifer shook her head. "That's putting it mildly. Let's just say, if she got hit by a bus tomorrow, I wouldn't be crying any."

That's it—she was off my Facebook friend list.

"I saw that bit she ran about you at the Martini Room," I said, goading her on. "So mean!"

Jennifer nodded vigorously, her blonde bangs bobbing up and down. "I know, right? She said I smoked 'Mary Jane'? I didn't even know what Mary Jane was. I had to google it!"

"But you *were* holding the joint," I couldn't help myself from pointing out.

Her face reddened. "Kinda, I guess."

"So . . ." I worded my next question carefully. "That party at the Martini Room, that was the night before last, right?"

She shook her head. "No, the after-party was the night before that. Two nights ago I was at Ashlee's housewarming party."

Bingo. Houston, we have an alibi. "Ashlee . . . Simpson?"

"Well, duh!"

I hated teenagers. "How late were you there?"

She shot me a look. "Why do you care?"

"Well . . . I was there, too! Just wondering how we missed each other."

Jennifer shrugged. "I dunno, maybe one. All the champagne gave me a headache."

The perils of being a star.

Unfortunately, one was late enough. Okay, it wasn't totally outside the realm of reality that she could have snuck out, made the call, then snuck back in. But I found it unlikely she could have done it at the party without someone noticing the robotic voice emanating from the next room. I remembered the way Max had poked his head up over the partition when I used it. It wasn't something you heard every day. Never mind the fact that the call had come from PW Enterprises and not "Jen's Cell Phone."

A PA picked that moment to pop his head out the stage door. "Miss Wood? They're ready for you."

Jennifer sucked the last of her latte through the straw, then set her empty cup down on the ground. "Gotta run," she said. "Catch you later, Sylvia."

"Samantha."

She gave me a bored look that clearly said, "Who cares?" then pulled open the side door.

"Nice meeting you!" I called after her.

But she was already inside.

Automatically, I picked up Jennifer's cup and tossed it into the nearest garbage can.

"Any luck?" Cal asked, joining me as I walked back toward our golf cart.

"Not much." I filled him in on Jennifer's story. "So far all I know is people aren't fond of me and everyone goes to better parties than I do."

"Cheer up. It's not everyone who has their own stalker." Cal threw an arm around my shoulders. It was a casual gesture, but it made me acutely aware of the heat coming off his skin.

"Gee. I feel much better now," I countered, trying to decide whether I liked or disliked that heat.

Before I could come to any solid conclusions, he pulled away and hopped in the golf cart again. I joined him and held on to the white roll bar as he deftly maneuvered through the sets.

"Okay," Cal said, "so Katie doesn't own a computer—"

"So she says."

"—and Jennifer was at Ashlee's house."

"So she says."

"Any way to check that out?"

"I was just about to do that." I grabbed my cell, quickly dialing Marco's number. He picked it up on the third ring.

"Fernando's salon, how may I help you?"

"Hey, Marco, it's Tina. Listen, party at Ashlee Simpson's two nights ago. Know anything about it?"

"Does Coach make handbags? Of course I do!"

"Were you there?" I asked, mentally crossing my fingers.

"Well, no," he conceded. "But my friend Maddie's friend Dana's boyfriend Ricky was. He's in Ash's latest video."

"Perfect! I need to know if Jennifer Wood was at the party. Think you can find out?"

"I'm on it, dahling!"

"Love ya," I said, doing a smooch into the phone before flipping it shut. Then I turned to Cal. "Alibi checking in motion."

"Great. Who's next on our list?"

I looked down at my watch.

"Uh, actually, I think I need to call it a day."

He raised an eyebrow at me. "Got a hot date?"

I scoffed. "Hardly. I have to get home to my aunt."

"The lady with the tracksuits?"

"You *were* spying on me last night!"

"I was keeping an eye on you."

"Through binoculars."

"Yes."

"Aimed at my windows."

"Yes."

I shook my head, indignation oozing from every pore. "That is such an invasion of privacy."

"That's my job," he calmly replied, pulling the

golf cart up to the lot and switching it out for the Hummer.

"Well, then your job sucks!"

"Says the girl who publicly trashes people for a living."

"Hey, those people deserved to be trashed. You do stupid stuff, someone's gonna point it out," I replied, hoisting myself back into the truck.

He shot me a look. "Remind me to behave around you."

"Yeah, well you can start by ditching the binoculars, buddy," I shot back.

We rode the rest of the way home in silence. A long silence. It was rush hour in L.A. We were lucky to move an inch in twenty minutes. I was seriously jonesing for my Rebel when we got stuck behind a pileup on the 101. How easily I could have weaved between the cars and simply zipped my way home. Instead, I was stuck in a tank, getting dirty looks from every eco-friendly Prius driver who passed us.

By the time we pulled up to Oasis Terrace, I was tired, hungry, and really had to pee.

"Well, thanks for the ride," I said, throwing open the door and dropping the two feet to the ground.

"I'll walk you in."

"You really don't need to," I protested.

"I'd feel better if I did." And before I could stop him, Cal had beeped the car locked and was already following me up the front path.

"Look, I'm a big girl. I think I can walk myself to my front d—" But I trailed off as we approached the condo.

The door was open. The wood splintered near the handle as if someone had kicked the thing in. Hard.

I felt my heart jump into my throat, the breath suddenly knocked out of me as my mind latched on to one horrible thought.

Aunt Sue.

Chapter Seven

Cal reacted immediately. In an instant his gun was in his hands, held straight-armed out in front of him, his stance low and guarded, one hand holding me back as he slowly approached the door.

Not that I was going anywhere. In fact, my entire body felt frozen with dread, my feet suddenly encased in lead. My breath sped up as I watched Cal slowly push the door open and ease inside the condo.

God, if anything happened to Aunt Sue . . .

No. I didn't even want to think about that. I shut my eyes, giving myself a mental big-girl talk, then followed a step behind Cal, adrenaline backing up in my chest at what horrible sight might greet me.

The kitchen was trashed. Cupboards open, pots and pans strewn all over the floor, broken glass in the sink, an entire box of spaghetti noodles dumped over the counters. And the living room hadn't fared much better—coffee table overturned, vases smashed, sofa cushions slashed, the stuffing bulging grotesquely out their sides.

I watched as Cal slowly circled the room, then entered the bedroom on the left, Aunt Sue's. I held my breath, tension building in every part of me.

"What in God's name happened here?"

I jumped. And may have even peed my pants a little.

I spun around to find Aunt Sue standing in the doorway, her eyes bulging behind her bifocals.

"Oh, thank God!" I rushed her like a linebacker, squeezing her in a hug that had her making strangled little gurgling noises in the back of her throat. "You're okay!"

"Of course I'm okay," she mumbled, disentangling herself.

I sniffed back a tear of relief. "Where were you?"

"At Hattie's. I was trying to get her lasagna recipe, but the old bat wouldn't let it go. Said her mother brought it from the old country. Baloney. I know for a fact she got that sucker off the back of a Ragu jar."

I couldn't help it. I hugged her again.

"What happened here?" she asked, her gaze pinging around the room, unsure where to focus.

"I don't know," I answered honestly. "I think someone broke in."

"Wait, what was that?" Aunt Sue asked. "That sound?"

I froze. But before I could answer her, Aunt Sue picked up a frying pan off the counter and lunged toward me, screaming like a banshee.

On instinct, I ducked.

Unfortunately, the guy behind me didn't.

"I got him!" Aunt Sue yelled, a sickening crunch filling the apartment as her frying pan connected with his nose.

"No!" I grabbed Aunt Sue's arm, pulling her back.

Cal grabbed his nose. "Sonofabitch!" he groaned.

"Oh, God, Aunt Sue, that's not the intruder. That's Cal."

She cocked her little pink head to the side. "Who's Cal?"

"My bodyguard." I grabbed a towel from the kitchen, quickly pressing it to Cal's nose, which was oozing red stuff all over the linoleum. Not good.

"Are you okay?"

"I think she broke it," he said, sounding like he had a cold.

"Why do you need a bodyguard?" Aunt Sue asked.

I snatched the frying pan from her hand. "Because someone's been threatening me. Do you need to sit down?" I asked Cal.

He shook his head. "Ice."

I picked my way over the broken debris on the floor, filling another towel with cubes from the icemaker.

"Who'd want to threaten you?" Aunt Sue asked, her wary gaze still ping-ponging between the frying pan and Cal.

"Someone who doesn't like my column. Here." I handed Cal the icy towel. As he switched them out, I got a good look at his nose. Yikes. Marcia Brady had nothing on this guy. He was right. I think she broke it.

Cal winced as the cold hit him. "Thanks."

"Sorry," I said. Then nudged Aunt Sue in the ribs.

"Sorry," she echoed.

Cal looked from Aunt Sue to me, to the frying pan. "That's it. I'm charging Felix double."

Three hours later we'd eaten pizza for the second night in a row—much to Aunt Sue's delight—managed to clean most of the broken glass off the floor, and I'd explained as best I could to Aunt Sue what was going on with my creepy caller turned vandal. Not that I was entirely convinced she'd remember by tomorrow.

After promising that I'd call a locksmith to fix the front door, I tucked her into bed with Tom Brokaw in the background to lull her to sleep.

I came back out into the living room to find an open bottle of wine, two full glasses, and Cal trying to shove the stuffing back inside the sofa cushions.

"It may be time for a new couch," he said.

"Ya think?" I sank down onto the only unmolested cushion, leaning my head back against the wall. If this day had been any longer, it would qualify for Guinness.

"Thought maybe you could use a drink," he said, handing me a glass.

Oh, mama, could I. Gratefully, I sipped at it. "Thanks."

"You okay?" Cal asked, righting the coffee table in front of me. I put my feet up on it.

"I will be."

"Nothing's missing. No one was hurt. Chances are whoever did this just wanted to scare you."

I nodded. Though I hated to admit just what an effective job they'd done. While my heart rate had slowed, my hands were still shaky enough that my merlot was bouncing in its glass.

"I'll be fine," I repeated. Hoping I'd believe that at some point.

"Right," he said. "But, just as a precaution, I'd feel better if your aunt wasn't here alone tomorrow."

I nodded. "I'm sure I can find someone to sit with her."

"Good." He paused, picking up a bent picture frame from the rug. He looked down at the image inside, his lips curling into a lopsided smile. "This you?"

He held it up. A little girl with dark hair and pigtails sat on a pink Big Wheel. Wearing a tutu, cowboy boots, and a plastic Viking hat.

I nodded. "Yep."

"Cute." He placed it on the coffee table. "Even then you had your own style, didn't you?"

I looked down at my funky T-shirt. Was he making fun of the way I dressed? "So sue me if I'm not an Abercrombie zombie."

Cal put both hands up in a surrender gesture. "Take it easy, Bender. I didn't say I didn't like it."

I bit my lip. "Sorry. Guess I'm a little on edge."

"Apology accepted. And I'm glad you're on edge."

"Gee, thanks."

"I'd be worried if you weren't. When you're on edge, you'll be careful."

I nodded. "Right," I croaked out, my throat suddenly clogged with emotion at how real this whole situation had become. Annoying phone calls and emails were one thing, but this guy had actually broken into my home. What would he have done if he'd found me, or worse yet, Aunt Sue?

"The guy your father?" Cal pointed to another photo, this one of my pigtailed self and a dark-haired man in khakis beside a palm tree.

Grateful for the change of subject, I cleared the thickness from my throat. "Yeah. He and my mom are both archeologists. When I was little, I used to travel all over with them."

"Must have been fun." He sat down on the sofa next to me.

"It was. Most of the time."

"Only most of the time?" He shifted to face me, the movement causing his thigh to rub against mine. Making me acutely aware of just how close he was sitting. It stirred a feeling in my stomach that was somewhere between incredibly uncomfortable and kinda excited. I tried to shrug it off.

"Well, it was cool being the only kid in third grade who'd been in an actual Egyptian pharaoh's tomb. But the traveling meant I didn't exactly have an ordinary childhood."

He cocked his head, his eyes assessing.

It was kind of unnerving, and I felt myself fighting the urge to fidget. I took another sip of wine.

Finally he said, "An ordinary childhood would have bored the shit out of you."

I laughed. "Yeah, you're probably right."

He gave the picture one more glance before reaching across me to set it back on the end table . . . and I felt his arm brush against my chest. I bit the inside of my cheek against the not-completely-unpleasant feeling. How sad was it that was the most action I'd gotten in months?

"Tell me more," he prompted, completely unaware of my body's alarms going off beside him. He leaned casually back into the sofa cushions.

"Uh, more?" I cleared my throat, my voice suddenly husky. Jesus, who was I, Lauren Bacall? It was an accidental touch. I needed to get a grip.

"About your childhood. You spent time in Egypt. Where else?"

"Oh. Um . . . well, there were the catacombs in France. That was a fun summer. Then the year we spent in Peru excavating Incan ruins."

"Your parents had eclectic tastes."

"They're both forensic anthropologists. They specialize in figuring out how people died. Everywhere you find ruins, there are dead people."

"Kind of morbid."

I shook my head. "Not at all. It was fascinating. Learning about how they lived, how they worked, how they died. It was all connected. It was like a private glimpse into their lives."

"Hence your fascination with other people's lives."

I grinned. "I guess I've always been interested in gossip, huh?"

"What about your life?" Cal asked, cocking his head at me.

"What about it?"

"There don't seem to be any photos past the age of pigtails. For all your fascination with other people's lives, I don't see evidence of much of a life of your own."

"Ouch."

He grinned. "I didn't mean it that way. What do you like to do?"

"Work, I guess."

"What do you do on the weekends?"

"I don't know." I shifted in my seat, the sudden Dr. Phil analysis unnerving me. I wasn't sure I really liked looking that deeply into myself. Let alone letting someone like Cal look. "Ordinary stuff."

He leaned in close, so close I could feel the heat radiating off his chest, smell the faint scent of wine on his lips. His eyes went dark, intense, like he could, in fact, see right into my psyche. Then his voice went low and intimate.

"I have a feeling there's nothing ordinary about you, Bender."

For a second I was terrified that he was going to kiss me. Terrified, because I had no idea whether I'd kiss him back.

Luckily, before I had a chance to decide, he stood, picking up another abused cushion from the floor.

"I think I should sleep here tonight."

My breath caught in my throat. Shit, had my thoughts been that plain on my face?

As if he could read my mind, the corner of his mouth quirked upward. "On the couch."

Right. I cleared my throat. "Um, yeah. Sure, yeah. That would be fine."

I got up, wiping my sweaty palms on my jeans, and grabbed a couple blankets from the hall closet, throwing them down on the sofa.

"So, um, bathroom's in there, fresh towels under the sink if you need them."

Cal nodded. "Thanks."

"So . . . good night." I did an awkward little wave in his direction.

He smiled, his eyes still giving me that look like he could see right through me. "'Night, Bender."

I quickly hightailed it to my bedroom, ignoring the mess of clothes and papers and files the intruder had made of my floor. Instead, I kicked off my shoes, stripped off my jeans, and jumped in bed. I slipped under the covers in my T-shirt, feeling just how tired the drain of earlier adrenaline had left me. I closed my eyes, letting the distant sounds of the freeway lull me to sleep.

It wasn't until I was just drifting off that I realized I'd completely missed my cyber date with Man in Black.

I awoke the next morning to the sound of Matt Lauer's voice coming from my living room full blast. Reluctantly, I peeled myself out of bed and stumbled though the bedroom door. I'm not exactly what you'd call a morning person. I'm more of a don't-talk-to-me-until-I've-hooked-up-my-coffee-IV person. Preferably after noon.

"Jesus, what is that racket?" I asked, stumbling into the living room.

On the sofa sat Aunt Sue, clad in a fuzzy powder blue bathrobe and matching slippers, and beside her Cal, arms folded over his chest, hair still wet from his shower, his nose just slightly swollen still. Light stubble lined his jaw, telling me he'd been too macho to use the pink razors in the bathroom. Though the five o'clock shadow was a good look on him. Instinctively, my hand went to my bed head, trying in vain to smooth the errant strands.

On the end table was the source of the full-blast *Today* show airing—Aunt Sue's hearing aid, conspicuously *not* in her ear.

"You're going to wake the entire neighborhood," I pointed out, crossing the room. Cal's eyes followed me, and I suddenly wished I'd stopped to throw on a pair of jeans first. Instead, I tugged at the hem of my T-shirt, willing it to cover my butt.

It almost complied.

"'Morning, peanut," Aunt Sue said, her eyes riveted to the cooking segment.

"'Morning."

"What?"

"I said, 'morning,'" I yelled. "Why aren't you wearing your hearing aid?"

She gave me a blank look.

"Your hea-ring ai-d," I repeated, pointing to it.

She waved me off. "I don't need that thing. I can hear the TV just fine."

"So can Canada. Can you turn it down?"

"What?"

"Down! Turn it down!"

"Actually, yes, I'd love some coffee, thanks."

I threw my hands up. It was useless. "I'm gonna take a shower," I muttered instead.

"With cream," Aunt Sue shouted after me.

I ignored her, instead shutting the bathroom door behind me with a click.

The room was still warm and steamy from Cal's shower, a lingering scent left behind that was subtle yet very clearly male. As I stepped into the spray of water, I couldn't help thinking that just moments ago his naked body had been where mine was now. An odd awareness tingled in my belly.

Yeah, I really needed to get laid, didn't I?

I shook it off, opening the tiny window over the bathtub to let the steam out as I lathered my hair.

Twenty minutes later I was washed, dried, dressed in jeans, a pair of hot pink converse (yes, I owned them in multiple colors), and a white button-down shirt. I swear it had nothing to do with the way Cal had looked at me last night that I matched it with a hot pink bra that showed just the slightest bit underneath. Nothing at all.

I emerged from my bedroom to find Aunt Sue now engrossed in *Regis and Kelly*, a cup of java in hand. Cal was manning Mr. Coffee, and as soon as he saw me, he pulled down another mug, filling it to the brim with sweet life-giving liquid. I'll admit, I was beginning to warm to the guy.

"My fault," he said, gesturing to Aunt Sue.

"What is?"

"I told her she looked too young to need a hearing aid."

I rolled my eyes. "Way to go, Romeo."

He grinned. "Sorry."

"Apology accepted. But," I warned, "only because you made coffee."

As soon as I was semicoherent, I pulled out my cell, called a locksmith, then began running through my address book for someone who could sit with Aunt Sue that day. Unfortunately, my cousin Brad had to take his dog to the vet. Aunt Sue's daughter, Catherine, was at Magic Mountain with the kids. My uncle Don was going golfing. Suddenly everyone had dentist visits or dry cleaning to pick up or belly button lint that needed removing. Apparently word had spread of my aunt's cooking.

In the end, there was only one person on the list who had the day off and was willing to spend it watching Game Show Network at top volume. Aunt Sue's older sister, Millie.

"Tina, look how much you've grown," Aunt Millie

said half an hour later when I answered the front door. She immediately began pinching my cheeks and making clucking sounds at how skinny I was.

Millie was dressed in a frilly turquoise blouse, turquoise slacks, and a pair of huge white sneakers fastened by Velcro. A turquoise cap studded with rhinestones sat on top of her white hair, tiny wisps escaping on the sides. Her face was such a series of wrinkles it was hard to tell where her chin ended and her neck began, and the top of her head only came to about my shoulders. It was as if someone had taken a normal-sized person and left her out in the sun until she'd shriveled into this raisin of a woman. A pair of very dark eyes squinted behind the thickest glasses known to man, bouncing from me to Cal.

Cal raised a questioning eyebrow my way.

"Cal, I'd like you to meet my aunt Millie. Aunt Millie, this is Cal."

Millie looked up at him, her eyes magnified to twice their size behind her super glasses. "He's hot."

I could swear I almost saw Cal blush.

"So, where's my baby sister?" she asked, eyes scanning the condo.

"In the living room." I took Aunt Millie by the shoulders, pointing her in the right direction.

"I see her." Millie nodded, then shuffled up to a floor lamp and started making conversation.

Cal grabbed me by the sleeve. "Okay, what's granny doing here?"

"I told you I'd get someone to watch Aunt Sue today."

"*This* is your bodyguard?"

"I never said bodyguard."

"She's a hundred."

"She's only eighty-nine. And she's very sharp."

Cal threw his hands up. "Oh, well then!"

"Look," I said, "she's all I could get on short notice."

"May I remind you that someone broke in here last night? What about taking this threat seriously?"

"I know she's no Rambo. But she's very spry. Aunt Millie was an Olympic fencer in her day."

"And which century would that day be in?"

"She's sharp," I repeated.

"She's talking to a lamp."

I pursed my lips together. "Okay, she's a little nearsighted. But she's got a mind like a steel trap."

He ran a hand through his hair. "I don't have a good feeling about this."

I followed his gaze, watching as Aunt Millie navigated around the lamp and bent down to pet one of Aunt Sue's fuzzy slippers, murmuring, "Nice kitty."

"I *really* don't have a good feeling about this," he repeated.

"Hey, you said yourself, it was probably just someone trying to scare me. What are the chances I'll get scared twice?"

Cal didn't look entirely convinced. Especially as he watched Aunt Millie greet her sister.

"Sue, darling, when did you get a cat?"

Aunt Sue cocked her head to the side. "What?"

"The cat. When did you get the cat?"

"Speak up."

"Cat! I like your cat!"

"Oh. Why, yes, I did notice your hat."

Cal shot me a look. Then shook his head, mumbling, "God help the guy who tries to break in here."

* * *

"So, what's the plan today?" Cal asked, once we'd left the gruesome twosome happily chatting about Sudoku and blood pressure medication.

"Well, Blain Hall's next on our list," I replied.

"Blain Hall," he rolled the name over his tongue. "Where's he drying out?"

"Sunset Shores. It's a chi-chi place in Malibu."

"You think they'll let us in to see him?"

I scoffed. "Not a chance. But if he's our guy, he had to have hired someone else to make that first call. The PW number was a landline and, I already checked, it's not associated with Sunset Shores."

"That's pretty risky. Hiring someone to do your dirty work in a town where everyone squeals to the press eventually."

"Yeah, well, Blain isn't exactly known for his brilliant decisions. Hence the rehab."

"You think he called this accomplice and told him what to say?"

I shook my head. "No, all calls coming in or going out are monitored. It would have had to be someone who visited Blain in person. We need to get a look at his guest log."

"They'll let you do that?"

I gave him a wink. "Oh, I have my ways."

Chapter Eight

Malibu is about thirty-five miles north of L.A. proper, along the historic Pacific Coast Highway, which hugs the California coastline in single lanes. And which between the hours of three and eight resembles a parking lot. Thankfully, at ten in the morning, things were relatively free of traffic heading north. Relatively. We were still stuck behind a slow Mercedes (hybrid of course—this was, after all, L.A.) the entire way. Though, in the towering oil hog, we were a good three feet above the car, a completely unobstructed view of the morning sun glinting off the ocean as we snaked past crab shacks, brightly colored sushi joints, and towering glass-walled mansions.

Half an hour later we rolled up to the Sunset Shores rehabilitation clinic. Of course, the term clinic was completely misleading. This was nothing like the crowded waiting room of the place that gave out free condoms in Burbank. This looked like something out of a Club Med brochure. Only nicer.

Huge glass windows spanned the front of the building, capitalizing on the natural California sunshine. Dark woods framed the structure, punctuated by palm trees and flowering agapanthus circling the perfectly manicured lawn. A small slate fountain with three coy fish circling in the pond at its base sat off to one side of the ornately carved front doors.

Cal did a low whistle. "Nice place."

"No kidding. It has a nice price tag, too. Rumor has it, two weeks here is more than my yearly salary."

"I'm in the wrong business."

Cal pulled up the circular drive and handed his keys to the valet before we pushed inside the impressive mahogany doors.

The interior smelled faintly of lavender and Pine Sol as we made our way across the expanse of marble floor to the large granite counter spanning reception. A young woman dressed more like a cruise director than a nurse sat behind it, typing away at a computer. She looked up as we approached, a name tag reading "Sandy" visible on her lapel.

"May I help you?" she inquired in a soft, evenly modulated voice that I'm sure the patients found very soothing.

"I hope so," I answered. "My name is . . . Laura. Laura Petrie. This is my associate, Rob," I said, gesturing to Cal. "We work with Blain Hall's publicist."

The receptionist nodded. "How can I help you, Laura?"

"Well, we're trying to head off a little potential trouble before the media gets wind of it. We'd be extremely grateful if you could help us, Sandy."

Her brows furrowed, creating teeny lines on her forehead that suggested she'd yet to hit that thirty-year mark when, in Hollywood, Botox became as necessary as flossing. "What sort of trouble?"

"I'm sorry," I said, straightening my spine. "We're not at liberty to discuss that."

Sandy looked disappointed. "Oh. Well, I'm not sure how I could help."

"We need to know if Blain has had any visitors recently. Say, in the past three days? You do keep logs?"

She nodded slowly. "Yes, we do," she agreed hesitantly. "But they're private."

"I understand, I really do. But this could mean the end of his career if this got out. It could be, well, tabloid suicide. And, I'm sure you can agree, that's the last thing he needs right now when he should be focusing on his recovery."

She nodded. "I understand. But the records are private and . . ."

"Let me level with you, Sandy," I said, leaning both elbows on the desk. Instinctively she leaned back a fraction. "If I have your word that you won't tell a soul—I mean a single solitary soul—I'll tell you what we're dealing with here."

Sandy immediately perked up, nodding vigorously. "I swear." She leaned in close. "What is it?"

"Okay." I made a big show of looking over both shoulders, then leaned in again. "A woman has come forward claiming that she's pregnant with Blain Hall's baby."

"No!" Though I could see her eyes light up like Christmas.

No one is immune to the power of good gossip.

I nodded. "Yes! This certain woman claims she's been seeing Blain for the past year, that they're currently an item. Well, I tell you this is the first I've heard of it."

"Who is she?" Sandy asked.

I shook my head. "I can't say."

"Oh." Her shoulders slumped.

"But I will tell you . . ."

She leaned in again.

". . . she *rocks*."

Sandy gave me a blank stare.

"And she's like a *dog* with a bone with this *dirty* story."

Again with the blank stare.

I mentally threw my hands up in surrender. "It's Cherry Chase. The Dirty Dog's bassist?"

Sandy gasped. "No!"

I nodded. "Yes." Okay, a total fabrication. As far as I knew Cherry and Blain were the proverbial "just friends." But she'd totally denied me an interview backstage at their latest concert, so I only felt the teeniest bit guilty throwing her under the gossip bus now.

"Wow, no wonder they have such chemistry on stage," Sandy mused.

"But you didn't hear it from me," I reminded her.

"Riiight." She winked at me.

"Anyway, we need to know if there's any truth to this before it gets out to the media. And having Blain's visitor records sure would help us out a lot."

Sandy nodded. "Absolutely."

"You can see why this is a very delicate matter that must be handled with the utmost discretion."

She nodded again. "Totally. Let me see if I can find those records for you. Hang on."

"Thanks," I shot back as she disappeared behind a pair of heavy oak doors.

I stood up to find Cal shaking his head at me.

"What?"

"You're good."

I grinned. "Thanks."

"I'm not sure it's a compliment. Does the truth ever fall between those lips of yours?"

I shrugged. "It's fifty-fifty."

He shook his head again.

A beat later Sandy reappeared with a wide notebook, lines of dates and times written on it.

"He's had two visitors." Sandy stabbed at a line halfway down the page. "Three days ago, his manager, Jerry Leventhal, and yesterday a Tak Davis."

I stared at the signatures. Tak was the drummer of the Dirty Dogs. The perfect friend to bring Blain contraband coke in rehab or threaten his enemies in the media. Unfortunately, our mystery call had come in two days before his visit.

Which left Jerry Leventhal.

"Does this help?" Sandy asked, her eyebrows raised expectantly.

I nodded. "It does. Immensely, Sandy. You've been an incredible help."

Cal and I turned to go.

"But, does that mean the baby isn't his?" Sandy hounded.

I bit my lip. I couldn't help it. Blain was too easy a target. "Oh, it's his alright. But, shhhh, don't tell anyone, 'kay?"

Right. I gave it five minutes before she was on the phone to every girlfriend she had. Poor Blain. If he wasn't such a douche, I might have felt sorry for him.

"So, I gotta ask," Cal said as we pushed through the front doors and handed the valet our ticket, "where do you get these names?"

"What?"

"The fake names you keep giving people."

I grinned. "Sixties sitcom stars. Jeannie, Samantha Stevens from *Bewitched*, Laura and Rob Petrie from *The Dick Van Dyke Show*."

Cal threw his head back and laughed. "Aren't you worried someone will catch on?"

"You didn't."

"Touché." He gave me a sidelong grin as we climbed back into his tank. "So, this Leventhal character? You know him?"

I frowned. "Not really. Reps maybe half a dozen acts, but they're mostly small time. Except for the Dogs."

"Know where to find him?"

"No, but—"

"Let me guess, you know someone who does?"

I grinned. "You catch on quick, Cal."

I pulled my cell from my purse and immediately started dialing. By the time we hit L.A. again, I'd cleverly bartered premier night tickets to Katie Briggs's new movie for the unlisted address of Leventhal's offices on Wilshire.

I was about to plug it into Cal's GPS when my cell rang again in my hand.

"Bender?" I answered.

"Think maybe you wanna show up for work sometime today?"

Felix. And he didn't sound happy.

"I'm . . . working in the field today."

"Cal with you?" he asked.

"Yes."

"Good. Then both of you can get back here."

"Look, you gave me three days," I reminded him.

"I also gave you Pines."

"And?"

I heard the sound of teeth gnashing together on the other end. "Don't you read the news?"

"Uh . . ."

"Jesus, Bender! That kid who was in Pines's last movie? Came forward this morning saying that Pines asked him to pose for inappropriate photos while on the set."

"Sonofa—" I caught myself just in time, remembering I was fresh out of quarters for the Swear Pig. "—goat."

"No kidding. Allie's been hounding his publicist for a comment all day."

I cringed. The blonde was showing me up big time. "I'll be right there."

I flipped my phone shut, shoving it back into my purse. "Change of plans," I told Cal. "We're going back to the *Informer*."

He raised an eyebrow my way. "Everything okay?"

"Peachy."

He shot me a look. "I notice you didn't tell Felix about last night's break-in."

"No. I didn't. And I'd appreciate it if you didn't either."

"He's going to find out sooner or later."

"Let's hope for later. Like after I've scooped Barbie."

Again with the look. But, thankfully, he didn't ask, instead, making a U-turn (no small task in a Hummer) on Pico and flipping back toward Hollywood.

Ten minutes later we were riding the elevator to the second floor. The doors slid open, and immediately I could feel the energy of a hot story crackling in the air.

Cam was laying photos out on the conference room table, Cece running back and forth from cubicles to the boss's office with all the latest developments, Felix shouting orders in rapid succession, threatening jobs if someone didn't get him an exclusive. And everywhere phones rang one after the other as reporters tried to get hold of the boy's publicist, his other co-stars, the parents, the tutor, the former nanny, anyone who could be quoted as an "intimate source." It was a race to find the winning angle that would land you above the fold.

Immediately I plopped myself in front of my computer and went to work, booting up my address book and sending emails like a mad woman to my network of informants. Even as I hit send on the third one, replies started to trickle in. As one after another popped into my inbox, it became clear the news was buzzing all over Hollywood. And I felt like a total lout for being the last to know the latest developing break on my own story. Felix was right—what kind of reporter was I?

"Hey, Bender," Max said, poking his head up over the top of his partition.

"Yeah?" I asked, though I didn't take my eyes from the screen as two more emails popped in.

"You know that guy in the movie with Pines and the kid? Jake Mullins? The one who played the kid's dad?"

"Yeah, sure," I replied.

"Turns out he died last month."

I paused, giving the old man my full attention. "No shit?"

"Just found the obit in my archives."

"How'd he go?"

"OD'ed. Prescription sleeping meds."

"Wow."

"You gotta be careful how many of those things you take."

"You ever taken them?" I asked.

He shook his head, jowls wiggling with aftershocks. "Not me. Bourbon does the trick."

I'll bet. "Anyone look into this death?" I asked. "Was there an investigation?"

Max shrugged. "Don't know. ME called it an accident at the time, but I doubt any official ruling has been made yet."

"Bender!"

My head snapped around at the sound of Felix hailing me from the conference room.

"Thanks for the tip, Max," I called over my shoulder as I jumped to the boss's call.

The surface of the conference room table was covered with photos of Pines (publicity shots, poses at last year's Oscars, his mug shot) and pics of the boy who'd starred in his last movie, a short kid with light hair and freckles across his nose. A regular Dennis the Menace. In the center was a candid photo taken on the set of the film last spring. Pines had a big smile pasted on his face, his arm around the boy as they posed next to a camera. Yesterday, it would have been a completely innocent photo of a boy and his mentor. Today, it took on a sickly sinister quality.

"We're leading with this," Felix said, pointing to the photo. "Cam's going to try to get a couple more of the kid today. She's staking out his school later."

Cameron nodded in agreement, her eyes solemn as she stared down at the boy's face.

"We need a piece to run beside it. Allie's been working the co-stars angle, trying to get info on how much time Pines spent alone with the little guy."

"Great, I'll take over," I said.

Felix gave me a hard look. "Allie's already working this story."

I put my hands on my hips. "But it's *my* story."

"You were sharing it. And today you were nowhere to be found, leaving the new girl to pick up all the slack. Allie's working it."

"You are not giving my front-page story away to a pair of tits you just hired!" I yelled.

Felix clenched his jaw, his eyes going hard beneath his brows.

Oops. Maybe too far? "Look, Felix—"

But he'd heard enough from me, cutting me off mid-sentence. "She's a good reporter. You, on the other hand, made a major blunder today. You didn't even know what was going on with *your* story."

"Well, excuse me. I guess getting my condo broken into kept me a little goddamned busy!"

Two heads whipped my way.

"Oh, hell."

"Someone broke into your condo?" Felix growled, a little vein in his forehead starting to pulse.

"Uh . . . well, *broke* is a strong word. Maybe they kinda just . . ."

"Did you know about this?" he asked.

I turned around to find Cal standing in the doorway behind me.

He looked from me to Felix. Then slowly nodded.

"Christ," Felix swore, running a hand through

his unruly mop of hair. "No one tells me anything anymore."

"There's really nothing to tell," I protested. "I mean, they hardly even touched anything."

"That true?" Felix asked over my shoulder.

Again Cal's eyes bopped between Felix and me. Only this time he shook his head in the negative.

Great. Thanks a lot.

"Alright, I want all the details." Felix crossed his arms over his chest. "What happened, Bender?"

So, I told him. Which wasn't much. The door had been forced. Nothing taken, that I could tell, everything trashed.

"It was just a warning," I said, repeating what Cal had said the night before. "I'm fine."

Felix didn't answer, just stared, that vein pulsing double-time.

"But you can see how I've been a little preoccupied this morning."

"Which is exactly why you should hand this whole thing over to the cops and do your job."

I bit my lip. "I have two more days."

"Right. Two days, in which Allie will be running with the Pines headline."

"But—"

"Unless you've got another lead . . . ?"

I bit my lip, watching my career flash before my eyes in one blonde-haired, blue-eyed, Barbie blur. "Murder!" I blurted out before I could stop myself.

This time three heads whipped my direction, all with matching eyebrows-to-the-ceiling expressions.

"Murder?" Cam asked.

I nodded vigorously. "Max said one of the kid's co-stars on the film died last month. Jake Mullins."

"Jake Mullins." Felix mulled over the name. "I thought he died of an overdose."

"Sleeping pills," I conceded. "But what if it wasn't an accident? What if it was murder? What if it has to do with Pines and the kid? Maybe Mullins saw something inappropriate, and Pines silenced him?" Talk about reaching. Even I was aware that was a whole lot of "if"s. But at the moment, I was ready to invent any story to save my front-page slot.

Felix gave me a long, hard look. Then finally, "Run with it."

I felt a grin break out across my face.

"On it, chief!" I said with a mock salute. I turned to go.

"And, Bender," Felix called.

I turned around.

"Swear Pig. That was at least fifty cents."

As soon as I got back to my desk, I divested my purse of the quarters and popped them in the ceramic pig. Then put in a call to a source at the morgue. Just because the official word was "accident," that didn't mean foul play *couldn't* have been involved. If there was even the slightest chance Mullins had been killed on purpose, I needed to know. I left a message with my favorite former reality show contestant turned morgue technician, then pulled open a search engine, ready to track down my next lead.

"He's right, you know."

I turned to find Cal hovering just over my shoulder.

"Right about what?"

"The police."

I sighed. *Et tu*, Cal?

"Look, I'm fine. I have you, remember?" I said, gesturing to his gym-honed biceps.

"Tina, I don't want you to get hurt."

I bit my lip, telling myself that was not real emotion backing up behind his eyes. I was a client to him. A job. If I got hurt, it meant his reputation went down the toilet, that's all.

"So, do your job," I said, purposefully turning away and focusing on my computer screen. "And let me do mine. In case you didn't notice back there, my butt is on the line."

I tensed for another argument but, instead, looked up to find Cal walking away. He tucked himself behind a desk a few feet away, an unreadable expression masking his face.

Good.

Great.

This whole shadow gig he had going was cramping my style anyway.

I turned back to my screen, trying to ignore how foolish I felt for wearing this hot pink bra, and brought up the main site of the *L.A. Times*.

While the *Informer* was L.A.'s premier tabloid (And, yes, I'm not above stating the obvious. We're not an entertainment magazine, or a media outlet, or a women's periodical. We report on celebrity scandals. Hollywood rumors. Which movie star's beach bod has the most cellulite. We're a total tabloid.), when it came to getting just the facts, ma'am, the *Times* was your best bet.

I pulled up their archives page.

"Hey, Max," I called over the partition.

Max's head popped up again. "Yeah?"

"What was the date on that Mullins obit?"

"Lemme check," he said and disappeared behind the carpeted wall. Two beats later he popped back up. "August. The twenty-sixth."

"Thanks," I called, turning back to my screen and typing the date in. After scanning through several unrelated articles, I finally hit pay dirt with a piece buried in the Arts and Entertainment section.

Turns out Jake Mullins was a character actor best known for his portrayal of the "stern father" in a variety of family films. He'd done a few guest shots on *Law & Order* and *CSI*, but he hadn't rated high enough on the Hollywood food chain for his passing to be front page news. Instead, the little six-inch article stated the bare bones of his overdose, the fact that the preliminary ruling was accident, and the highlight of his short-lived career—playing supporting actor in the latest Pines film. At the end of the article, the reporter noted that Mullins was survived by his wife, Alexis, who was best known for being a child star in the seventies TV show, *The Fenton Family*, about a blended family of musically inclined kids.

Immediately I typed the name "Alexis Mullins" into my People Finder database and came up with an address in Echo Park near Dodger Stadium. I copied it down on a Post-it and grabbed my Strawberry Shortcake purse.

"Where are we going?" Instantly, Cal was at my side. For such a big guy, he had that speedy stealth thing down pat.

"To see Jake Mullins's widow."

"The guy 'if' Pines murdered?" he asked, following me to the elevator.

"Can the sarcasm. Trust me, I know a long shot when I make one up."

"The nice thing about long shots is when they pay off, they pay off big."

I turned on him, expecting to see a mocking smirk on his features. Instead, that same unreadable expression.

"Hmm," I said, making a noncommittal sound in the back of my throat. "Let's hope you're right."

Because there was no way I was letting Barbie win.

Chapter Nine

Echo Park is a quiet suburb off the 5 freeway in the hills near Dodgers Stadium. Quaint little fifties bungalows and seventies apartment buildings clung to the hillsides, dotted with fragrant eucalyptus trees and hearty daisy clusters, flowering despite their proximity to the state's most traveled highway. Alexis Mullins lived in an eight-unit complex behind a Ralph's grocery, just a block up from Sunset. The paint was a dull beige, and the thick shrubbery helped hide the years of smog-induced grime coating the stuccoed walls. A Saturn hybrid and two electric cars sat at the curb. Cal did a U-turn and opted to park his Hummer in the Ralph's parking lot.

"You know, I'd pay good money to see you try to parallel park this thing," I told him.

He grinned. "I'd take your money, Bender, but I know all you carry around in that lunchbox of yours is quarters."

I stuck out my tongue. What could I say? He brought out my mature side.

"By the way," I said as I jumped down from the passenger seat, "thanks for having my back there with Felix."

He beeped the car locked. "The cat was already out of the bag. What did you want me to do, lie for you?"

"Yes!"

He shook his head. "Sorry, Bender, that's your gig."

"Well, then you'd better let me do the talking here."

Alexis's unit was the second on the bottom, wedged under a dark stairwell that had "don't forget your mace" written all over it. I rapped on the door, inhaling the scents of stale curry and cigarette smoke that seem to pervade every pre-1990 apartment complex in California.

I saw a shadow cross the peephole. A few seconds later the door opened a crack, the chain still in place.

"Yeah?" asked a voice, still gravelly with sleep, despite the fact that it was well past noon.

"Hi," I said, doing what I hoped looked like a friendly wave. "My name's . . . Mary Ann. Mary Ann Summers."

"And?" the voice asked. Through the crack I could just make out frizzy blonde hair and a yellow robe.

"I'm . . . an author. I'm writing a book about Hollywood stars who have been taken too young in life. I was wondering if I could talk to you about your husband?"

"Jake?" the woman asked, clearly surprised.

"Yep. Jake. I absolutely loved his work in that last Pines film. What a loss to the acting community."

There was a pause. Then the door shut, and I heard the sound of the chain being slid from the lock before it opened again, this time revealing the occupant behind.

She was taller than me by at least a head, long and lean, and, like 90 percent of Hollywood, her C cups were obviously not natural to her frame. She had green eyes, rimmed in dark circles as if she hadn't slept much lately. An oversized Van Halen T-shirt hung on her bony shoulders while a yellow robe was draped around her, the sash loosely tied in front. And her blonde frizz rivaled my bed head any day.

I guess it had been a while since she'd flashed her girlish dimples on *The Fenton Family*.

She gestured toward a futon-slash-sofa thing, and Cal and I sat as she shut the door, sliding the chain back into place behind us.

"Uh, coffee?" she asked. Then shot a furtive glance at her kitchen, as if having second thoughts about whether or not she actually had coffee.

"No thanks," I quickly said.

"Sorry, I work nights," she said, gesturing to her pajamas. "At the twenty-four-hour deli near the Sunset Studios? It's handy when last-minute auditions come up." She took a seat opposite us on an orange La-Z-Boy chair. It creaked as she tucked her long legs up underneath her.

"You still act?" I asked.

She shrugged. "Here and there. Things have been picking up a bit lately. I've got a callback for a cable movie next week, and VH1 has offered to put me in some celebrity reality series. My agent says all the child stars are staging comebacks these days."

"That's great," I said. Though I was having a hard time picturing her doing the red-carpet glamourista thing at the moment.

"So, what do you want to know about Jake?" she asked. "He was a good actor, but it's not like he's on the walk of fame, you know? He mostly took bit parts."

"Except for the Pines movie."

She nodded. "Yeah. He was stoked about that one."

"How did he land the job?"

"Bastard got lucky." She let out a sharp laugh. "Came into the deli to see me one day and sits down next to this guy eating a turkey on rye. Turns out, the guy is casting director for Pines's latest flick. Jake chats him up, and the next thing I know, he's got the part."

"How did he and Pines get along?"

She shrugged. "Great. They palled around on the set."

I felt my internal radar perk up. Jake was a two-bit actor—guys like Pines were way too high up the Hollywood food chain to waste their time on him. So, what was the common bond that prompted Pines to buddy up with the likes of him? An affinity for kiddie porn, perhaps?

"Did Jake talk about Pines?"

She cocked her head to the side. "Sure. Just the normal stuff. How he was a great director. How the film was going to be phenomenal once they were done."

Hmmm . . . If they had bonded over something shady, it was clear Jake hadn't shared it with his wife. "How long had you and Jake been married?"

"About seven years."

I did a low whistle. Wow. In Hollywood that constituted a silver anniversary. Any marriage that lasted longer than six months was considered a success in this town.

"Can you tell me what happened on the night he . . . passed," I said, trying to sound as compassionate as possible.

She licked her lips, pulling her robe tighter around

her middle. "I was at a party. A friend's birthday. Jake had planned on going with me, but he got an audition for the next morning, so he didn't want to be out late. Instead, he said he was going to go over his lines, then get to sleep early." She licked her lips again. "I should have stayed with him."

"I'm sorry, I know this must be hard."

She nodded. "I'm still not used to him being gone, you know? Like, any second I just expect him to walk in that door. I have to remind myself every day that he won't."

"I'm sorry," I repeated, at a loss for what else to say. I couldn't imagine loving someone that much, then having him suddenly taken away like that. I could tell by the look in her eyes that what she'd felt for her husband was something much deeper than I'd ever experienced. Sure, I loved Aunt Sue, but this was a whole different kind of being wrapped up in someone. And, even though it was currently breaking Alexis Mullins's heart, I couldn't help feeling just a little jealous that she'd known that kind of connection, albeit briefly.

"Shouldn't you be writing this down?"

"What?"

Alexis pointed a finger at me. "For your book. Shouldn't you be writing this down somewhere?"

"Oh. Uh . . ." I looked to Cal for help.

Unfortunately, he just raised one eyebrow at me, as if daring me to come up with a good lie to get out of this one. What women saw in the strong, silent type, I'll never know.

"Uh . . . I'm recording it," I said, quickly pulling my pocket recorder out and holding it up. I hoped she didn't notice it was switched off.

Luckily, she didn't. "Oh. Right."

"You don't mind, do you?" I asked her.

She shook her head. "Whatever."

"The papers said that Jake died from an overdose of sleeping pills. Did he take them regularly?"

"Sometimes. Usually when he had to get up early, like for a shoot or audition. He didn't want to short-change himself on sleep, so he'd take the pills, go to bed early, wake up fresh for the camera the next morning."

"How many pills did Jake usually take?"

"One or two."

"How many did he take that night?"

"I don't know for sure. The police said it looked like he'd taken a handful, at least."

I leaned forward, realizing just how important the answer to this next question was. "Alexis, do you think Jake would have done that? Accidentally taken so many more pills?"

She shrugged. "Look, Jake was no rocket scientist. It's possible he panicked about the audition and took too many."

"Who else knew your husband took sleeping pills?"

She toyed with a piece of lint on the armchair. "I don't know. He didn't exactly keep it a secret."

"Would, say, his coworkers have known? People he was filming with?"

"Probably."

Like Pines. It wasn't exactly conclusive evidence, but it didn't disprove my theory either. Which was a start.

"Who else is in the book?"

"Excuse me?" I asked.

"The book you're writing? Which other deceased stars are in it?"

"Oh . . . uh . . ." I drew a total blank. Where was Max when I needed him? "I wish I could tell you, but my publisher wants me to keep a lid on it until they're ready to put out a press release. You understand."

"Oh." Alexis nodded, even though it was clear she didn't.

"Just one more question," I said, feeling like I was losing my audience here. "Did Jake ever mention anything about the boy who played his son?"

"I guess so. I mean, he said the kid was cute."

"Really? Did Pines think so, too?"

She narrowed her eyes. "Look, I know he's been in some trouble with the law lately, but Pines is still the most powerful director in town. It would be career suicide to say anything negative about him."

I hated to say it, but from the looks of her, it was clear her career had jumped off a tall bridge years ago.

Unfortunately, it was equally clear that if Jake had told his wife about Pines's little fetish, she wasn't sharing.

"Thank you, Mrs. Mullins. I appreciate you taking the time to talk to us," I said, rising.

Cal followed suit, Alexis unwinding herself from her perch to walk us to the door.

"Hey, let me know when the book's out, 'kay? I'd like to have a copy."

"I'll send you one," I lied as she shut the door behind us.

"So," Cal said as we crossed the Ralph's parking lot, "Jake died just like the papers said. Accidental overdose."

"Hello? Did you hear the wife? Pines knew he took sleeping pills. He could have easily poisoned Jake."

"Bender, people make mistakes with this kind of medication all the time. They take a few pills, get drowsy, forget how many they've had, and take a few more."

"A handful? They take a handful more?"

He shrugged, conceding the point. "Okay, so what now?"

I leaned against the Hummer's door, looking out at the busy shoppers pushing carts full of screaming kids and ground chuck.

"Think there's any way we could get in to see Pines?"

"Don't tell me you don't have a prison connection?" Cal teased.

"Very funny. But I'm not exactly sure I'd be on the list of approved visitors."

"Lucky for you, I happen to have a few friends in law enforcement." Cal pulled out his phone. "Let me see what I can do."

Five minutes later he hung up, a look of triumph on his face.

"So?" I asked.

"So, we can see Pines at five."

I looked down at my watch. Two twenty.

"Let's go back to the office." As much as I was dying for that Mullins lead to land me on the front page, I still had a daily column to write. And since Pines wasn't going anywhere, this seemed like an excellent time to do it.

I climbed into the Hummer as Cal beeped the doors open.

"So . . . Mary Ann Summers?" Cal asked, roaring the beast to life.

I grinned. "From *Gilligan's Island.*"

Cal laughed as he slid his shades on. "I guess that makes me the Professor, huh?" He winked at me.

I didn't have the heart to tell him he was more the Skipper type.

As soon as the elevator doors opened at the second floor, I ducked behind a partition, purposefully taking the long way around the office. The way that didn't lead past Felix's glass-walled office. While I was sure I was making headway tying Mullins's death to Pines, I was far from having copy ready yet. And copy was the only language Felix understood.

I plopped back down at my desk (Unseen. Yes!) and listened to my voice messages for any hot tips I could spin into a quick column. Luckily I had four. The first one from my morgue guy telling me that, as Max had said, there was no official ME ruling on Mullins's death yet. Bummer. But no ruling meant no one had ruled our murder yet, right?

As I listened through the next three messages, I realized they were all about the same story—Blain Hall allegedly fathering Cherry Chase's baby. Mental forehead smack.

So, I tried to spin what I'd gleaned from my celebrity interrogations for column fodder.

THE GOOD, THE BAD, AND THE UGLY

BAD: JENNIFER WOOD GETS A NEW TITLE THIS WEEK TO ADD TO REIGNING QUEEN OF TWEEN— LITTERBUG. TURNS OUT SHE NOT ONLY PUTS TRASH ON TV, BUT ON THE GROUND, TOO, LEAVING A TRAIL OF LATTE CUPS IN HER WAKE.

GOOD: KATIE BRIGGS WAS SEEN AT A CHARITY EVENT IN THE VALLEY LAST WEEK. HER DATE? HERSELF! TRUST ME, IT'S TRUE LOVE.

I bit my lip, tapping a pencil on the desk, trying to come up with an "Ugly" to round the column out.

UGLY: RUMORS ARE SWIRLING THAT HOLLYWOOD WILL SOON BE SEEING THE LOVE CHILD OF REHAB ROCKER BLAIN HALL AND HIS DIRTY DOGS BASSIST, CHERRY CHASE. ALL I CAN SAY ARE MY CONDOLENCES, MISS CHASE—IF BABY LOOKS ANYTHING LIKE DADDY, LET'S HOPE HIS TRUST FUND INCLUDES A PLASTIC SURGERY STIPEND.

"Don't tell me you're seriously printing this?" I looked up to find Cal reading over my shoulder.

"What? It's true. The rumors *are* swirling."

"But you started them."

I waved him off. "Semantics."

"Aren't these three on our suspect list?"

"So?"

"So, assuming one of them is your stalker, you really think it's a good idea to piss them off like this?"

I swiveled in my chair to face him. "Look, this is what I do, Cal. I poke fun at celebrities. And these are the only celebrities I have at the moment."

"So, maybe you should take a break from printing the column until this whole thing dies down."

I lifted my chin. "I'm a writer, Cal."

"I know."

"A good one."

"And humble."

"Look, laugh all you want. I know what I am and what I'm not. I'm not pretty like Cam, I'm not stacked like Allie, I'm not a born leader like Felix. But I am a damned good writer. I can make an entire story out of nothing and word it in such a way that you're dying to know more when I'm done. That is a skill. And I'm not letting some buttmunch with a voice disguiser take that away from me. I'm stronger than that."

"You're wrong," Cal said.

I opened my mouth to argue, but Cal cut me off before I could get it out.

"You're very pretty."

I shut my jaw with a click, my cheeks instantly going hot. I looked down at my shoes, clearing my throat. "Look, why don't you make yourself useful and go get us a couple of sandwiches, huh?" I asked.

"You're trying to get rid of me, aren't you?"

"I have work to do, and I can't do it when you're all hovery." I snuck a look up at him through my bangs. His eyes were laughing at me—I could feel it.

"What kind of sandwich you want?" he asked.

"Salami."

Cal grinned, the laugh transferring to his lips. "I thought you hated salami."

"In case you haven't figured it out by now, I'm a big fat liar."

The grin widened. "Yeah, you are. Alright, I'll be right back."

I watched him walk away, fanning my cheeks as soon as his back was turned.

Work.

Right. I had lots of work to do.

I hit spell-check, loaded my column into an email for

Felix, and had just hit the send button when a new window popped up.

Hey, Bender.

That familiar flip hit my stomach. Man in Black.

Hey.

Missed you last night.

I scrunched my nose up. Right. Last night.

Yeah, sorry about that. Something came up.

There was a pause. Then, *No problem. You okay?*

I took a deep breath.

Kinda.

Tell me.

I wondered how two simple little words could convey such concern. But they did. I suddenly felt the entire weight of the last few days crushing down on my shoulders and realized I was dying to unburden it on someone. So I did, spilling everything that had happened in the past two days, from that first weird phone message to the break-in last night and my tenuous position here at the *Informer* ever since Miss Jugs walked in. When I finally finished, I had paragraphs of text filling up my little IM window. I hit send and sat back, watching the cursor blink, waiting for his reaction.

Wow.

No kidding.

You okay?

My first reaction was to say yes. But somehow my fingers typed the word *No* instead. *I'm scared.* Which, as I stared at the words on the screen, was true. I know, I know, I'd played macho for Felix, because, frankly the idea of losing all the contacts I'd made in the last three years since I started here scared me even worse. But that didn't mean that having someone break into my home hadn't shattered my illusion of safety and security into a million little pieces.

You think maybe you should go to the police? he asked.

I shook my head at the screen. *No. I can't lose my informants. No police.*

You sure?

I have Cal.

There was a pause. Then, *The bodyguard?*

I nodded at the empty room. *He's good.*

I thought about the way he'd searched our condo last night, gun drawn. The way he made me ride around in his tank, shadowed me like a puppy everywhere I went. There was no way anyone was going to get the jump on me with Cal around.

I trust him, I typed.

Again with the pause. *Then I do, too.*

Thanks.

Be careful, Bender.

I will.

We on for tonight?

I wouldn't miss it for the world.

Be good, he typed.

Bye.

And then he signed off.

I stared at the little "offline" icon blinking back at me. I'm not sure how long I sat there feeling inexplicably lonely, but I was roused from my thoughts by a sandwich falling onto my desk.

I looked up to find Cal, a Coke in hand.

"Salami on sourdough." He handed me the soda. "And a Coke."

"Thanks."

Cal pulled a chair to my desk and straddled it backwards, digging into his own sandwich. Something with lots of veggies on whole wheat. Probably lots healthier than my salami with extra mayo. Probably a lot less tasty, too.

"You finish your column?" Cal asked around a bite.

I nodded. "Yep."

"Good. Now what?"

"Now," I said, popping a pickle into my mouth, "we go see Pines."

Chapter Ten

The Men's Central Jail in Los Angeles is the largest correctional facility in the world, housing over five thousand inmates at any given time. Located near the courthouse, its main inhabitants are those awaiting or appealing trial. A big, concrete building with a double layer of chain-link fencing surrounding the grounds, it was nothing special to look at.

Cal parked his truck in the visitor's lot and cut the engine.

I looked up at the gray building. "Look, I really think I should go in alone this time," I said.

Cal froze, his hand on the door handle. "No way."

"It's a prison. Nothing's going to happen to me in there. I'll be perfectly safe. Besides, I just think Pines might talk more readily to me."

"And why is that?"

"Besides the fact that you look like The Rock and Hulk Hogan's love child?"

He shot me a look.

"Because you suck at this whole lying thing. And if I'm going to get an exclusive, let alone information about Jake Mullins from this guy, I'm gonna need to bend the truth. A lot."

He narrowed his eyes at me, chewing the inside of

his cheek as he contemplated this. His gaze went up to the gray building. Then back to me. Then narrowed even further.

"Fine."

"Fine?"

"But be careful."

I nodded. "Scout's honor," I promised, hopping out of the car and making my way inside. I felt Cal's eyes on my back the entire way up to the door. To be honest, it was kind of reassuring.

If the exterior of the building was uninspired, the interior didn't offer much more in the way of aesthetics. Dirty beige walls, dirty beige floors, gunmetal gray desk where I had to show my ID and be checked into the visitor's system. Then a guy who looked like he could just as easily be on the locked-down side of the prison bars instructed me to empty my pockets and turn my purse inside out. After ascertaining that I didn't have any files baked into cakes with me, and after making me remove my shoelaces (the ultimate weapon), he let me into the visiting room, which consisted of two rows of tiny little cubicles with telephones on each side, between a layer of bulletproof glass.

I sat down at the station the guard indicated on the end of the first row. The glass was smudged with something I did not even want to speculate about. Instead, I clasped my hands in front of me, trying hard not to touch anything.

I waited, listing to the muffled sounds of the other conversations in the room. A man telling his brother that Mom was not sending any more gum unless he took his GED course seriously. A woman telling a prisoner that if he didn't start writing every weekend, she was gonna start seeing Joaquin, and there ain't nothing he could do about it.

Finally, after what seemed like an eternity, a figure in an orange jumpsuit approached my window. Hunched over, shuffling, gray skin, pronounced wrinkles, three days past needing a good shave.

Pines.

He sat down slowly, then gave me a long look as if trying to decide if he should know me, before picking up the telephone extension on his side of the glass.

I did the same, listening to his ragged breath on the other end.

"Hiya," I said, doing a little wave.

He stared at me just long enough to hammer home what a ridiculous greeting that was, then answered back, "Who the hell are you?"

I cleared my suddenly dry throat. "Uh, I'm . . . Daisy."

"Daisy what?"

"Moses."

"Bullshit."

"Excuse me?"

"Daisy Moses was the granny's name on *The Beverly Hillbillies*."

I was impressed. He knew his classic TV.

"Okay, fine. I'm not Daisy."

"Obviously."

"But it's not important who I am. It's important what I can do for you."

He narrowed his eyes. "And that would be?"

"Look, I . . . have a friend . . . who works for a major publication here in Los Angeles."

"Great, a fucking reporter." He pulled the phone away from his ear and moved to get up.

"Wait!" I shouted, banging on the glass.

"Don't touch the glass!" the guard behind me boomed, prompting both the gum-less brother and Joaquin's new lover to glance my way.

"Sorry," I said, holding both hands up.

But, luckily, it had gotten Pines's attention, too. He sat back down, putting the receiver to his ear again.

"What." More of a threat than a question.

I swallowed that dry lump again. "Look, I can help you. At the moment, the public is ready to write you off. Let them hear your story."

"I could give a shit what the public thinks," he said. He was surprisingly spunky for a billionaire who had just spent the last week in jail.

"Fine. But the studio heads read the papers, too. You think you're ever going to get a job in this town again? Let alone work with child actors?"

"I never touched no kids," he argued.

I wagged a finger at him. "Don't be naïve," I shot back. "You know as well as I do that it doesn't matter what you've done. It matters what people *think* you've done. Guilty until proven innocent. And," I added, "it's my job to tell people what to think."

He paused, seeming to digest this for a moment. "What paper you work for?"

"The *Informer*."

He narrowed his eyes at me, recognition slowly setting in. "I know you," he said, his jaw clenching. "You're that damned gossip columnist."

"Uh . . ."

"I'll tell you what you can do for me, Tina Bender. Go fuck yourself." He slammed the receiver into the set.

"No!" I banged on the window again.

"Don't touch the glass!" The guard's hand hovered over his firearm.

I threw both hands up in surrender. "Sorry!"

But I was glad to see Pines hadn't walked away. He stood, his arms crossed over his chest, glaring.

I gestured to the telephone and mouthed the word, "please."

I attributed it to the fact that waiting back at his cell were hours worth of nothing that he reached for the receiver again.

"You have some nerve coming here," Pines growled into the phone. "You've been crucifying me since day one."

"I never printed anything that wasn't true."

"You wouldn't know the truth if it bit you in the ass, girl. You print rumors."

I cocked my head to the side. "So, tell me a rumor, Pines."

He shook his head back and forth, a big, creepy smile spreading across his unshaven face. "You know how many reporters, *legitimate* reporters, would give their left nut to get an exclusive with me? You think I'm just gonna give it to you?"

I took a deep breath. It was now or never. "Jake Mullins."

"Who?"

"He was in your last film. Played the dad. OD'ed on sleep medication a couple of months ago."

Pines paused. Then nodded as if reluctant to admit

any connection. "Yeah. I remember. What about him?"

"I heard you two were pretty chummy."

"We *worked* together."

"But you knew he took sleeping pills?"

Pines narrowed his eyes. "So what if I did? The guy took one too many. It was an accident."

"He took one *handful* too many. Where were you the night he died?"

"So you wanna pin this on me, too?" he asked, throwing his arms up.

"What I want is to know how well you knew Mullins."

He paused. Then a slow grin spread across his face. "Well enough to know that he got what he deserved."

My heart sped up. "What's that supposed to mean?"

He leaned forward, his face inches from the grimy glass. "Look, kid, I think I've told you enough. You want to know about Mullins? I want something in return."

"I told you I'll print a positive story about—"

But he cut me off, waving his hands in the air. "No, no, no. I want something tangible. Something now."

I bit my lip. "What?"

"Porn."

I did a mental eye roll. "No way. I am not bringing you pictures of naked kids."

He shook his head. "Boys, girls, men, women—I don't care. I just need some porn! Look, I'm dying in here, all right? The hottest thing I have to look at are *National Geographics* with all the tits blacked out. I need something to get me through the day."

I chewed my lower lip, doing a backward glance at the guard by the door. I was pretty sure that nudie magazines were up there with shoelaces on the prison no-no list.

However, I could just imagine the look on Barbie's face when I waltzed in with an exclusive from Pines . . .

I leaned in close. "*Playboy* or *Hustler?*"

"So, how'd it go?"

I slid into the passenger seat of the Hummer.

"He knows something about Mullins."

Cal raised an eyebrow my way. "And?"

"And, if I want to know what it is, I have to bring Pines porn."

"They allow that in jail?"

I shook my head. "He wants me to bring it to the preliminary hearing tomorrow afternoon. He says he can slip me in as some sort of counsel."

Cal gave me a hard look. "I'm not sure I like that."

"Relax. It's a courthouse. His lawyer will be there. It's perfectly safe."

"It may be safe, but I still don't like it."

I looked down at the dash clock. "Well, Felix isn't going to like it if I don't get this story typed up pronto. So less talking, more driving."

Cal grunted something that sounded suspiciously like a dirty word but complied, pulling the Hummer back out onto the street.

Unfortunately, it was after five in Southern California, which meant all freeways and major arteries in the city became virtual parking lots, the average speed topping out at ten miles per hour. Not surprising, it was dark by the time we finally reached the *Informer*'s offices again. Immediately, I hit my computer, pulling up a word processing program to type up my Pines interview. I had just gotten the first sentence down when a breathy voice interrupted.

"Tina?"

I spun around to find Allie standing behind me, squinting at the screen over my shoulder.

Instinctively, I hit the "off" button on my monitor. "Did you want something?" I asked, pointedly.

She straightened up, focusing on me. "Felix said I should get with you on where we are with Pines."

We. I hated that word.

"I am looking at a possible angle involving a co-worker," I said, emphasizing the pronoun in question.

"Who?" Without invitation, Allie pulled a chair up beside my desk.

The last thing I wanted to do was give Reporter Barbie my inside scoop. On the other hand, Felix had been pretty clear about us working together. And I had a feeling where I was concerned, lately his patience was thinner than an Olsen twin. So, I made a compromise.

"I talked to Pines."

Allie's eyebrows went north. "He gave you the exclusive story? I've been trying to get his publicist all day, and the best I got was 'no comment.'"

"Well . . . it's not exactly what I'd call a full exclusive . . ." I hedged, remembering the way he'd clammed up. "But he did tell me that he never touched any kids."

Allie's nose crinkled. "He's not accused of *touching* kids."

Picky, picky.

"Look," I said, "I know you're new here. But when we

have a direct quote of any kind, we have a story. All we have to do is make a story around the quote."

Again with the crinkle. I had to admit it was adorable. You know, in a unicorns-farting-out-rainbows kind of way that made me want to hurl.

"That doesn't really make sense," she protested. "I mean, is there a story or not?"

I shook my head. "So young. So naïve. Watch and learn, honey." I cracked my knuckles and flipped my computer screen back on.

PINES PROTESTS INNOCENCE

FROM HIS JAIL CELL IN THE LOS ANGELES COUNTY CORRECTIONAL FACILITY, DIRECTOR TURNED FELON EDWARD PINES GAVE AN EXCLUSIVE INTERVIEW TO—

"Wait." Allie held up a hand. "I thought you said it wasn't technically an exclusive."

I shrugged. "I sure didn't see any other reporters there."

Allie cocked her head to the side. "Isn't that lying?"

"I'm on the blonde's side," Cal piped up, coming up behind me and resting his butt against my desk.

"You would be," I mumbled. He was male, she was stacked—you do the math.

I ignored them both, continuing with my article.

—AN EXCLUSIVE INTERVIEW TO THE *INFORMER.* CLAIMING INNOCENCE, PINES TOLD OUR REPORTER THAT "HE NEVER TOUCHED NO KIDS." THE BELOVED DIRECTOR'S LATEST FILM, STARRING CHILD ACTOR REED HARRISON, WAS A HOT PROPERTY AT THE BOX

OFFICE, EARNING A WHOPPING $85 MILLION IN ITS
OPENING WEEKEND—

I heard a low whistle from Cal. "Is that number
right?"
I nodded.
"I am so in the wrong business."
"You and me both."

—WHEN ASKED ABOUT HIS RECENT TROUBLES
WITH THE LAW, PINES SAID THE MEDIA WAS
"CRUCIFYING" HIM.

"Wait," Cal interrupted again. "Didn't he say *you*
were crucifying him?"
"Yeah, and I'm a member of the media."
He shook his head. "You have a way with words."
"Thanks."
"I'm not sure that was a compliment," Allie
pointed out.
"Quiet. I can't concentrate with all this talking."

PINES IS SCHEDULED TO APPEAR IN COURT FOR
A PRELIMINARY HEARING THIS AFTERNOON ON
CHARGES OF POSSESSING CHILD PORNOGRAPHY. ALL
PINES HAD TO SAY? "IT WAS AN ACCIDENT."

"Pines said the magazines were an accident?" Allie
asked.
"Well, not exactly. But, he did say those words during our interview." I didn't mention that they were in
reference to Mullins's overdose.
"They're out of context? That's so unethical."

"That's how we do it at the *Informer*."

Cal shook his head, mumbling something about journalistic integrity. Allie just stared at the screen, her nose permanently crinkled.

"When did you get this interview?" she asked.

"Today."

She cocked her head to the side. "Felix said we were supposed to work together on this story. Why didn't you tell me about it?"

"I'm telling you now."

"And if I hadn't wandered over here? Whose name would have been on the byline?"

"Both of ours?" I said. Though it came out more like a question. One that did nothing to convince Allie of my honorable intentions.

Probably because I didn't have any.

She stuck her hands on her round hips and narrowed her big blue eyes at me.

"Look, I know you don't like me very much."

I opened my mouth to protest.

"Spare me," she said, plowing ahead. "I'm not stupid. I can feel you shooting daggers at me from across the room."

I shut my mouth. What can I say? Subtlety was not one of my finer points.

"That's fine," she went on. "I'm not here to make friends. I'm here to make news. Pines is big news, and you're not blowing this story for me. Not by printing half-truths and quotes that may or may not be taken completely out of context. From now on, I want to hear the context myself. I'm going with you next time you talk to Pines."

"Like hell you are."

She thrust her chest out toward me in a combative stance. "Oh, I am. Or I'm going to Felix."

I ground my teeth together. While being shadowed by Barbie sounded about as pleasant as a root canal, I knew she had me. I was on shaky ground with the boss as it was. Any shakier, and I just might find myself replaced entirely by Miss Jugs.

"Fine," I finally spat out. "Two o'clock. Before the trial. I'm meeting Pines at the courthouse."

Her perfect ocean blue eyes lit up, and she smiled so wide I could see all five hundred of her bleached white teeth. "Great, see you then. Partner," she added with a wink.

It was official. I hated blondes.

By the time I emailed *our* story on Pines to Felix, hopped in Cal's Hummer, and braved the L.A. traffic home, it was late, I was beat, and nothing sounded sweeter than a long, hot meal followed by a long, cool swim.

"You coming in again?" I asked Cal as he pulled the Hummer down Oasis Terrace.

He shrugged. "You need me to?"

Yes.

"No."

Okay, did I *need* him? No. Had I enjoyed having someone in the house last night who carried a big scary gun? Yeah. A lot more than I wanted to admit.

"I'll hang here for a little while, then," he said, adjusting his seat back and flipping the radio on.

"Suit yourself," I replied, trying to keep the disappointment out of my voice. "But," I added, "no binoculars this time."

He grinned. Then leaned his head back and slipped on his shades.

I left him at the curb and made my way up the walkway. Unfortunately, as I walked into the house, I quickly realized that whole hot meal thing was a pipe dream.

"What's that smell?" I asked, wrinkling my nose as I followed the offending odor to the kitchen. On the stove a muddy brown mixture bubbled to a boil in a large pot.

"Your Aunt Sue made goulash," Aunt Millie proclaimed, shuffling into the kitchen, Aunt Sue a step behind. Millie squinted down into the pot behind her monstrous glasses. "It looks delicious to me."

That wasn't saying much.

I got closer to the pot and sniffed. "What did you put in it?"

"All the usual stuff," Aunt Sue answered. "Onions, potatoes, paprika."

That didn't sound so bad.

"Oh, but we were out of beef, so I dumped a can of Spam in instead."

I felt a gag reflex kick up in the back of my throat.

"Actually, I'm really not that hungry tonight. I think I might just go for a swim."

"You're too skinny. You need to eat," Millie protested.

I looked down at her shrunken form. "I'll eat later," I promised.

"Suit yourself," Aunt Sue replied. "Millie and I are going down to the community room. They got bingo tonight."

"You sure that's a good idea?" The idea of the hear-no-good, see-no-good twins gambling didn't strike me as stellar.

But she waved me off. "Don't worry, I only got ten bucks in my pocket. The way I play, I'll be home by the time *Jeopardy!* comes on."

"Have a ball," I said.

"What?"

"Have a ball!"

"Well, sure you can go to the mall! Honey, you're an adult, you don't need to ask my permission anymore." She kissed me on both cheeks.

Swell.

I saw them out the door, then slipped into my bedroom. It was still in a state of mild disarray from the night before, piles of clothes off their hangers, two slashed pillows facedown in the corner, the top of my dresser littered with the entire contents of my desk. I ignored it all, the sight just adding more tension to my already overtaxed shoulders. Instead, I waded through the chaos to my dresser, threw open the top drawer and, after digging only a few minutes, found my pink, polka-dotted bikini. I threw it on, added a pair of cut-off shorts, flip-flops and a towel and headed out, locking the front door behind me.

I slipped out the back, not wanting another confrontation with Cal, and headed toward the pool.

The Palm Grove complex consisted of thirty-three units, set in a series of connecting lanes that made a circular pattern. In the middle was a community center where senior yoga was taught in the mornings, watercolors in the afternoons, and movie nights and bingo in the evenings. Next to the center was the swimming pool that was largely occupied by aqua aerobics by day, but once the sun went down and the temperature dipped below eighty, was virtually abandoned. Like now.

I stepped out of my flip-flops, tossed my towel on a folding chaise, and ditched my shorts. I dipped one toe into the shallow end, testing the water. Crisp, cool. Perfect.

I walked around to the twelve-footer mark, raised my arms up, and dove in headfirst. The cool water washed over me, blocking out all sight, sound, and feeling but the energizing water. It was total sensory deprivation, and I loved it.

I surfaced, sucking in a long breath of air, then dove back under, kicking my legs behind me. Immediately I fell into a familiar rhythm. Arms pumping, legs kicking, steady, even breath breaking the surface in measured time. I reached the side, flipped around, then did it again.

Five laps in, I was beginning to hit my stride. My muscles felt relaxed for the first time in days. In the pool there was no threat, there was no boss, there was no perky Barbie doll vying for my stories. There was just me, the cool sensation, and muscles pumping in time to the steady rhythm of my breath as my body sliced through the water.

I'm not sure how many laps I did, but by the time I surfaced, I was breathing hard and the strain had seeped out of me, replaced by a lax, loose feeling that left my body sighing in relief.

One that, unfortunately, didn't last for long.

I looked up to find Cal standing at the end of the

pool, a lopsided grin creasing his face in the sparse moonlight.

"What?" I asked, wiping the chlorine out of my eyes.

"Cute bikini."

Despite the cool water covering my skin, I felt my cheeks flush. "Can it," I said, pulling myself out of the water. Self-consciously, I wrapped a towel around my middle. "What are you doing out here?"

"Watching you." His eyes roved to my midriff as if to illustrate the point.

The flush kicked up a notch, and I tugged my towel higher. "I'm fine."

"You are not fine," he argued. "There's a reason Felix hired me. So, next time you leave the house, ask me first, okay?"

"No." I felt my chin tilt up a notch.

Cal's left eyebrow hitched in response. "No?"

"No." I crossed my arms over my chest. A slightly childish gesture, I'll admit. But the truth was, I was tired of being bullied. By Felix, by Allie, by Cal, by the freak show who was threatening me. Even Pines was ordering me to buy him porn! I wanted some say in my own life again. And I was taking it.

Even if it was with childish defiance.

"No. I don't need your permission to live my life, Cal."

Cal rolled his eyes. "Bender—"

But I wasn't finished. Not by a long shot.

"I'm sick and tired of being treated like I can't take care of myself, like I can't think for myself. I know you think I'm some ridiculous little chick—"

"That's not true."

"—but I got along fine on my own before you came along, and I'll get along fine well after your taillights fade into the distance. I can handle this. So you can quit ordering me around like I'm your German shepherd or something. 'Sit, stay, beg to leave the house.'"

"I know this arrangement wasn't your idea."

"No, it wasn't. And I'm sick and tired of people thinking they know what's best for me."

"Maybe we do know what's best for you. Look, I know you're angry, and I know you're scared by all this—"

"I'm not scared!" I protested.

"Well, I am," he shouted back.

Which shocked me into silence. Looking at his compact build, sleek reflexes, gun bulging from his jeans (at least, I'm pretty sure that bulge was a gun . . .) I couldn't imagine Cal being scared of anything.

"You are?" I asked quietly.

He took a step closer. Instinctively, I tried to take one back, calves coming up against the side of the lounge chair.

"Yes, I am. You're reckless. You're dishonest. You're stubborn. You make enemies wherever you go."

"Gee, way to flatter a girl."

"You're also vulnerable. Alone. And too smart for your own good."

I swallowed, suddenly having to concentrate on the most automatic of body movements.

"I'm scared something's going to happen to you," he said, his voice low. Intimate. Close.

I shivered in the cool night air, goose bumps brewing

along my arms as his gaze moved slowly over me, resting on my face.

His hand came up. I held my breath as he brushed a strand of wet hair from my forehead, tucking it behind my ear.

I licked my lips, wondering what he'd do next. Wondering what I *wanted* him to do next.

His eyes went dark, his features soft. He leaned in until I could smell the coffee on his warm breath as it grazed my cheek.

"Tina," he whispered.

My heart was racing, my breath stuck in my throat, anticipation and fear mixing an uneasy cocktail in the pit of my stomach. Yet it was the best feeling I'd felt in a long time. Was he going to kiss me? Did I want him to?

I stood on tiptoe, leaning in.

But I never got the chance to find out.

Sirens erupted behind me. Muted at first, but gaining intensity at a rate that completely broke the moment, both of us turning to watch as an ambulance screeched into the Palm Grove complex.

Quite frankly, ambulances here were not an unusual sight. Considering the average age of the residents was high enough to put half of them on the Grim Reaper's waiting list, we were on a first-name basis with at least three local paramedics.

But the way this one tore through the complex, zipping up Paradise Lane, I could tell something wasn't right. Something that became even less right as it turned onto Oasis Terrace.

And pulled to a halt right outside my condo.

Chapter Eleven

I froze for a full ten seconds before adrenaline flooded my system, and I sprinted toward the flashing lights of the ambulance. I felt Cal a step behind me, his heavy boots thumping along the pavement in time to the slap of my bare feet. Somewhere near Haven Circle I lost my towel, but I didn't care. My entire being was focused on my home, where a police car had just joined the ambulance, a pair of uniformed officers following the paramedics through my front door.

Aunt Sue. Millie.

I should never have left the house. I should have made Cal come in with me. I should never have written those damned columns, should never have taken this damned job, should never have butted my nose into other people's business. If anything happened to Aunt Sue . . .

Flashing red and blue lights painted the scene in garish hues, bouncing off our stoic pink flamingo. I felt a choking sob escape my throat as I hit the front door.

A uniformed officer held out an arm, barring my entrance.

"I need to get inside. My aunt," I cried, desperation slurring my speech, making me sound like some hysterical horror movie heroine. Behind him I could make out the shapes of two paramedics, heard the sounds of *Jeopardy!* blaring from the TV.

"She lives here. What's going on?" Cal asked, coming up behind me.

The uniform looked from me to him, his expression unreadable. Which did absolute nothing to quell the fear rising in my throat.

"You'd better take her away," the uniform finally told Cal.

Like hell.

I shoved at the officer's arm, pushing my way into the foyer.

Which was far enough to see just what had prompted the guy's poker face.

Laying on the living room carpet, facedown, was a figure clad in a blue polyester track suit, her pink scalp visible between her tight, white curls. And beneath her, an ugly red stain spread on our beige Berber.

I heard a scream and was only vaguely aware that it might be coming from me. My legs collapsed, and I landed in a heap on the floor. Two arms instantly went around my middle, lifting me up and dragging me back outside. I closed my eyes, shaking my head defiantly from side to side as a strong chest pressed against my face. It couldn't be. I refused to believe it. Aunt Sue was fine. That scene, it hadn't just happened. This was a dream. A very bad dream that I'd wake up from any minute now.

"I'm sorry," Cal whispered into my hair. And I realized I was sobbing, tears soaking the front of his shirt as he held me tight. So tight I almost couldn't breathe. So tight I wasn't sure he'd ever let go. Then again, I wasn't sure I ever wanted him to.

I don't know how long we stood like that, but it felt like an eternity. I began to shiver in the cool breeze, my wet bathing suit clinging to my skin. I felt Cal drape his jacket around my shoulders. It was warm and smelled like soap and leather. I shut my eyes, inhaling the scent. Trying to focus on just that one scent, trying to block out the horrible flashing lights still bathing our neighborhood in ominous light.

"What's going on here?"

My head shot up, my voice catching in my throat. I spun around.

To find Aunt Sue and Millie striding across the lawn.

I launched myself at them, tackling Aunt Sue around her middle. Huge tears flowed down my cheeks. Only this time, they were in relief.

"Ohmigod, you're alive."

"Well, of course I'm alive. It was just bingo," she shot back, detaching me. "And you've got my shirt all wet. Where are your clothes?"

I choked back a laugh, relief replacing the grief which had replaced the fear, which all had me feeling limp, tired, and amazed I could even stand up still.

"What's going on?" Aunt Millie asked, squinting at the flashing lights through her glasses. "You having some sort of party?"

"I thought she was dead. The body. Our carpet. It's red." I realized I was babbling. I stopped. Took a deep breath. Then hugged Aunt Sue again.

"I have no idea what you're saying, peanut," she confessed, "but, I hope you're as glad to see me when I tell you I lost fifty bucks."

"I don't care," I mumbled into her curls as I squeezed her midsection.

"I'll be right back," Cal said, moving away from our group to talk to the uniform, his brow drawn in concern. Which I didn't blame him for. As I released Aunt Sue, I realized that even though my loved ones were still alive and well, things were not hunky dory. There was a dead body on my living room floor. If it wasn't Aunt Sue or Millie, who the hell was it?

I tugged Cal's jacket tighter around my shoulders, watching as he pulled some sort of identification from his back pocket, presenting it to the officer. After a brief moment examining it, he and Cal exchanged a few words, the officer gesturing behind himself every few seconds. When they were done, Cal's expression wasn't any less grim.

"Well?" I asked as he returned to the group, almost afraid of the answer.

"It's your neighbor. Hattie Carmichael."

Aunt Sue sucked in a breath, her hand going to her mouth.

"It looks like she was in the living room, near the television. She was struck from behind with a metal bookend."

"This is all my fault," Aunt Sue moaned. "I forgot to shut off the TV before we went to bingo. Hattie was always complaining about it playing too loud."

"Did Hattie have a key to your house?"

I shook my head. "No, but we always kept one in the planter near the door. Hattie knew it was there."

"Would she have just let herself in?"

"This is Hattie Carmichael you're talking about,"

Aunt Sue said. "She was nosier than a bloodhound." She paused. "God rest her soul," she added, quickly crossing herself.

"A murder at the old folks' village," Aunt Millie said, then jabbed me in the ribs. "There's a story for ya, huh?"

It certainly was. And, were it anyone else this was happening to, I would have already been mentally constructing a salacious headline for the morning edition. As it was, I pulled Cal's jacket tighter around my shoulders.

Someone had been in my home. Someone had been seen there by Mrs. Carmichael. And someone had killed her. If anyone was to blame for this, it wasn't Alex Trebek at top volume. It was me.

My caller turned vandal had just turned murderer.

Since our condo had officially become a crime scene, Cal insisted that Aunt Sue and I come stay at his place for the night. For once, I didn't protest. As soon as the officers let me, I slipped into my bedroom, carefully avoiding looking at the black tarp-covered mound on my living room floor that used to be my neighbor. I changed out of my cold, wet bikini and packed a few necessities in a bag. I crossed the hall and did the same for Aunt Sue before meeting them back outside.

Cal, Aunt Sue, Aunt Millie, and I hopped into his Hummer and rode through the dark streets in silence, each of us lost in our own thoughts. We dropped Millie home at the Sunset Palms retirement village in Glendale, then hopped on the freeway, where the steady rhythm of the wheels turning beneath me suddenly caused the physical toll of the day to catch up to me. Big time. So much so that by the time we pulled up to Cal's place in West L.A., I was half asleep and Aunt Sue was snoring in the backseat.

Cal cut the engine, the silence settling over our trio as I stared up at the one-story craftsman in front of us.

"You okay?" Cal asked, turning to me.

His face was guarded, shadowed by the light from the streetlamp outside.

I nodded. "I will be." Which was more than I could say for poor Mrs. C.

"The police are going to want to talk to you tomorrow."

"I know.

"Do me a favor and don't lie to them, okay?"

I nodded again.

"I mean it." He paused. "You can do that, right?"

I shot him a look. "Yes."

"Good. Tell them everything. They need to know about the calls, the break-in. Everything."

Full disclosure was not exactly in my nature. However, in this instance, I had to agree with Cal. Someone was dead. And it was all my fault.

I nodded in the darkness once more.

"Good."

He got out of the car. I roused Aunt Sue, and we followed him up the walkway to a dark porch where he fumbled with the keys for a second before letting us inside.

As soon as he switched on the lights, I fell in love with the little house. It was small even by L.A. standards, a tiny living room in front, a kitchen/dining area to the left and hallway visible in the back. But the low beamed ceilings and dark, hardwood floors gave it a cozy feel instead of being cramped.

A red leather sofa hugged the back wall, chrome legs curling under it like claws. Beside it, black, lacquered end tables squatted, one of them holding a lamp with a hula girl painted on it. Two *Jetsons*-looking white, futuristic chairs flanked the fireplace, and the sign over the mantel read, "Eat at Joe's" in bright neon lettering. The floor was covered in a zebra-striped rug, and, to the right, the kitchen was tiled in black and white checkers, an old, turquoise fifties-style stove sitting in the corner.

Despite the day I'd had, I felt the corners of my mouth tilting upward. Who knew Cal had such personality?

"Guest room's down the hall," he said, dropping his keys in an olive green ashtray near the door as he led the way. "Sue, you can take that one," he offered. "Tina can sleep in my room."

I felt my cheeks rush with heat, instantly remembering how close together our lips had been earlier that night. "Oh, I'm not sure that's—" I started.

"I'll take the couch."

Oh. Right.

"No, I don't want to put you out. I'm fine on the couch, thanks," I protested.

But Cal ignored me, taking my bag and leading the way to a room at the end of the hall. He flipped on the light.

I'm not sure what I had expected Cal's bedroom to look like. Maybe a few guns, posters of Rambo on the walls, camouflaged bedding. But, instead, I found myself in your average bachelor bedroom. A comforter in dark navy, a black dresser in the corner, hamper just slightly overflowing with dirty laundry. The only thing that wasn't average was the larger than life fuzzy velvet portrait of Elvis on the wall.

I smirked.

"You have something against the King?" Cal asked.

I shook my head, not trusting myself to speak without giggling.

"Good." He grinned. "I'll put some fresh towels in the bathroom. Let me know if you need anything else."

With that, he backed out of the room, shutting the door behind him. I could hear him rummaging in the linen closet as I slipped out of my jeans and turned off the light, sliding between the sheets.

Cal's sheets.

They were cool and smooth beneath my skin, and I was suddenly hyper aware that *Cal's* bare skin had touched this same place.

I got up and put my jeans back on, then slid in again. Not that it helped. I could smell his aftershave on the pillow. Subtle, just a whisper of woodsy scent. But there. So very there. I inhaled, burying my face in it. And felt myself relax, the tension, adrenaline, and worry of the day slipping away as I melted into his pillow.

I was swimming. The water cool and smooth, enveloping my limbs. I peeled through the water. Long, even strokes, legs pumping, arms reaching, lungs burning. It felt great. Wonderful. I was in a lane that seemed to go on for miles. No matter how hard I pumped, I was still swimming, never seeming to get closer to the end, never hitting that wall. I pumped harder, faster, pushing with everything I had. If anything, the wall seemed to get farther away.

And then it happened.

The water started to cloud. Red. Swirls of bright red liquid surrounding me like tendrils as they mixed with the chlorinated water. I reached out to touch one, watching the wisps of colors slide over my fingers. Then there was more. And more. Suddenly the entire pool was red. Bloodred.

I screamed. Long, loud, lashing in the bloody water, feeling it suck me down, down, down. Lower and lower until no one could hear my screams anymore.

"Tina!" A sharp voice barked out my name.

I shot awake, blinking up into the face beside me. Cal.

What the hell was Cal doing in my bed?

I blinked again, my eyes slowly focusing on the room around me until I realized this wasn't my bed, it was his. And his sheets were wrapped around my legs, tangled and twisted, his pillow clutched in my hands in a death grip.

"Hey, you okay?" Cal asked.

I looked down. And noticed that his hand was resting on my thigh. I gulped.

"Yeah. Just . . . a bad dream, I guess."

"Well, I'd say after last night, you're entitled to a nightmare or two."

I sat up, shrugging Cal's hand off and rubbing my eyes. "Aunt Sue up?"

He nodded. "Yeah, she's in the kitchen making French toast."

That woke me up. "She's cooking?"

"Don't worry. I'm supervising closely." He looked down at my jeans as I jumped out of bed. And smiled.

"What?"

"You always wear jeans to bed?"

"I was cold," I said. Even though the feel of Cal's silky sheets on my bare skin had left me anything but.

"Well, let me know next time. You can borrow some sweats," he said, rising from the bed and leading the way to the kitchen.

I found Aunt Sue at the little turquoise stove, manning a pan of egg-battered bread, a cup of coffee in one hand.

"'Morning," I said, giving her a quick peck on the cheek as I rubbed the sleep from my eyes.

"What?" she asked. I noticed her ears conspicuously absent of hearing aids.

"Goo-d morn-ing," I enunciated.

"Huh?"

"Good morning!"

"Oh. Well, good morning to you, peanut. But there's no need to shout, I'm right here."

I rolled my eyes. "Right." I leaned over and inspected the pan. Right color, right smell, no charred edges—so far so good.

"I took the liberty of calling your Aunt Millie," Cal said, handing me a cup of coffee. Black with sugar. Perfect. I took a grateful sip. "She agreed to come visit with Sue again today."

I nodded. "Good plan."

"We're going over to Hattie's," Aunt Sue said. "God

rest her soul," she added, then crossed herself. "Her only family's some nephew in Hoboken, so I figured we'd pack up her place for her."

The guilt from last night hit me full force. "That's nice of you."

"It's the least we could do. You know, considering . . ." Aunt Sue trailed off. Cal cleared his throat. I stared down into my mug. It was unanimous—we all thought I was guilty.

Aunt Sue pulled a plate from the cupboard and transferred a slice of French toast onto it before shoving it in my direction. "Here. Eat something," she directed.

While food was the last thing I wanted, I obliged. Mostly because the fight had been guilted out of me. I sat down at the tiny dining table, digging into the toast and shoving a forkful into my mouth.

And nearly choked.

I spit the bite back onto my plate, gulping down coffee to put out the fire that had exploded on my tongue.

"What did you put on this?" I finally managed to ask. Though it came out more like, "ut id ou ut in is?" since my tongue had somehow swollen to twice its size.

At first Aunt Sue gave me a blank look. Then she shrugged. "I couldn't find the cinnamon. So I used cayenne instead. Gives it a bit of a kick, huh?"

I shoved the plate away. "A hell of a kick."

At least now I was wide awake.

Chapter Twelve

Just as I was finishing my coffee—sans volcanic French toast—my cell rang. It was the LAPD, as predicted, asking Aunt Sue and me to come down to the station to give an official statement about last night. While reliving the scene was the last thing I wanted to do, as Cal had said, I didn't have much choice in the matter now. I told the officer I'd be there as soon as I could, finished my coffee, and the three of us loaded into Cal's Hummer.

Three hours later, I had completely spilled my guts to a homicide detective who was the spitting image of Kojak, and Aunt Sue had given a somewhat coherent statement to his partner, a woman with the most severe ponytail I'd ever seen. By the time we were finished, I had renewed purpose. I was going to find this guy if it was the last thing I did.

And I was going to start where we left off yesterday—Blain Hall's agent.

As soon as we dropped off Aunt Sue at Millie's, I plugged the agent's address into Cal's GPS.

"What's that?" he asked.

"Address of Jerry Leventhal's place."

Cal narrowed his eyes behind his shades. "And why do we need that?"

"I never got a chance to question him about his visit to Blain in rehab."

"I thought we agreed to leave this to the police."

I shook my head. "I agreed to *talk* to the police. Do you have any idea how many homicides have taken place in L.A. County this year?"

"Two hundred and four."

I raised an eyebrow his direction. Okay, so he *did* know. I was impressed. "Right. The police have their hands full. I, on the other hand, have all the time in the world to devote to catching this asshole."

I turned to find Cal grinning at me.

"What?"

"Remind me never to piss you off."

"Does that mean we're going to Leventhal's?"

Cal flipped a U-ey. "You're the boss, Bender."

A mere hour later we'd made our way onto Wilshire, a long street winding through the heart of Beverly Hills and flanked on each side by exclusive boutiques, towering penthouses, and high-rise office buildings that housed the movers and shakers of the big screen world. The Wilshire corridor was about as high dollar as real estate could get. Leventhal's office was on the sixth floor of a huge glass and chrome building shared with a law firm, a cable network, and about fifteen other talent agents. Leventhal's office was the last one on the right as we got off the elevators.

A slim, waiflike girl with unnaturally black hair sat behind a low reception desk as we walked in. Obviously an actress slash receptionist. Not that that was an anomaly. In L.A. almost everyone was an actor slash something. Even the janitor in our building had done a guest spot on *House* last season.

Actress Slash Receptionist was applying lip gloss in a little compact as we approached. "Can I help you?" she asked without looking up.

"We're here to see Mr. Leventhal," I told her.

"Do you have an appointment?"

"Uh . . . no."

"Names?" she asked.

"Douglas. Lisa and Oliver," I said.

"I'll see if he's in," she said noncommittally, rising from the desk and crossing to a hallway behind her.

As soon as she was out of earshot, Cal leaned in. "Oliver and Lisa Douglas?"

"From *Green Acres*."

I felt him smirk as the receptionist returned.

"Yeah, go ahead," she said, waving us in the direction she'd just come from.

"Thanks."

The hallway was short, a copy room on the left, an office on the right, and a dead end in a window that overlooked the Wilshire traffic below. The door on the right read "J. Leventhal."

I quickly pushed through.

Jerry Leventhal sat behind a large oak desk, every inch of which was covered in papers and CD cases. He perched on the edge of an enormous leather chair that made me think of a throne, upon which the gatekeeper to fame sat. His skin had an unnaturally tanned look, as if he seldom saw the real sun but was a devotee of the spray-on variety. Dark hair covered his head—well, most of it. A large thinning patch sat on top, though I could tell by the obvious plugs that he was doing his best to fight nature. A Bluetooth was implanted in his ear, and he spoke seemingly to the air as we entered.

"Baby, you're great. You're a fucking John Lennon, a Bob Dylan, a Kurt Cobain. You speak to the generation. No one can touch you, baby. You're king, got me? King. Call me when the tour gets to Baltimore. Keep rockin', baby."

He touched a button on his ear, then turned his attention our way.

"Prima donnas. Fragile artist egos, need all the help they can get. Poor kid, probably won't make it past Philly. So, what can I do for you?" he asked, leaning forward onto his desk, hands clasped in front of him.

"Uh, hi. I'm Lisa, and this is my colleague Oliver."

He nodded, motioning me to go on. Unless our names were Brad and Angelina, it was obvious he could care less.

"We're . . . freelancers for *Rolling Stone*," I lied. "We're doing a piece on Blain's brave battle with addiction."

Leventhal shook his head. "I'm sorry, Blain's not up for interviews at the moment."

"Oh, I completely understand. His treatment has to be paramount. We actually wanted to talk to you."

"Me?" He raised an eyebrow, leaning back in his chair. "I'm not sure what I can tell you."

"You recently visited Blain in rehab, didn't you?"

"Yes," he hedged slowly. This was a man who'd dealt with the fickle media before and was not going to let some juicy quote slip out unnoticed.

"What did you discuss?"

"I'm sorry, but that conversation was private."

"Did you talk about his treatment?"

"Some."

"His plans when he gets out?"

"A bit."

"How does he feel about what the media's been saying? I hear that Tina Bender at the *Informer* has been roasting him?"

He narrowed his eyes. "Exactly what are you getting at?"

"Where were you last night?"

Leventhal stood, planting both hands on his massive desk. "Okay, that's it. This conversation is over. I want you both out, or I'm calling security."

Shit. Too far.

But Cal stood up, matching Leventhal's height and then some. "I don't think you want to do that," he said.

"Oh really?" He crossed his arms over his chest. "And why not?"

"The truth is we're working with the police. We're investigating a murder, and your client is a suspect."

All the color drained from the agent's fake tan.

"Murder? Are you serious?"

"As a heart attack," Cal said, holding the man in his steely gaze.

Slowly, Leventhal sank back into his chair. "Jesus, when the tabloids get wind of this . . ."

Little did he know.

"Look," he continued, "I don't know anything about any murder, but Blain's been in rehab the past four weeks. He couldn't have killed anyone."

"Blain has plenty of resources. He could have had someone else do his dirty work," I pointed out.

"Like who?"

"Where were you last night?" I repeated.

If it was possible, Leventhal paled further. "Me! You have got to be joking. You don't seriously think I killed someone for Blain, do you?"

Neither Cal nor I answered, both giving him the cold stare.

"I was here," Leventhal finally squeaked out.

"Alone?"

"The cleaning lady saw me. She can vouch for me. Maria. Or Juanita. Something like that. I was brokering a deal for my latest act, a punk band from Milwaukee. Here, you guys want a free CD?" He shoved two unmarked discs at Cal and me.

"Has anyone else been to see Blain?" I asked. I knew the guest book had been free of signatures, but I was desperate here.

But Leventhal shrugged. "I don't know. Look, he's under pretty tight surveillance. Trust me, Blain's not your guy."

"Maybe we should ask Blain directly," I said.

"No!" Leventhal jumped in his seat at the suggestion. "No, you can't talk to Blain."

"Why not?"

"He's in treatment."

"We'll be gentle."

"Please. I know Blain isn't your guy."

Cal leaned forward, narrowing his eyes at the man. "You seem pretty anxious to divert attention from your client."

"It's bad publicity."

"I don't buy it," Cal said. "He's a rock star. The badder he seems, the more records he'll sell."

Leventhal swallowed audibly.

"What's the real reason?" Cal pressed.

Leventhal licked his lips.

I leaned forward.

"Alright. I'll tell you. But it goes no further than this room."

I crossed my fingers behind my back. "I swear."

Leventhal took off his Bluetooth, dropping it on the table as if someone might hear him through the device. "Blain's not really in rehab for drug addiction. We floated the story to stave off the media."

Cal cocked his head to the side. "Floated?"

"They spread the rumor themselves," I explained. Unfortunately, it was something studios did all the time to protect the real secrets of their stars. "Remember how many times Lance Bass was linked in the media with some supermodel or another before stepping out of the closet? All floaters."

"Okay," Cal said, addressing Leventhal, "so, you're saying he's not even at Sunset Shores?"

"Oh no, he's in rehab alright," Leventhal assured us. "Just not for drugs."

"What then?" Cal asked. "Alcohol? Gambling? Sex addiction?"

"World of Warcraft."

I blinked. "Excuse me?"

"Poor kid got caught up in this online game, World of Warcraft. It's this whole virtual reality world with these complicated plotlines and battles and all kinds of crazy characters. Blain started playing it on the road. At first it was a nice way to relax, wind down from a show. But then he got so into it he started missing gigs."

Leventhal shook his head. "Poor kid became obsessed. He couldn't focus on anything else. He was playing up to twelve hours a day. So I checked him into Sunset to help him break the addiction."

I bit my lip to keep from laughing. The big bad rock star was a closet gamer nerd. I would have given my firstborn to run with the story.

Though, sadly, it also cleared Blain of motive to want me out of the picture. The longer I kept reporting the floater story, the safer Blain's secret really was. It was in his best interest to keep me writing, not stop me.

"Mr. Leventhal, does the name PW Enterprises mean anything to you?" I tried not to sound as desperate as I felt to make some connection here.

He scrunched his forehead up. "PW?"

I nodded. "They're local."

He snapped his fingers. "Production company! They were interested in an act of mine to do a soundtrack at one point. I think they're in Hollywood somewhere."

"Got any idea who runs it?" I asked, perking up.

"Sure do." He nodded, clearly pleased to be talking about something other than his client. "The owner is Edward Pines."

Mental forehead smack.

It had been Pines calling me all along! Which, now that I thought about it, made perfect sense. Who else had that kind of time on their hands? Thanks in part to my column, the public thought he was total scum. And I'd just visited him yesterday, trying to dig up more dirt, before someone had broken into my house and killed Hattie. It fit like a dream.

"There's just one problem," Cal pointed out as we

hopped back into his gas guzzler and I told him my theory.

"What's that?"

"That first call was made from the PW number, not the L.A. County jail."

I waved him off. "Simple. Pines is a director, people are used to taking orders from him. He could have easily had one of his flunkies do his dirty work."

"But why would he go through all that trouble to disguise his voice, then call on a number that links directly back to him?"

I chewed my lower lip. Beats me. I looked down at the dash clock. One thirty p.m.

"Let's go ask him."

We made tracks toward the courthouse, stopping at a newsstand along the way just long enough to pick up copies of *Playboy*, *Penthouse*, and some magazine called *Naughty Bits* that Cal swore Pines would love.

"It's the best," he said.

I cocked an eyebrow at him.

He shrugged. "You know, so I've heard."

"Uh huh."

"Come on, we don't want to be late."

I paid for the magazines and hopped back in his Hummer, making our way through town to the courthouse. We pulled into a spot in the lot and quickly jogged up the steps and through the metal detectors. I felt my cheeks heat as the guy manning the x-ray machine got a load of the stash in my bag, but we cleared security and hit the lobby at two on the dot.

As did a perky blonde in a miniskirt and knee-high boots with four-inch heels.

Right. I'd forgotten about Allie.

"I'm not late, am I?" she asked, all breathless like a porn star.

I shook my head. "No." Unfortunately.

"I just talked to the clerk. Pines is in conference room 4A with his lawyer," she informed me.

"Great. Let's go talk to him."

We made our way up the stairs and past the courtroom, where shortly Pines would be sitting behind the defendant's table, to a small wooden door to the right that served as chambers for the prisoners to meet pretrial with their counsel. A bailiff stood outside 4A, a sure sign that a prisoner was inside.

I threw my shoulders back and walked up to the guy like I owned the place.

"Excuse me," I said, doing my best imitation of a Harvard Law grad. "My client is inside. I need to speak with him."

His eyebrows ruffled. "He's already with his counsel."

"Right. I'm second chair."

"And I'm third," Allie piped up behind me.

Cal had the good sense to remain quiet, instead taking a seat on a bench against the wall.

The bailiff shrugged, then stepped aside and let us through the door.

Pines and his weedy-looking lawyer were sitting at a large oak desk, papers strewn across the top. Both were deep in conversation as we walked in, and again I was struck by how pale and thin the lawyer was. I almost couldn't tell which of the men had spent more time locked in captivity.

The lawyer's head popped up as we entered the room, his expression immediately contorting into outrage.

"What the hell are you doing here? This is a private meeting room. I'm here with a client."

He jumped out of his seat, but Pines put a hand on his arm, calming the man down. "Don't worry," he said, a slimy grin taking over his features. "They're here for me. You got what I asked for?" Pines asked, nodding to my bag.

I set it on the table and pulled out the magazines, sliding them across to him.

"What the hell is this?" his attorney cried. "Jesus, you know how much trouble I could get into for bringing you contraband?"

"Relax," Pines told him, greedily flipping through the pages. "You didn't bring it, they did."

Which didn't seem to make the man feel a whole lot better, as he began pacing the room.

"I held up my end, so now it's your turn, Pines," I said, taking a seat at the table across from him. "Start talking."

Pines took a moment, licking his lips as he eyed the cover of *Naughty Bits*. Apparently Cal was right. It seemed to be a winner.

Finally he looked up. "What do you want to know?"

Everything. Why he was threatening me. Why my neighbor was dead in my living room. And how to steal a front-page story from Allie McTiny Top.

"Let's start with the kid."

"I told you I never touched him."

"Did you ever take compromising pictures of him?"

"Don't answer that," his attorney said, swooping in.

Pines looked from him to me, then finally shrugged. "Sorry, can't answer that one. Try again."

"Jake Mullins. You said he deserved what he got. What did you mean by that?"

"Just what I said. He was a slimy sonofabitch, and I hope he's rotting in hell."

"What did he do?" Allie piped up beside me, gel pen hovering over her little floral notebook, a little frown of concern between her perfectly plucked brows.

Pines shifted his gaze, letting it rest somewhere in her double D region.

"Tried to blackmail me."

Pines attorney jumped up. "I have to strongly suggest that you not talk to these women."

But Pines waved him off. "Relax, Paul. I didn't go for it. The guy comes at me saying he found some kiddie mag in my trailer. What the hell he was doing in *my* trailer, I don't know. But he says he wants a hundred K or he's going to the media. I told him, good luck. He could try, but he'd never work again in this town, I'd see to it."

"And what did he do?"

"Nothing. What could he do? I steered clear of the little prick after that."

"How long before his death was this?"

"A couple weeks."

I mulled that over. If Mullins had been so strapped for cash that he'd jeopardize his big break, he may have tried the same tactic on someone else. And maybe they weren't as confident as Pines that he'd go away on his own.

"Where were you last night?" I asked, switching gears.

He gave me a blank stare. "Are you fucking kidding me? Same place I've been every night since that judge denied my bail. A cell."

Right. Stupid question. I cleared my throat. "Did you have any visitors?"

"No."

"Call anyone?"

"As a matter of fact I did. My mother. Why the hell do you care?"

"Because someone killed my neighbor last night."

He blinked, then leaned forward, clasping his hands in front of him. "What the hell does that have to do with me?"

"PW Enterprises. Your company?"

"Yeah. So?"

"Someone from your company threatened to kill me if I didn't stop printing stories about them in my paper. Two nights ago, someone broke into my home. Last night, my neighbor was murdered in my living room. Quite a stretch to claim coincidence, huh?"

At the word "murdered," Pines's lawyer began shoving papers into his briefcase. "That's it, this conversation is over!"

"You're kidding, right?" Pines asked me. "This is some kind of joke to get me to give you some shit quote to print in your paper, right?"

I shook my head from side to side. For Mrs. Carmichael's sake, I wished it were just a joke.

Pines swallowed, his Adam's apple bobbing nervously up and down. "How do you know the caller was with PW?"

"I traced it to a number owned by your company."

He shook his head. "That could be dozens of people.

I started PW to back my last movie. The one before didn't do so great at the box office, so I needed to re-create myself. Financially speaking."

I nodded. That was standard op in Hollywood. Pro-duction companies came and went faster than the Santa Anas. "Go on."

"That's it. We've got an office on the Sunset Studios lot manned by a couple assistants and an intern. But anyone could have used the phones. The place isn't even locked during the day."

Which meant any one of my celebrity suspects could have had access. Katie was a regular at the studios, and Jennifer was there every day. Blain could have conceiv-ably called in a favor to an actor friend on the set. And even if Pines was telling the truth, as I'd pointed out to Cal, he could have easily had an assistant do his dirty work. I felt myself mentally slumping in my chair, feel-ing like I was taking one step forward only to take two back again.

"Let's go back to the case at hand," Allie said, scrib-bling in her notebook. "You're being charged with pos-session of child pornography. How do you—"

But Pines's lawyer held up his hand. "We cannot comment on an open case."

Allie shut her mouth with a pretty little pout. Then shifted tactics. "How do you feel about the public call-ing you a pedophile, Mr. Pines?"

"Look, honey," Pines told her breasts, "people like to rubberneck at accidents. They all wanna see what's go-ing on. Doesn't mean they're gonna go crashing their cars into each other on purpose, now, does it? Just be-cause I like to look now and then doesn't make me some child molester."

I had no idea if he was telling the truth, but I suddenly felt like I needed a shower. Or ten. No matter how he spun it, it was clear that lurking just beyond his flashy Hollywood exterior lay the heart of a diehard pervert.

"Why did you plead not guilty?" Allie asked.

Pines cocked his head at her. "What are you, the brains of the outfit? Because I'm *not guilty*."

"The cops found the magazines in your car."

"They were planted," Pines said. Though I could tell by the look on his face, even he was having a hard time believing that lie.

"Edward," his lawyer warned. "Be careful."

"What? I can't tell the truth?"

"So," Allie said, furiously scribbling, "you're saying you were framed?"

"That's right."

"By whom?"

"The cops. They have it in for me. Did you see the movie I did about police corruption? I get a parking ticket every week now. Fuckin' pigs."

Persecution complex much? But I was happily dancing in my seat, picturing the headline that went with that quote: PIGS PERSECUTE PINES OVER PARKING.

"I think we're done here," the lawyer said, jumping in before Pines could do any more damage.

Both men rose, prompting Allie and I to do the same.

As we walked out, Allie was still jotting down notes. "I might suggest investing in a digital recorder," I told her.

She looked up, a frown of concentration on her forehead. "What?"

"It's a lot easier than trying to write down everything they say."

"Do interviewees usually let you record conversations?"

I smirked. "I don't actually ask."

"But you have to disclose that you're recording, right? Otherwise, well, that would be unethical, wouldn't it?"

I shook my head. "Wow, do you have a lot to learn about working at a tabloid."

When we got back to the *Informer* with our mega story, I stopped at Max's desk first thing. "Hey," I said, leaning over the fabric partition.

Max looked up, the droopy bags under his eyes a testament to his night with Jim Beam. "Hey, Bender. What's up?"

"I was wondering if you'd do me a favor. I'd like to see an obit for her." I handed him a slip of paper with Hattie Carmichael's name on it. "Think you can dig up some stats?"

Max took it, frowning at the name.

"Who was she?"

"No one famous," I told him. But before he could protest, I added, "But she was a friend. It would mean a lot."

Max nodded. "I'll see what I can do," he promised.

I thanked him, glad I could do something for Mrs. Carmichael. I know, it wasn't much. But at least it was something.

One time when I was sixteen, I was visiting Aunt Sue's house in Long Beach and she'd let me take her station wagon out to a party. I'd had a little too much to drink and, instead of driving it home, I'd parked it overnight at the beach and took a cab. I'd had two parking tickets by the time I went to retrieve it the next day. Or, more accurately, Aunt Sue had two tickets. On her perfect, never even a speeding ticket or fender bender DMV record. I'd worked the rest of the summer at Togo's to pay off the fines, but I still felt incredibly guilty about blemishing the perfect record she'd been so proud of.

Let me tell you, that guilt was nothing compared to what I was feeling now. This was guilt supersized. And it was a bitch.

I plunked down into my chair, cueing up my computer screen to type up my Pines interview. I was halfway through when an IM window popped up.

I missed you last night.

Man in Black. Shit. I'd completely forgotten about him last night. Again. Though, in my defense, a dead body was a pretty good excuse.

Sorry. Long night.

Hot date?

No!

Though even as I typed it, I remembered just how close Cal's lips had been to mine and how hot things might have gotten had circumstances not intervened.

Good, Black typed. *I'm not a guy who likes to share.*

I grinned. *Sorry. I know that's two nights in a row I've stood you up.*

If I wasn't such a stud, I might start to worry. Then, *Tell me about your long night.*

I paused. Usually, I told Black everything. But he was likely to run for the hills the second I started talking about dead bodies.

I don't even know where to begin, I typed.

You okay?

I nodded at my empty cubicle. *Yeah.* And I guess I was. Surprisingly. I thought back to last night and how much I'd leaned on Cal to get me through. I'd leaned so hard, my IM date with Black had been the last thing on my mind. I felt a little twinge of something. My good friend guilt again? Which was ridiculous because Black was a fantasy and Cal was a rent-a-goon. In reality nothing was going on with either of these guys.

I've missed you, Black typed.

I bit my lip. Nothing. Right. Then why was my chest suddenly clenching as I stared at those three little words on my monitor?

I typed back a simple, *Me too.*

I'm not making a date for tonight, because I hate being stood up. But type at me when you can.

I will, I promised, meaning it. Okay, so maybe he was just a fantasy, but Black was the one person who really *got* me. He always knew just the right thing to say—or type—to make me feel better. Let's face it, my internet crush knew me better than anyone.

Jesus, I needed to get a life.

Chapter Thirteen

I was just finishing up my story when my cell rang from Strawberry Shortcake. I pulled it out, glancing at the caller ID. Marco.

"What's shaking?" I asked.

"Dahling, did I come through for you, or did I come through for you!"

"You got Jennifer Wood's alibi?" I asked.

"I did."

I grabbed a pen. "Shoot."

"Well," Marco started, and I could tell he was going to give me the long version. "I met up with my friend's friend's boyfriend at a party in the Hills last night, and he said that he did, in fact, see Jennifer at Ashlee's housewarming."

I felt my heart sink. One by one my suspects were falling. I could feel myself slowly being dragged back to square one again. "Did he see what time she got there?" I asked.

"No. But he said he was there at eleven, and she was already drinking appletinis with a Jonas brother."

"How long was she there?" I asked.

"She did a table dance in Ashlee's dining room at two."

Shit. "Did she leave the party at any time?" I was so grasping here.

"Sorry, dahling, no idea. Ricky didn't keep that close tabs on her, ya know."

"Right. Thanks anyway." So, Jennifer had been telling the truth. Granted, there was a slight chance she could have snuck out of the party, booted up her computer, used the Audio Cloak software to disguise her voice and play it back into a phone to leave me a threatening message before slipping back into the party. But, considering the phone was on the Sunset Studios lot, that chance was *very* slight.

"Hey, before you hang up—whose party were you at last night?" I couldn't help the gossip hound in me from asking.

"Oh, honey, it was to die for! A birthday party for that kid who plays the brother on that medical drama. He turned twenty-one, and man, does that boy know how to throw down."

"Sounds fun." I tried to remember the last time I'd gotten an invitation to a birthday party. I think it was Aunt Millie's. And we'd all had pudding cups instead of cake 'cause she'd cracked her dentures.

"Oh, it was, doll. Everyone was there. The Kardashian girls, Jessie Simpson, Katie Briggs."

That's it, my social life officially sucked. "Anyone get drunk? Make out? Cat fights?" I asked, mentally preparing tomorrow's column.

"Well . . . Kim K. and Jessie showed up in the same dress, and of course Jess looked better in it, so that almost turned into a wrestling match. But luckily that guy who does the Mac commercials was there to break it up. Oh, and Katie, she totally lost her iPhone in the pool when one of the Playboy bunnies bumped into her. She was pretty pissed about that. Apparently those suckers sink."

"Wait," I said, my mental hamster stopping in his tracks. "Did you say Katie Briggs has an iPhone?"

"Well, she did. It's toast now."

I narrowed my eyes. So much for Katie's rebelling against modern technology. Was that whole speech she'd given me a line of bull? If so, maybe she did have a computer. And maybe my suspect list wasn't so depleted after all.

"Is she scheduled at the salon today?" I asked.

"She'll be here in half an hour."

"Thanks, Marco. Hey, be a doll and keep her there as long as possible, 'kay?" I said. Then added, "There's a backstage press pass to Clay's next concert in it for you."

I heard Marco do a happy squeal as I hung up.

I grabbed my purse and stood.

"Where are we going?" Cal asked, suddenly at my side. He was licking the remnants of a protein bar off his fingers.

"Katie Briggs." I headed for the elevators, my shadow a step behind me as I quickly passed Allie's desk. She was scrunching her nose at her computer screen, no doubt trying to figure out how to spell "guilty." She looked up as I hustled past, but I ignored her.

"I thought we already talked to Katie," Cal protested.

"We did. And apparently she really is an Oscar-worthy actress, because it turns out her whole aversion to technology was a fake." I quickly filled him in on the conversation I'd had with Marco as we waited for the elevator.

"So, you think Katie was lying about owning a computer?" he asked.

"Could be. Look, Blain has no motive, Jennifer has an alibi, and Pines was in jail. Katie's our best bet at the moment."

We rode down two floors, then Cal beeped open his Hummer, and I hoisted myself inside, cueing up his GPS as soon as he cranked the engine over.

"What's that?" Cal asked, watching me input the address.

"Katie's house."

"I thought you said she was at Fernando's."

I grinned. "She is. Which means we only have an hour at best to search her place for a computer with Audio Cloak installed."

Cal cut the engine. "You're joking."

"What?"

"We are not breaking into her house."

"There's no way I can trust Katie to be straight with us. The only way to out her as a murderer is to find that computer."

"Then let the cops search her place."

I put my hands on my hips. "You really think my word is enough probable cause for a search warrant?"

He bit the inside of his cheek. Obviously he saw my point. "You're making it very hard for me to do my job, Bender."

"Your job is to protect me from bad guys. No one said anything about keeping me from bending the law a little."

Cal narrowed his eyes at me. Then finally muttered an, "I need a raise," and turned the car back on.

I tried to hide my smirk of triumph.

"And quit smirking."

Okay, fine. I didn't try *that* hard.

As soon as we were on the freeway, I grabbed my cell and dialed Cameron's number. She picked up on the fourth ring.

"Cameron Dakota."

"Hey, Cam, it's me," I told her. "Listen, where are you right now?"

"Afternoon baby bump watch on Melrose. Why?"

"I need a favor. Think I can steal you away for a couple hours?"

"Are you kidding? You'd be doing me the favor. It's like a hundred degrees out here, and I've already downed three Frappucinos. What's up?"

I quickly filled Cam in on our little mission and gave her the address to Katie's place in Beverly Hills.

When I hung up, Cal still had that I'm-going-to-live-to-regret-this look on his face.

"You're dragging Cam into this, too?"

"She's got a telephoto lens that can spot cellulite at a hundred yards away. She's our lookout."

Cal just shook his head again. "A *big* raise."

At six square miles, Beverly Hills is actually one of the smallest towns in California. But the wealth in those miles could buy a small country. Several times over. Designer boutiques, oversized homes on acres of prime real estate, and more Mercedes per capita than anywhere on the planet, it is a haven to the elite of L.A. society. Manicured, buffed, shined, and pleasant in every aspect, Beverly Hills is the sparkling gem of L.A. County. There isn't even a hospital or cemetery to remind residents of the unpleasant thought of mortality. It's said that technically, no one is actually born or dies in Beverly Hills.

Katie Briggs's place was on a wide, tree-lined street full of homes on steroids. Big, bold, and fairly bursting from their lots. Katie's was a two-story Mediterranean style, complete with adobe-colored shingles and wrought-iron balconies filled with brightly overflowing flowerpots. A narrow front lawn separated the house from the street, all wrapped up tight behind a large security gate that spanned the length of the property.

Cal parked at the curb in front of a faux Tudor across the street. "Now what?" he asked. Clearly not really wanting to know.

I ignored him, picking up my cell, dialing Cam's number, and putting it on speakerphone.

"Yeah?" she answered.

"You in place?"

"Yep."

I looked down the block. Cam's Jeep Wrangler was parked at the corner, her camera to her eye.

"Any sign of security?"

"None that I can see. Bodyguard's probably out with her."

"Weak point?"

"I'd try the south side. There's a bunch of trees shielding it from the road, and it leads right into the backyard."

"Perfect."

"You're not seriously going through with this, are you?" Cal asked.

I hopped out of the car.

"Of course I am."

"It's breaking and entering. You could be arrested."

"If I don't figure out who's behind the threats, I could end up dead."

Cal clenched his jaw together. "This is crossing a line, Bender. I don't feel good about it."

"Fine. Wait here, then. I'll be right back."

And before he could argue any further, I was jogging across the street to the small grove of trees separating Katie from her neighbor. I cautiously looked both ways, then stepped behind a thick palm and eyed the fence. It was at least eight feet high, brick topped with decorative iron scrollwork. I lifted my arms as high as they would go and tried to get some traction with my feet. I scaled a full two inches up the wall before dropping to the ground again. The bricks were too uniform; there was nothing to hold on to.

I glanced around the yard, looking for anything to boost me over. Flowers, bushes, strategically placed decorative rocks. Shit.

Then I spotted it. A metal planter with a skinny little lemon tree sticking out. It was only a couple feet high, obviously a newbie. With one more over the shoulder glance, I dug my fingers into the soil around the little tree and lifted it, roots and all, out of the planter. I laid the baby tree on the ground, then flipped the planter over and shoved it up against the wall. I stepped up on top of it. It was just high enough that I could reach the iron scrollwork. I curled my fingers around it, planted my feet against the brick, and hoisted myself up on top of the wall. Quickly, I twisted over the top and dropped down the other side. As soon as I landed on Katie's flagstone patio, my cell buzzed to life with a text. I looked down at the readout. Cam.

Way to go Spidergirl.

I grinned, shoving my phone back in my pocket as I quickly tippy-toed to a pair of French doors at the back of the house. The interior was deserted, large pairings of overstuffed furniture the only occupants. Gingerly, I tried the handle on the back door. Locked. I quickly made my way along the house until I hit another pair of French doors. These looked like they led to a guest room, a colorful throw on the bed, but no personal photos or touches. Again, I tried the door. Locked tight as a drum.

Okay, obviously I wasn't going to get that lucky.

I slipped my hand into my pocket, rummaging for anything that I could use to pick a lock. Gum, movie stub, ballpoint pen. Sigh.

I looked at the glass panes on the door. They were small, but large enough to slip a hand through. If I could smash the one near the handle . . .

I bent down and picked up one of Katie's decorative rocks and lifted it over my head.

But someone grabbed it away before I could use it.

"Jesus, Bender!"

I spun around to find Cal glaring down at me. "What the hell are you doing?"

"I was gonna smash the windowpane."

Cal dropped the rock back on the ground. "I can't take you anywhere." Then he proceeded to pull a long, thin thing that looked a dentist tool from his pocket. He inserted it into the keyhole and jiggled it.

"What's that?"

"Lockpick."

I raised an eyebrow at him. "How is it a guy that 'doesn't feel good' about breaking and entering owns a lockpick?"

He shrugged. "I don't always have to feel good."

I grinned.

My cell buzzed in my pocket. Cam again.

Cal's coming in after you.

Gee, thanks for the heads-up.

"There." I heard a click, then Cal turned the handle, pushing the door open. "We're in."

I shoved my phone back in my pocket and brushed past him into the guest room.

It was on the small side, expensively furnished, but in an understated way. A queen bed, dresser, and matching set of nightstands. A large oil painting hung above the bed depicting the Tuscan countryside, and a vase of fresh flowers sat on the dresser.

"Guest bedroom," Cal said, voicing my thoughts.

"Let's go find hers, then."

I opened the bedroom door, peering out. Two more doors, then the hallway opened up to the large living room I'd seen through the first set of French doors. Quickly I tried the other two rooms, only to find similarly furnished guest rooms. Beyond the living room was a tall, winding staircase, leading to another hallway. I motioned for Cal to follow and jogged up, hoping like hell that my shoes didn't muck up Katie's bright white carpets.

At the top of the stairs were three more doors. The first two contained a home gym and a study. The third, a master bedroom bigger than the entire offices of the *Informer*. Large canopied bed, two walk-in closets, and a crystal chandelier hanging from the ceiling.

"So, this is how the other half lives," Cal whispered beside me.

No kidding.

I spied a Victorian writing desk in the corner. And on top of it? A laptop.

Gotcha.

"No technology my ass . . ." I mumbled as I crossed the room, flipping the top open and powering the sucker up.

"You know, just because she has a computer doesn't make her a killer," Cal pointed out. "Lots of people have computers."

"Yeah, but why would she lie about it?"

"To impress a fan? To seem deeper than she is?"

I shrugged him off, watching the welcome screen flicker on. I went through the motions of booting up her system, then quickly started scanning her list of programs for Audio Cloak. But, of course, I still wasn't that lucky.

"Maybe she deleted it," Cal offered, reading over my shoulder.

I checked her trash folder. Empty.

"Got any other ideas?" I asked him.

He shrugged. "Sorry, not a computer genius."

Unfortunately, neither was I. What I was dying to do was take this back to the office, to the one person I knew who was a computer genius. Felix. Only, if I did that, I'd also have to tell him whose it was and how I got it. Not exactly a conversation I was dying to have.

"What about her browser history?" Cal suggested. "If she had to go through the website, it should show up there, right?"

"Brilliant." I pulled up an Internet Explorer window, then checked her history. A list of websites came up. An online shoe store, two spas, a bank, *Variety* online.

And Match.com.

I snorted. "Looks like we just found Katie's dirty little secret." I clicked the link. And immediately a profile popped up on the screen for "Kate B.," a single, "friendly, outgoing" woman in the L.A. area looking for a "confidant man who doesn't mind sharing the spotlight."

"Is this for real?" Cal asked over my shoulder.

I scanned through her profile. "Sadly, it looks like it." I thought back to the lonely look in her eyes as she'd told me about her night home alone. Could it be that Katie was really that hard up to find a good man?

Cal shook his head. "Finding love online. What a myth."

I cringed, my thoughts instantly bounding to my own dirty little secret and Black. "Not necessarily. I'm sure some people hook up that way," I countered. "There's no shame in looking for love online."

Cal raised an eyebrow at me. "Ninety percent of the guys on there are losers or perverts."

"Well, that still leaves a girl with a 10 percent chance," I mumbled.

I looked at Kate's picture. It wasn't a headshot or studio airbrushed job, but a candid photo of her sitting at a park, an ice cream cone in one hand as she laughed at something off camera. I had to admit, it was nice. Okay, she was a movie star, there was no way any pic of her was going to look hideous. But it was more natural, fresher, than I'd ever seen her.

Unable to quell my curiosity, I clicked her mailbox to see who'd written to her. Three profiles came up. A guy carrying a "few extra pounds" in Omaha who loved dogs and rodeos. A guy who listed himself as five feet tall, but promised that "good things came in small

packages." And a seventy-five-year-old who listed himself as "very young at heart."

Wow. Talk about depressing. If this was the response
someone like Katie was getting, what kind of chance
did the rest of us have?

"What does this have to do with your stalker?" Cal
asked, glancing at his watch. Clearly he was feeling less
"good" the more time we spent in Katie's house.

"Nothing. But, it's the best gossip I've hit on all year.
LONELY HEART MOVIE STAR SEEKS CYBER RO-
MANCE."

"I thought you said there was no shame in looking
for love online."

"There isn't. But it makes for awesome headlines."

Cal opened his mouth to respond but was interrupted by my cell ringing from my pocket. I slipped it
out and saw Cam's number light up the screen.

"What's up?" I asked.

"You've got company."

I froze. "What do you mean?"

"I mean someone is coming up the walkway."

I ran to the window, hiding behind Katie's heavy
curtains as I peeked out the front.

Sure enough, I could see the back of someone's head
as he stood at the front door.

"Who is he?" I asked, praying she said the UPS guy.

"The tree's in the way. I can't see his face," Cam
protested.

Which, I realized as the front door creaked open,
didn't much matter. Because whoever he was, he'd just
entered the house.

Chapter Fourteen

I froze, adrenaline coursing through my body as I heard the sound of the front door shutting behind our mystery man. Then footsteps coming up the stairs.

Shit.

We had to hide. Now!

I grabbed Cal by the arm, making for the large, walk-in closet. I shoved aside a rack of designer gowns (OMG—I think that was Katie's 2009 Oscar dress!) and wedged myself behind them. Cal opted to stand behind the door, his hand on the butt of his gun.

Two beats later the footsteps made their way into the bedroom. I closed my eyes, praying to the saint of breaking and entering that whoever it was saw Katie wasn't home and left quickly.

But, by this point, we all know how great my luck is.

I heard the man walk around Katie's canopied bed, to the window, and back again. What was he doing, pacing?

And then my luck got worse. Footsteps heading straight toward the closet.

I crossed my fingers, bit my lip, and mentally chanted "please go away, please go away, please go away."

The door flew open, narrowly missing Cal, and I was face to face with mystery man.

"Bender, what the hell are you doing?"

Felix.

I let out a breath so big it made Katie's dresses flutter.

"Jesus, Felix, you scared me half to death."

"I scared you?" Felix put both hands on his hips. "I hear one of my reporters is breaking into an A-lister's house and *I'm* the one who scared *you*?"

I stood up, disentangling myself from Katie's couture, and pushed past Felix into the bedroom again. Out of the corner of my eyes I noticed Cal holstering his gun.

"And you," Felix said, turning on him. "You're supposed to be keeping an eye on her."

"I am," Cal answered truthfully.

"This is hardly what I call keeping her out of danger. Do you know what would happen if anyone caught you two here? God, the lawsuits alone would cost us millions."

"Your concern is touching," I said, brushing hundred-thousand-dollar lint off my sleeve.

"What the hell are you even doing here?" he asked, his gaze pinging from me to Cal.

"Katie has a computer," I answered.

He gave me a blank stare.

So, I quickly filled him in on Katie's so-called techno aversion, the fact she was lying, and the computer sitting on her desk.

"No sign of the Audio Cloak software?" he asked when I was done.

Reluctantly, I shook my head.

"And no sign she's even been to the website?"

Again, I shook in the negative.

"Then really all you have is the fact that she's not fond of appearing in your column."

"And she lied!" I pointed out again. "And just because the software isn't there now, doesn't mean that she didn't delete it after using it. What we really need is to scan her computer for any possible deleted files."

Felix narrowed his eyes at me. "*We?*"

I batted my eyelashes at him. "Please? I know it would only take you a second."

"That's all it would take for someone to see us here and call the cops, too," he pointed out.

"Don't worry. If anyone comes, Cam will tell us."

His eyes narrowed again. "Cam's in on this too?"

Oops. Sorry, Cam!

"Uh, sorta."

Felix ground his teeth together, probably thinking about five bucks worth of dirty words. Finally he spat out, "Fine," and crossed the room to Katie's laptop. "But only because the sooner we find this person, the sooner I can have my paper back to normal."

"Amen to that!" I agreed as Felix started typing in strings of letters and numbers that made the screen turn black. He bypassed Windows, going into some directory that housed information in a completely foreign language. I tried to keep up with his commands, but it was all Greek to me. Instead, I peered out the window, scanning the street for any sign of other cars, hoping that Katie needed a long touch-up today.

It seemed like hours passed while Cal and I listened to the keys clack in silence, but in reality it was probably a matter of mere minutes before Felix finally shut the computer down and lowered the top. "Sorry. There's no sign Audio Cloak was ever used on this computer."

I felt my shoulders sag. My one good lead, crushed. "Well, maybe she has another computer. In another room!"

Felix shook his head, his face stern. "No way. We're out of here, Bender."

"But—"

"No buts. This has gone far enough."

"He's right," Cal said.

I shot him a mutinous look.

"The longer we stay, the greater chance someone will see us," he reasoned.

Two to one. I was sorely outnumbered. "Fine," I conceded, crossing my arms over my chest as Cal led the way downstairs, Felix bringing up the rear as if afraid I might bolt into another room if he let me out of his sight. (Which, honestly, I might have.) I was about to turn back into the guest room with the open lock when Felix gestured toward the front door.

"We should go out the front. Less conspicuous."

I narrowed my eyes at him. "Okay, how did you get in the front? Wasn't the door locked?"

He shrugged. "I carry picks."

Jesus, was everyone more experienced at breaking and entering than I was?

We quickly filed out the door, clicking it shut behind us, and crossed the street to where Felix's beat-up Dodge was parked behind the Hummer. And behind him was Cam's Jeep, Cam sitting on the tailgate.

"Some lookout you are," I mumbled as I passed her.

She mouthed, "sorry," at me.

"It wasn't Cam's fault," Felix said, unlocking his car.

I paused. That statement suddenly begged the question—whose fault was it?

"Soooooo, how *did* you know we were here?"

"Allie told me."

I felt my jaw clench, remembering the way her eyes had followed Cal and me to the elevators. She must have eavesdropped on the whole conversation. When I got my hands on that blonde . . .

"Speaking of whom," Felix continued, unaware of the rage building in my gut, "she tells me you interviewed Pines today?"

I swallowed my temper, telling myself to save it for the blonde. (I was out of quarters anyway.) "We did. And have we got a scoop on the Mullins guy." I filled him in on how Pines had alleged Mullins was trying to blackmail him just before his death. "If he tried it with Pines, maybe he tried it with someone else who wasn't as confident, and they killed him."

Felix listened with his poker face in place, mulling this over. Finally he said, "I like it. I want to know who else Mullins might have been trying to blackmail. Start with his co-stars. Find out who else was on the film with Pines and Mullins."

"On it!" I promised.

The first thing I did when I got back to the office was head straight for Allie's desk. Only to find out she was taking a late lunch. I hoped she enjoyed it. Because there was a distinct possibility that meal would be her last.

It also served to remind me I hadn't eaten yet either. Cal offered to go get us sandwiches again, and I plunked down at my desk.

Max's head popped up over the top of the partition. "That you, Bender?"

"Hey, Max."

"I got that obit typed up that you wanted," he said, handing me a sheet of paper.

I took it, scanning the highlights of Mrs. Carmichael's obituary. Apparently she'd been crowned Miss Venice Beach back in the forties. She'd owned two racehorses, one that had come in fourth in the Kentucky Derby in the sixties. She had penned a romance novel in the eighties that even sported Fabio on the cover. She'd been widowed three times—by a plumber, a car salesman, and a window washer. She'd been a certified scuba diver, had a pilot's license, and a black belt in judo. And, according to Max's fine reporting skills, she'd been the very first person to ever play Mickey Mouse at Disneyland.

Immediately a deep sense of sadness hit me. While she'd been a pain in the butt as an old woman, I'd had no idea of the kind of life she'd led before Palm Grove. I suddenly felt sorry that I hadn't taken the time to find out until now.

"That work for ya?" Max asked.

I nodded, not trusting myself to speak as I handed the sheet back to him.

I turned my watery-eyed gaze back to my computer screen, forcing the lump from my throat. Focus. I had work to do. And sitting here feeling guilty wasn't going to help Mrs. C. at this point.

Trying really hard to believe my own pep talk, I

booted up IMDB and focused on finding out who else had been in Pines's picture with Mullins.

The Internet Movie Database has all the info on every movie or TV show ever made. Plot, production status, cast, crew, and every agent associated with it. It's a huge network of who's who in Hollywood. You know that you've truly made it in this town when you have your own entry on IMDB.

I plugged in the name of Pines's last film and came up with a page that held the meager plot, a movie poster, and list of participants. Pines, of course, and a handful of other crew whose names I didn't recognize. Mullins was listed, as was the kid who'd played his son and allegedly posed for Pines. But as I scanned the names of the rest of the cast, one fairly jumped out at me.

Jennifer Wood.

Apparently she'd had a small part as the kid's babysitter. Huh. Small world. Well, considering "Samantha" was already pals with Jennifer, it was a place to start.

"Salami on sourdough." Cal dropped a sandwich on my desk. "Extra mayo." He gave me a wink.

I had to admit, I could get used to this lunch delivery thing.

An hour later we were parked outside the Sunset Studios lot, watching as one flashy BMW after another was waved through by a security guard who looked like he'd started shaving yesterday.

"So, how are we going to get in this time?" Cal asked behind his shades.

I stared out the passenger side window. Across the street were a liquor store, a souvenir shop and a Krispy Kreme.

I grinned. Now, this I could use . . .

Ten minutes later Cal and I were at the front gate, facing the baby security guard with two dozen glazed donuts.

"Who did you say you were again?" he asked, pulling out his list of those-cool-enough-to-be-allowed-entry.

"Crafts service. For the *Celebrity Diet Wars* show."

He frowned, his baby-fine brows drawing together. "It says here crafts service already came in at noon."

I nodded. "Yeah, I know. But, see, they didn't anticipate how much those chubby celebs like their pastries." I held up the Krispy Kreme box. "We had to go get more supplies."

The guard nodded. "Oh. Right." He consulted his clipboard again. "Okay, well, um, I guess go on in."

I gave myself a little mental pat on the back for my fabulous acting skills as Cal maneuvered the SUV through the gates.

Five minutes later we'd ditched the tank for a golf cart and were speeding our way toward the *Pippi Mississippi* set. We parked outside, near a row of white trailers, and made our way onto the sound stage. Today's filming was taking place in Pippi's "bedroom," a three-walled set decorated in more pink tulle than the entire cast of *The Nutcracker*. I tried not to gag on the cotton-candy-colored overload as Cal and I hung back.

In the center of the scene, on a ruffled pink daybed, sat Jennifer and her co-star. Jennifer was texting someone as a makeup artist powdered her forehead. The brunette was listening intently as the director gave her instructions.

"Okay, Lani, this is where Chloe confesses to Pippi

that she has a crush on her boyfriend. So, I need you to look really contrite, okay?"

The brunette nodded seriously. "Okay."

"You can do that, right?"

She rolled her eyes. "Julius, I'm a classically trained Shakespearean actress. I think I can handle 'contrite teen,' okay?"

"Right." I saw the director's nostrils flare as he took in a deep breath. Then he shouted, "Back to one, everyone," causing the crew to scatter like mice that had just heard the kitty coming.

The guy with the clapboard yelled, "Speed," someone yelled, "Rolling," and a loud bell sounded, signaling that shooting was under way.

"Nick totally asked me to the dance at lunch today," Jennifer said.

"Oh." Lani did an exaggerated "sad" face.

"What, Chloe? I thought you'd be happy for me."

"Oh, it's nothing," Lani said. "I just . . . well, I was kind of hoping that Nick would ask—"

"God, she's doing it again!" Jennifer interrupted.

"Cut," the exasperated director yelled. I could feel the collective groan ripple through the crew. "Doing what, love?" he asked.

"She's going off script."

"I am doing no such thing!" Lani protested, throwing her shoulders back.

"Are too. The line is, 'I *wondered* if Nick was going to ask me.' Not, 'I was *hoping* Nick would ask me.'"

The director closed his eyes, and I could imagine him mentally chanting whatever mantra his therapist had given him that week. "Jennifer. Honey. Darling. It doesn't matter. It's close enough. Let's just finish the scene so we can all go home, okay?"

"What do you mean it doesn't matter?" Jennifer yelled. "I memorize my lines, but Lani can get away with messing hers up?"

"It's called ad-libbing, Jenny," Lani protested. "If you'd ever taken an acting class in your charmed little life, you'd know that."

"Snob!" Jennifer stuck her tongue out at Lani.

"Twit!" Lani gave Jennifer the finger.

"Enough!" The director put both hands out in a stop sign motion. "Look, let's just . . . just call it a day," he said with a resigned sigh. "We'll work this out tomorrow, okay?"

"Fine," Jennifer said.

"And, Lani," the director added. "Could you please go over your script again tonight?"

Jennifer sent Lani a smirk. The brunette narrowed her eyes, mumbling something about a donkey and Jennifer's mother under her breath as she stalked off set.

"Are all teenage girls this catty?" Cal whispered to me.

I shrugged. "I wouldn't know. I'm pretty sure I was never a teenager. There!" I pointed as Jennifer walked off the set. "I'm going in."

"Good luck," Cal mumbled to my back.

Jennifer stepped outside, immediately going to one of the white trailers and shutting the door behind her. I did a quick glance over my shoulder, then followed, knocking on the metal door.

"What?" I heard from inside.

Gingerly, I turned the knob and pushed my way inside. "Hello? Jennifer? It's me, Samantha."

The interior of the trailer was, like Pippi's bedroom, done in all pink—pink walls, pink carpeting on the floor, pink velvet sofa. It was like a cotton candy machine threw up. To the right sat a small table and chairs, pink vinyl on shiny chrome. On the side table a film script sat open-faced, as if abandoned mid-read.

The queen of all things pink herself sat on the sofa, her legs curled up under her, eyeing me over an iced latte. (I had to find out where she was getting those!) "You're who?" she asked, clearly not recognizing me.

"Uh, Samantha. Stevens. You know, from the Bochco drama."

Jennifer blinked, trying to place me. Then finally shrugged as if it didn't really matter that much to her anyway. "Yeah. Sure."

"Uh, I was wondering if you had a few minutes?"

"I'm actually kinda busy right now," she said, taking a long, noisy sip from her drink.

"It'll just take a minute."

She rolled her eyes. "Whatev."

I took a seat on the sofa next to her, trying not to covet her caffeine fix too deeply. "A little trouble with your co-star?" I asked.

She cocked her head at me.

"I watched that last scene you shot," I explained. "The brunette seemed to be giving you some trouble."

Jennifer nodded. "Lani. She thinks she's so hot just because she's taken a few acting lessons. She doesn't understand that some of us are just naturals, ya know?"

"I thought I read in the *Informer* that you and Lani were friends?"

"Well, sure," she said, slurping away. "But she's, like,

totally the Nicole Richie of the friendship, you know? She's just riding my coattails."

"Right." Ah, Hollywood loyalty.

"So, I heard that you worked on that last Pines movie?" I said, getting down to business.

She nodded, licking coffee off her lips. "Yeah. What of it?"

"Well . . ." I leaned in close. "Someone told me a rumor about Jake Mullins, and I was wondering if you could confirm if it's true."

She raised a perfectly plucked eyebrow at me. "What kinda rumor?"

I took a deep breath, mentally crossing my fingers. "That he tried to blackmail Pines."

The other eyebrow shot up. "Seriously?"

I nodded.

"Wow, that's so not cool."

"You didn't know anything about it?"

Jennifer shook her head, her blonde locks brushing her shoulders. "Nope. Man, you think you know someone."

"Any idea if he approached any of your other co-stars?" I asked.

"No. Why?"

"Who did Mullins talk to? Pal around with on the set?"

"You're awfully nosey," Jennifer said, narrowing her eyes as she bit down on her straw.

I suddenly had a bad feeling that the blonde might not be as dumb as she played on TV. So I decided to level with her. Hey, at this point, what did I have to lose?

"Okay, here's the deal," I said. "I'm not really an actress."

"I know," Jennifer said.

Which took me off guard. "You know?"

"Duh." Jennifer rolled her eyes. "That hair. Who would hire an actress with purple hair like that?"

I bit my tongue, promising myself I could crucify her in tomorrow's column. "Right. Well, I'm actually a reporter," I confessed.

Jennifer froze, straw dangling from her lips. "A reporter?"

"With the *L.A. Informer*. Tina Bender."

She slammed the latte down on the side table. "You! What, trying to dig up more fake dirt on me? Those marijuana lies weren't enough?"

"Hey, I just wrote what I saw."

"Right." She crossed her arms over her chest, glaring at me like a two-year-old facing a plate of broccoli.

"I'm sorry," I conceded.

"Yeah, well, check your facts next time," she spat out. "I don't smoke."

"Duly noted. Look, actually, I'm investigating Mullins's death."

"I thought that was an accident? Overdose or something?"

"Sleeping pills. But I'm not convinced it was accidental. I think he may have tried to blackmail someone else on the set and been killed for it."

Her eyes went big. "Dude."

"No kidding."

"So, what do you want to know?" she asked, curiosity starting to override her initial anger.

"Anything you can tell me about Mullins. His behavior on the set, who he hung out with, what he might have dug up on his co-stars."

Jennifer pursed her lips together. "Jake was really creepy. Always keeping to himself, kinda slinking around the place like he had some secret. I don't think he was really close to anyone. There was always something a little greasy about Jake, you know? Like he was just a little too desperate. But blackmail . . . Wow. I had no idea he'd be that stupid."

A great quote that I mentally tucked away for later use. However, not really helpful in finding out anything further about Mullins's potential killer. I bit my lip, trying to come up with anything else that might make this trip not for nil. My eyes rested on the script beside her.

"A new film opportunity?" the gossip columnist in me had to ask.

She followed my gaze. "Kinda."

"What's it about?"

"Oh, it's one of those boring Oscar films with a micro-budget that no one goes to see but sweeps all the awards. But it's not for me personally," she said, scrunching up her nose at the idea of doing anything less than a summer blockbuster. "It's for my production company. My manager thinks it will be good publicity."

I froze, gears clicking into place.

"You own a production company?"

She nodded. "Co-own, at least."

"That company wouldn't happen to be here on the Sunset lot, would it?"

Again with the nod, her blonde hair bobbing up and down.

Mental forehead smack.

"PW Enterprises?"

Her shoulders sagged, and her mouth dropped open into a surprised little "o." "Yeah! How did you know?"

"Lucky guess," I mumbled. It all fit, and I felt foolish for not putting it together sooner. The company was on the same studio lot as *Pippi Mississippi*, Jennifer had been in the one and only film they'd produced so far, and if Pines was the "P," it was suddenly painfully obvious who the "W" had to be. Jennifer *Wood*.

I cocked my head to the side, sizing Jennifer up as a suspect once again. Sure she had an alibi, but now that she was tied tighter than a Christmas bow to PW Enterprises, I wondered, how hard would it have been to get one of her "Nicole Richie" hangers-on to make the call for her?

"Did you know that someone has been threatening my life?" I asked.

"No way! Who?" she asked, leaning forward.

"I don't know yet. But I traced the threatening call to PW Enterprises."

Jennifer blinked at me, realization slow in coming. "Wait, you don't think that I . . . ? No way!" she repeated.

I nodded. "Way."

She shook her head back and forth so violently her hair smacked her perfectly powdered cheeks. "Nuh-uh. Not me. I would *so* not do that."

"You just admitted you're not my biggest fan."

"Well, yeah, but can you blame me?"

She had a point. "Who else would have access to the PW offices?"

She shrugged. "Anyone, I guess. I mean, everyone on

the lot knows where it is. And PA's are always coming and going."

"What about at night. Aren't they locked up?"

She shrugged. "I dunno. I mean, probably, but we're not like putting alarms and guard dogs on the place. Security on the lot is tight enough we don't really worry about it that much. They don't let just anyone into Sunset."

She was right. I thought back to how inventive Cal and I had to be to get on the lot. While it wasn't impossible the call was made by an outsider, chances were it was someone who actually belonged on Sunset property.

Unfortunately, that included half of Hollywood.

"Look, I totally swear I had nothing to do with this," Jennifer said again. "You have to believe me!"

Sadly, by the look of true fear of bad press in her eyes, I kinda did. I sighed, realizing just where that left me.

All the way back to square one. Again.

Chapter Fifteen

By the time we finished with Jennifer Wood, the sun was setting, my stomach was growling, and the traffic on the 101 was thicker than Kirstie Alley's waistline.

"Ready to call it a day?" Cal asked, inching forward behind an electric smart car. The driver looked nervously in his rearview mirror as if Cal's monster truck might crush his bumper any second.

I nodded. "I'm beat. But first, you think we could stop at a drive-thru?"

"I think your aunt said she was making enchiladas tonight."

"All the more reason to stop for food first."

He shot me a look.

"Trust me, it's survival."

He shrugged, then pulled off at the next exit, navigating the Hummer into the Carl's Jr. drive-thru. (Just barely—the top of the tank was mere inches from the clearance rod.)

I ordered three chicken sandwiches (one for me, two just in case), curly fries, onion rings, and a strawberry shake. Cal ordered a side salad and fried zucchini.

"Okay, I get the no beef thing. But are you going vegetarian on me now?" I asked, digging into my greasy bag.

"I don't trust their chicken."

"What do you think they put in it?"

"It's not what they put in it," he said, pulling back into traffic, "it's the chickens themselves."

I knew I was going to regret asking this, but . . . "What's wrong with the chickens?"

His eyes went from my bag to me. "You really want to know?"

No. "Yes."

He shrugged. "Okay. For starters, fast-food places have a very small profit margin on each item. So, they want the cheapest chickens out there. They go for the older ones, the sickly ones, the ones no respectable farmer will eat himself. You know what kind of chickens are in that patty?"

I looked down at my sandwich. "Yummy ones?"

"Poultry plants take the diseased chickens, cut out the infected parts, and chop up the rest for use in processed chicken products like nuggets and patties."

"Infected?" My appetite was quickly waning.

"Then there's the antibiotics. Chickens are routinely given these drugs in a vain attempt to keep them healthy, but guess where the drugs go? They're stored in the chicken's fat cells. When we eat the meat, we get a healthy dose of those drugs ourselves. Or, unhealthy, as the case may be."

I slurped my shake. "That's gross."

"That's why I don't eat fast-food chicken. Only organic."

I looked down into my bag. Maybe the enchiladas wouldn't be so bad.

* * *

Half an hour later we pulled into the driveway of Cal's place. The second I walked in, the scent of chilies and limes hit me square in the face, waking up my growling stomach once again.

"I've got some work to finish up," Cal said, sinking onto the sofa in the living room and dropping a stack of files onto the coffee table. Which was fine with me. I had a one-track mind—or stomach, as the case may be. I followed my nose into the kitchen where Millie and Aunt Sue were standing at the oven, a half empty pitcher of margaritas in front of them as they giggled at some private joke.

"Smells good in here," I said.

"Oh, Tina, you're back. How was your day, dear?" Aunt Sue asked me.

"Good." I peeked in the oven. So far, nothing was charcoal colored. A good sign. "Yours?"

"Well, your aunt Millie and I spent the day going through Hattie's things."

I felt that familiar lump of guilt well up in my throat again. "I'm sorry to hear that."

"Oh, don't be. We had a ball. Hattie had such eclectic taste. Anyway, we're boxing it all up and sending it out to Goodwill tomorrow."

I nodded.

"And the coroner called," Millie added. "He said they're releasing her body tomorrow. She wanted to be cremated and have her ashes spread out in her favorite place. The mortuary said we could pick her up day after tomorrow, so we'll do it then. You want to come with?"

The last thing I wanted to do was stand downwind

while the aunts dumped Hattie Carmichael in her last resting place. But considering she was now resting because of me, I found that guilt answering with an, "Of course."

"Good." Aunt Sue nodded. "You want a margarita, honey?"

Did I ever. "Fill 'er up."

Aunt Sue poured me a tall glass, which I gratefully drank from as the aunts chatted about what to do with all of Hattie's photographs and scrapbooks.

Poor Mrs. Carmichael. I tossed the chicken patties in the trash and took another long sip from my margarita. It was strong, but not half bad. Could have used a little more salt.

As I watched Aunt Sue pull a tray out of the oven and sprinkle cheese on top, my thoughts wandered to who could have done in Mrs. C. My original suspect list had yielded nada so far. Was I on the wrong track entirely? Maybe this was just some random creep who liked to see journalists squirm. There was no way either Pines or Blain Hall could have killed her, both of them locked up at the time. But both Katie and Jennifer had alibis for when the original call was made.

Which left me where?

I took a long drag from my glass.

Nowhere. No suspects, no leads. The only thing I had was motive. Everyone in town apparently hated me.

Wow, was I the self-pity queen today or what? I downed the last of my drink, filling up the glass again.

"The enchiladas are almost done," Aunt Millie informed us, pulling a steaming pan from the oven.

"Good. I love enchiladas," I said. Though somehow it came out more like, "Good, I wuv eshiladas."

Aunt Sue looked from the nearly empty pitcher to me. "How many of those have you had, peanut?"

"One." I hiccupped. "And a half."

A deep wrinkle of concern formed on her forehead. "Well, you might want to slow down just a little."

I waved her off. "Ish juss 'cause I haven't eaten." I was sure after I dug into the enchiladas I'd feel better. In fact . . . I downed a few more gulps . . . I was beginning to feel better already. Better than I had in days.

Okay, so what if everyone in town hated me? That just meant I was doing my job well. No one loves a good reporter. And I was a good reporter, despite what Felix thought. So maybe I wasn't 100 percent sure of this creep's identity, but in the past week I'd single-handedly gotten the goods on Katie Brigg's secret online dating life, Blain Hall's real addition, blackmail on the set of Pines's last film, and kickass quotes from both Pines and Jennifer Wood. All things considered, I rocked. I was a superstar gossip columnist.

With that cheery thought, I dug into my enchiladas with relish, not even caring the slightest that they were just one jalapeno shy of being toxic.

Three margaritas later, I staggered into the living room to find Cal hovering over a stack of papers in a yellow manila folder.

"What's that?" I asked, plopping myself down on the sofa next to him.

"A new client. Wants me to watch his wife while he's out of town."

I looked down at the folder. A picture of a tall,

stacked blonde stared back at me. I hated tall, stacked blondes.

"She looks high maintenance," I pointed out.

He shot me a look, the corner of his mouth tilting upward in a grin. "Well, luckily, I don't have to date her. I just have to watch her."

I felt my cheeks flush. "Right."

"Anyway, I won't take it until I'm sure you're out of danger."

Something about the protective tone in his voice made my insides warm. Yeah, I know he was being *paid* to be protective, but that didn't make it any less comforting.

"Thanks," I said.

He turned to me. "For what?"

"For taking care of me. Nobody takes care of me."

His eyes softened. "You're slurring your words a little there, kid."

I nodded. "It's 'cause I'm drunk." I lifted my empty margarita glass as proof.

He grinned. "Yes, you are."

"It's okay," I told him. "I like being drunk. It means I don't have to think about anything."

"Such as?"

"Suspects, murders, Pines, the paper, Felix, you."

"Me?"

Shit. Had I said that out loud?

"I mean, the way you follow me around."

His eyebrows drew together. "Does it bother you that much?"

"No. I mean, yes, at first. But, no, that's not what I meant when I said you and you following me around. I meant, well, I guess what I really meant was . . . I mean, it's complicated, I mean . . ." Truth was, I had no idea what I meant.

Cal looked at me, concern lacing his eyes. Dark brown eyes. I'd never noticed before, but they were fringed in the longest lashes I'd ever seen on a man. I sighed. "You have nice eyes."

The corners of his lips tilted upward. "Thanks."

"And nice lips. They look like soft lips."

The grin grew. "Honey, you're *really* drunk."

I nodded. But somehow that knowledge didn't stop me from leaning in closer . . . closer . . . so close I could have licked his lower lip if I'd stuck my tongue out.

Which I did.

"Tina," he whispered.

But I didn't let him finish that thought, my mouth suddenly acting all on its own as it latched on to his.

I was right. His lips were soft. And sweet. And when they started moving beneath mine, gently nipping at my lower lip, I felt a moan curl up from my belly. Wow, he was good at this. *Really* good.

His goatee tickled my chin, his arms drawing around my shoulders, pulling me in tight against that body that could make anyone believe in the power of protein shakes.

I lost all sense of time, but after what felt like a blissful eternity, we finally came up for air. Cal pulled away, his eyes dark and unreadable, his breath coming as quickly as mine suddenly was. His voice was husky. "I think maybe we'd better get you to bed."

I grinned, biting my lower lip. "Anything you say, big guy."

* * *

A full brass band was playing in the next room, the tuba relentlessly thumping out note after note. My temples throbbed with each beat, my head threatening to explode. I covered my ears with a pillow, trying to drown out the noise. But the damned band kept on playing, louder if anything. God, how many margaritas had I had last night? Thirty? Forty? Okay, it was probably more like four. But that was four too many. Tequila was definitely not my friend this morning. I rolled over, giving up on the pillow, and stumbled to my feet, trying to get my bearings. Four-poster bed. Navy comforter. Fuzzy velvet Elvis on the wall.

Cal's room.

As the band played on, the night before came flooding back to me in one horrible ohmigod-what-did-I-do-last-night rush.

I remembered sitting on the sofa, saying something stupid about his eyes, and then we were kissing. Then he said something about going to bed . . .

I covered my mouth. Oh shit. Had I slept with Cal?

I looked down. I was wearing the shirt I'd worn yesterday and a pair of pink panties. Inconclusive.

I looked wildly around for any sign of Cal, but I was thankfully alone. Which could mean I'd dreamt the whole thing or that he'd already gotten up from our post-coital bliss to make me breakfast. Think, Tina, think! What happened last night? I wasn't sure. My memory was covered in a tequila haze. I licked my lips and swore I could still taste Cal there. I'd kissed him . . . Oh, God, I'd kissed him. I buried my head in my hands. How stupid could I get? And why the hell was that band still playing?!

I threw the covers off, willing my feet to hold me up.

One foot on the ground. Two. Okay, so far so good. I took a couple tentative steps, and, while my stomach wasn't thrilled with the idea of movement, last night's enchiladas stayed firmly put. Which I took as a good sign.

I threw a pair of jeans on, then opened the bedroom door. And the brass band grew louder. By the time I shuffled into the kitchen it was all I could do not to gouge my own eardrums out at the sound. I walked in to find Aunt Sue at a blender, throwing chunks of bananas in as she danced to the forties big band coming from a radio in the corner.

"Could you turn that off?" I pleaded, one hand on my head to keep my brains from oozing out my ears.

"What?" Aunt Sue yelled.

"Turn it off!"

She turned the knob on the radio, bringing with it blissful silence. "What did you say? I can't hear you with the radio on!"

I took a deep breath. Blew it out. Reminded myself how much I loved my aunt. "Coffee. Is there any coffee?"

"Here you go, tequila queen." I looked up to find Cal handing me a mug of steaming liquid.

His hair was still wet from a shower, his eyes crinkling at the corners, dancing with some secret knowledge. I sincerely hoped it wasn't about me.

Self-consciously, I took the cup. "Thanks."

"How you feeling?" he asked, sipping from a mug of his own. If he was feeling any hint of the awkwardness consuming me, he didn't show it, casually leaning against the kitchen counter as if it were the most natural thing in the world for him to get his clients drunk and take them to his bed.

Maybe it was.

A thought which did nothing to settle my angry stomach.

"Um. Good. Fine," I lied, sipping my coffee.

"You look like hell."

I stuck my tongue out at him. "Gee, thanks."

He grinned. "Hangovers are a bitch, aren't they?"

"Just shut up, keep the coffee coming, and no one gets hurt."

"You got it, sunshine," he said. Then gave me a wink.

My stomach rolled again, but this time I kinda liked it.

"So," I said, purposefully clearing my throat and turning to Aunt Sue. "What have you and Aunt Millie got planned today?"

Aunt Sue poured her thick banana shake into a glass and started sucking it through a straw. "Got more packing to do at Hattie's. Then we're shipping some boxes of photos to her nephew, and we're gonna hit up the lunch buffet at the senior center. Today's chicken dumpling day."

"Sounds thrilling."

"Felix called," Cal told me, dropping a piece of bread into the toaster.

I groaned. "What did he want?"

"Wanted to know when you might be coming in to work today."

I glanced at the clock. Eleven already. Geez, I'd slept half the day away. Curse you, tequila.

"Ten minutes," I said, downing the rest of my coffee.

I took the fastest shower on record (even though the

hot water on my hangover brain felt like heaven), then quickly dressed in a pair of jeans, pink converse, and a stretchy black top with purple rhinestones spelling out the words, "Yes, they're real," across the chest. I grabbed my notebook and purse and was ready to go just as Millie walked in.

"Sorry I'm late today," she said. "The bus wasn't running on time."

Last year Aunt Millie had driven her boat of an Oldsmobile right up onto the front lawn of St. Mark's Episcopal Church, nearly taking out the bronze statue of St. Mark himself in the process. To her credit, she promptly got out of the car and apologized to the statue. That is, until he didn't answer back, and she thought the rude man was giving her the cold shoulder, at which point she whacked him on the arm with her purse and started questioning what his mother would think of his ill manners. Needless to say, after this incident the DMV had decided that her twenty/one-fifty vision was not entirely safe for operating a motor vehicle. Since then, Millie had been riding the bus, and the rest of us on the streets had been breathing a little easier.

I quickly directed Millie to the kitchen and made for Cal's Hummer before Felix decided that the *Informer* could get along with one fewer gossip columnist on staff.

Luckily, by eleven thirty there was little to no traffic on the way into the *Informer*'s offices. Unluckily, the talent agency on the third floor was holding auditions for a role in the latest Spielberg movie, so there was no parking to be had for two blocks in either direction. Cal circled twice, finally finding a space six doors down.

By the time we'd hoofed it back to the office, I was sweating from places I didn't know even had sweat glands. I hated Indian summer.

Finally we rounded the building, cutting across the parking lot to the back entrance. We were halfway to the doors when I spotted my Rebel bike, parked in a space to the left of the entrance, just where I'd left it. Only, unlike the shiny, clean state I'd left it in, it was now covered in large splotches of white birdie doo-doo.

"Shit!" Literally.

I looked up to find two pigeons perched on the fire escape directly above my bike, looking innocent as anything. Damned birds.

"My bike is not a bathroom!" I shouted to them. I thought I heard Cal smirk behind me but chose to ignore him, taking my anger out on the stupid pigeons instead. "Stay the hell away from my bike. Got it?"

I swear to God, the fatter pigeon cocked his head at me. Then, as if to spite me, he flapped his no-doubt diseased little wings, sailing down from this perch and landing, you guessed it, on my bike.

"Oh, that's it. You're toast," I said, taking a menacing step forward.

Only I didn't get any farther. Suddenly a huge boom filled the air. Bright orange flames burst from my bike, tossing hot pink pieces of metal into the air, and sending me flying backward across the parking lot.

Chapter Sixteen

Instinctively, I threw my arms up, trying to shield my eyes from the instant sunburn. I felt my butt slam down on the macadam. Hard. Tiny pieces of debris that used to be my baby raining down on me.

From somewhere that sounded very far away, I heard Cal yelling my name. Only he must have been closer than I thought, because in an instant his arms were around me, pulling me to my feet and away from the smoldering black spot on the ground that used to be my bike.

"Tina, are you okay?" he asked, his eyes searching my face and limbs, hands feeling for broken bones.

I blinked, trying to take in what had just happened. "I . . . I think so." Which, as I wiggled my fingers, toes, arms, and legs, seemed true. My arms were red and covered in tiny scratches, and I was sure a big purple bruise was already forming on my butt, but other than that I was mostly unharmed.

More than I could say for my bike.

"It blew up," I said, lamely pointing to where the pigeon's bathroom used to be.

Cal nodded, his face grim.

And the full realization of what just happened hit

me. "Someone blew up my bike. Someone . . . tried to blow up me." I looked back to the charcoaled spot.

The first threat on my life I honestly hadn't taken all that seriously. Even the email had been creepy but not particularly scary. But with Mrs. Carmichael's murder and now this . . . This was so over the top I needed a new word for scary. I felt myself start to shake as Cal pulled his cell out, dialing who I presumed to be the police. In fact, I was trembling so badly that I slid to the ground against the wall of the *Informer*'s building.

"You okay?" Cal asked, the phone still to his ear.

I nodded. Apparently unconvincingly, as he crouched down on the pavement next to me. "Don't worry, we're going to get this guy," he said, putting a hand on my shoulder.

I nodded again. But didn't tell him that I wasn't trembling solely out of fear. I'd have to be a moron not to be freaked out by this, but, even more than scared, I was pissed. This guy had taken away the safety of my home, my neighborhood, my job. He'd turned my life upside down. And I was ready for it to end. I was ready to take my life back.

And as I stared at what could very well have been barbequed me, I vowed that I wasn't going to stop until I did.

Two hours later the cops had dusted, swabbed, and sprayed the entire parking lot for any trace evidence my would-be killer might have left behind. With no results. They said they needed to take it all back to the lab for more comprehensive testing.

As soon as the detective in charge said I could go, I bolted, leaving Cal to deal with the rest of the mess. I knew he could handle it. Me? Hangover plus explosion was more than I could take in one day. Instead, I marched up to the second floor and shoved myself in front of my computer. I pulled up a word processing file and immediately started typing.

GOSSIP COLUMNIST CALLS OUT HER MYSTERY STALKER

RECENTLY YOURS TRULY HAS BEEN THE RECIPIENT OF A NUMBER OF THREATS—

I paused. Then hit the backspace button.

—THE RECIPIENT OF A NUMBER OF *CHILDISH* THREATS—

There, that was better. I smirked as my fingers continued typing.

—*CHILDISH* THREATS FROM AN UNKNOWN SOURCE. THIS SOURCE PROMISED THAT IF I DIDN'T STOP PRINTING ARTICLES ABOUT HIM OR HER, I WOULD END UP DEAD. WELL GUESS WHAT, MYSTERY STALKER? THIS IS ONE REPORTER WHO IS A LITTLE CLEVERER THAN YOU BARGAINED FOR. I KNOW YOUR IDENTITY. AND IF YOU DON'T TURN YOURSELF IN TODAY, I'LL BE PRINTING IT IN TOMORROW'S PAPER. HOW'S THAT FOR A THREAT?

"What is that?"

I spun around to find Cam reading over my shoulder.

"It's my column for tomorrow."

Her blonde brows puckered in concern. "Are you sure that's wise? You're kind of taunting a killer here, Tina."

I looked back at the screen. "Trust me, I know what I'm doing." Which was the biggest load of false bravado ever, but I wasn't about to back down now.

"Are you sure about this?" she asked.

"Yes." No. "The only problem is going to be getting this past Felix. There's no way he'll print it."

"Felix is a smart man."

I chose to ignore that comment.

"What we need is a distraction. Final copy has to be in to the printer by six. If I can find a way to distract Felix and slip this in at the last minute, it might work."

Cam shook her head. "Don't look at me. I like my job here. No way am I going behind Felix's back with something like this."

I felt my shoulders sag. I'd actually secretly been counting on Cam to help me out.

"Please?" I begged.

But the resolved look in her eyes told me no amount of pleading was going to change her mind. "Sorry, Tina, but you're on your own with this one. Look, just submit it to him, and see what he says. Maybe he's feeling generous today."

I put my hands on my hips. "Hello? Have you met Felix?"

She gave me a sympathetic shrug. "Sorry." Then added as she turned to go, "And be careful, Tina, okay?"

I nodded. Really, I couldn't blame her. A week ago keeping my boss happy would have been at the top of my priority list, too. And I'd already gotten her in hot water over the whole lookout at Katie Briggs's incident.

Unfortunately, that left me still distraction-less. I let my gaze wander over the newsroom for another possible ally. Max, Cece . . . Allie.

I froze. If ever someone had distraction written all over her, it was Allie.

I clenched my jaw. I stood up. I sucked in a deep breath. And prepared to make a deal with the devil to save my skin.

"You're nuts, you know that?"

I nodded.

Allie shook her head at me, her blonde locks falling over her shoulder. "You're really going to call this guy out?"

I nodded again. "Look, I need you to distract Felix. Just for a second."

She narrowed her eyes. "And what's in it for me?"

I bit my lip. "That satisfaction of helping a co-worker?"

Her eyes narrowed further until they looked like a cat's.

Okay, so she was into satisfaction.

"Look, I'll . . . I'll introduce you to some of my contacts around town."

Her lip curled. And she shook her head. "Not good enough."

I threw my hands up. "Okay, fine. What do you want?"

"I want this story."

I blinked at her. "What story?"

"The story of the *Informer* reporter who's being

stalked by a murderer, threatens to expose him, then ends up getting herself killed."

I raised an eyebrow at her.

She shrugged. "It's one possible ending."

"Thanks for the vote of confidence."

"Do we have a deal?"

I ground my teeth together. The last thing I wanted to do was give Barbie an exclusive on *my* life story. On the other hand, if I didn't, said story was likely to be a whole lot shorter and have a much less pleasant ending.

Begrudgingly, I stuck my hand out. "Deal."

Allie shook it, the most evil grin I'd ever seen spreading across her cute little face.

I involuntarily shuddered.

"So, you're on Felix, then?"

She nodded. Then fluffed up her boobs. "Come six o'clock, he's all mine."

For a moment, I almost felt sorry for the boss.

Crisis One taken care of for the day, I made my way back to my desk, avoiding looking directly at Felix as I passed his office, lest he see the glint of guilt in my eyes.

As soon as I sat down, my cell rang.

"Tina Bender?" I answered.

"Tina, dahling," Marco cooed on the other end. "How are we this fine morning?"

Oh, boy. Loaded question. But I figured the short version would suffice. "Fine."

"Fab. Listen, hon, is it true that you've been talking to the police?"

Shit. My worst fears were confirmed. Word was

spreading through my network of informants that Tina Bender and the cops were *like that.*

"Um, sorta."

Marco made a tsking sound. "Sweetie, that's not good. You know loose lips aren't gonna wag your way like that."

I nodded at my cubicle. "I know. Look, it's just . . . temporary," I hedged, not willing to air all my dirty laundry for Beverly Hills's biggest gossip.

"Let's hope. For your sake, dahling."

"Thanks."

"In the meantime, I'm not a fair-weather friend, and has mama got some good d-i-s-h for you, girl."

I leaned forward. "I could use some good dish today. Lay it on me, Marco."

"Guess who came into the salon yesterday?"

I opened my mouth to respond, but he didn't give me a chance.

"Duke Donovan."

I drew a blank. "Who?"

"Duke Donovan! Ohmigod, girl, don't tell me you don't watch *Massexachusetts*?"

I had to admit, I didn't. But the name was starting to ring a bell. "He did that paranormal alien show for a while, right?"

"Yes! Gawd, I miss that show. Anyhoo, while Gia was doing his highlights I overheard him on his cell saying that he was slated to star in that new action film with the mondo budget. And, get this, his co-star— Tom Cruise!"

I raised an eyebrow. That *was* big news. If I remembered correctly, the last movie Donovan worked on had been . . . well, I couldn't actually remember the last movie he'd worked on. Then again, Donovan's sister had been murdered last spring, catapulting his name back into the spotlight and earning him that all important Hollywood sympathy vote.

Amazing how one little murder could make a has-been a household name again.

I froze.

Suddenly I felt the distinct *click* of puzzle pieces falling into place in my brain.

Jake Mullins's widow was a has-been child star. One who was desperate to get back into the business. Hadn't she mentioned she'd recently picked up a couple roles?

"Thanks for the tip, Marco. I gotta go," I quickly said into the phone, hanging it up and letting my fingers fly with lightning speed over my keyboard. I pulled up the IMDB website again, typing in the name "Alexis Mullins." Her credits as a member of *The Fenton Family* popped up (back when she was known as cute little Alexis Grant), but alongside them were three new projects: a Lifetime movie, VH1's *Celebrity Sorority House*, and an HBO TV series pilot produced by Tom Hanks. Not too shabby.

I chewed my pen top as I sat back in my chair. It was a long shot, but . . .

I grabbed Strawberry Shortcake and made for the elevator.

Unfortunately, as soon as I got there, the doors slid open to reveal Cal on the other side.

He looked down at my purse. "Going somewhere?"

"Jake Mullins's widow."

He raised an eyebrow.

"Let's just say I've got a hunch."

Cal looked like he was about to protest. Luckily, he

knew me better than that by now and, instead, shrugged, leading the way back into the elevator.

Half an hour later we were back in Echo Park, Cal's Hummer stashed in the Ralph's parking lot and the two of us knocking on Alexis Mullins's front door. A few beats later it was opened a crack by the widow herself.

This time she was fully dressed, sporting a pleather miniskirt, thigh-high boots, fishnet stockings, and a lacy top that left little to the imagination. Either she was headed for the casting couch or a street corner somewhere on Hollywood Boulevard.

"Hi," I said, doing a little wave at her. "Remember us?"

She wrinkled her forehead as if trying to. "Yeah. The writer, right?"

I nodded. "I had a few more questions about your husband. Do you mind if we come in?"

Her eyebrows drew together. Clearly, she did mind. But the allure of her name in print finally won out as she stepped back, allowing us entrance. "Sure. But I'm on my way to meet my agent for lunch, so if we could make it quick?"

"No problem," I promised her.

This time she didn't offer us coffee or a seat, instead standing near the door, antsy, shifting from one foot to another.

"So, what kind of questions?" she asked, biting a manicured fingernail between her two front teeth.

"You mentioned roles had picked up lately for you. When exactly did they start coming in again?"

Alexis blinked at me. "I dunno."

"Was it before or after your husband passed away?"

Her eyes darted once to the door. "After, I guess."

"Any particular reason things picked up for you?"

Again with the, "I dunno."

"I bet people were very sympathetic when they heard what happened to Jake."

She nodded. "Everyone has been very supportive."

"Your friends?"

"Yeah."

"Agent?"

"Sure."

"Casting directors?"

She chomped down on that fingernail again.

"It's because of Jake's death that you've been getting roles again, isn't it?"

She didn't answer.

"Look, it's okay. I know Hollywood loves a sob story. I mean, you practically have to be dead to get a cover of *Entertainment Weekly* these days, right?"

"I guess," she finally conceded, her eyes darting to the front door as if really wishing she hadn't answered it.

Cal must have noticed, too, as he nonchalantly moved so he stood directly between her and any chance of escape.

She shifted on her heels.

"I talked to a couple of people who worked with Jake on the set of his last film," I continued. "Did you know that your husband was trying to blackmail Edward Pines?"

"No!" Alexis vehemently shook her head, crossing her arms over her chest in a protective gesture. "That's not true. They're lying. Jake would never be that stupid."

"Why would they lie?"

She bit her lip, not sure how to answer that one.

"Pines said your husband tried to extort a hundred grand. He said he'd tell the world that Pines was into kiddie porn if he didn't pay."

Alexis shook her head again, but I could see doubt creeping into the gesture this time.

"Pines refused to pay," I went on. "He said he'd ruin Jake, make sure he never worked in Hollywood again."

Tears started to fill Alexis's eyes.

"You knew, didn't you?" I asked. "You knew your husband was making enemies, knew he was ruining his reputation at the studio, killing his career." I paused. Then mentally crossed my finger I was on the right track with this. "And he was taking you down with him."

"That bastard!" Alexis suddenly shouted. "Sonofabitch gets a chance at a real film—fucking Edward Pines!—and what does he do? He throws it away. Pines wouldn't have touched him again with a ten-foot pole. I've been waiting fifteen years to get back into the business, and just when I get a chance to walk those red carpets again, he goes and ruins everything. And he wasn't going to stop with Pines. He said he had even bigger fish lined up for the next time. The next time! God, how stupid could he get."

"So, you killed him," I slowly said.

"He had to be stopped! Look, you should be thanking me. Everyone in Hollywood should be thanking me. Who knows how many people he could have blackmailed. How many lives he could have ruined."

Sure. She was a regular Mother Teresa.

"But he was your husband," I said, feeling like a complete dope for ever having bought her grieving widow role. I had to hand it to her, the woman had mad acting skills.

She rolled her eyes. "Please. I did the world a favor. Did you see his last film? The man couldn't act himself out of a paper bag."

Ouch.

Out of the corner of my eyes I saw Cal dialing on his cell, probably calling the cops for the second time that day. (Hanging out with me lately, he'd be smart to put them on speed dial.)

Unfortunately, Alexis saw it, too. Her eyes cut to the door—still being guarded by Cal—and then to the bedroom, her body making a split second decision as she bolted toward the bedroom door.

I lunged after her, one quick step behind. Unfortunately, her legs were a hell of a lot longer than mine, and the door slammed in my face.

"I'll go around back," I heard Cal yell, throwing the front door open.

I jiggled the bedroom doorknob, but no luck. She'd clearly locked it from the inside. My eyes darted wildly around the apartment for anything I could use to break the thing down. Lamp, CDs, old copies of *Variety*. Damn.

Then I spied it. A Golden Globe award from 1983 sitting on the bookshelf.

I grabbed it, testing the weight in my hand. Stars weren't kidding in their acceptance speeches. The thing was hefty.

I lunged for the door again, raising the Golden Globe up over my head, and brought it down as hard as I could on the cheap renter's doorknob. The force knocked it sideways.

I heard shouting from the other side of the door. Cal's voice outside, Alexis screaming back, "Leave me alone! I'm a celebrity!"

I lifted the award for another go, slamming it down on the dented knob, knocking the brass thing to the ground with a clang. The lock fell away on the other side, and I easily pushed the door open, still brandishing the Golden Globe as a weapon.

"Freeze!" I yelled, suddenly feeling very *Law & Order.*

Though it turned out Alexis didn't have much choice. She had the screen off her bedroom window, one leg thrown over the sill, her pleather skirt around her waist, and her fishnets caught on the latch, capturing her halfway between Cal and me.

She was totally stuck.

And crying, "I want a lawyer. Get me Robert Shapiro. Get me Paris Hilton's lawyer. I'm too famous to go to jail!"

Chapter Seventeen

Three cups of coffee, two statements to the cops and four hours later, we were finally released from the police station for the second time that day. I swear the detective in charge was starting to look at me funny. Like I had some golden touch or something, but in reverse; whatever I touched eventually ended up in a homicide.

By the time we pulled Cal's Hummer back onto the freeway, it was five thirty. Prime traffic time. And I only had half an hour to get my threatening column into the printer behind Felix's back.

"Can't this thing go any faster?" I asked as we crawled up the 101.

Cal shrugged. "Sure. I'll drive on over the top of these other cars. I'm sure they won't mind."

Smart-ass.

I pursed my lips together. "Well then, maybe we should take surface streets, huh?"

He shot me a look. "What's the hurry, Bender?"

"Nothing. No hurry. I just . . . want to get back to work." I turned my face to the window so he couldn't read the obvious lie in that statement. If Cal had even a whiff of my plan, there was no way he'd let me follow through with it. Not that I'd normally *let* or *not let* anyone tell me what to do, but Cal was bigger, stronger, and I had a feeling he wasn't above using bodily force if the situation called for it. All in all, the less he knew the better.

So, even though I felt as antsy as a six-year-old on a double espresso as we inched forward, watching the minutes tick off on the dash clock, I kept my mouth shut. Trying not to do a little impatience dance in my seat.

At five forty-eight, the traffic miraculously parted as we neared Hollywood and exited the freeway. I held my breath as we hit two red lights in a row, losing precious seconds, then, of all the luck, got stuck behind a Beemer double parked outside a nail salon.

"I hope you get toe fungus!" I yelled out the window as we finally slipped into the left lane and passed.

Cal raised an eyebrow my way. "You okay?"

I shrugged. "What? Double parking is very rude. Oh, there! Right in front!" I pointed to the left as a cab pulled away from the curb, leaving an open space right in front of the *Informer*'s building. After making a semilegal U-turn, Cal maneuvered his tank into it, and I bolted, grabbing Strawberry Shortcake and flying through the lobby with a speed generally only seen in Olympic trials.

Giving up on the ancient elevator, I took the stairs, jogging up two at a time until I reached the second-floor landing, panting and holding my side. I looked up at the clock over Cece's desk. Five fifty-six.

"Jesus, Bender, where have you been?" Allie slipped behind me, whisper-yelling in my ear. "I thought you said six o'clock?"

"I [pant] did [pant]." I sucked in a big gulp of air,

shooting a glance at Felix's office. He was sitting at his computer, no doubt making all the last minute changes to copy before sending in final draft. "Give me five minutes," I said, hurtling toward my desk.

"You only have four!" Allie yelled. Then looked down at her watch and amended it to, "Three now!"

I ignored her, diving for my desk and pulling up the file I'd typed out earlier. No time to read over it. I prayed it was relatively typo-free.

I formatted it, logged it into the system, my finger hovering over the send button. Five fifty-nine.

I stood, glancing over the tops of the cubicles toward Felix's office. Allie sat on the edge of his desk, giggling. Legs crossed, thigh exposed, boobs inches from his face. He was one step away from drooling on his button-down shirt. God bless the little tart.

I pounded my finger down on the enter key, sending my column in just as the clock changed to six. I held my breath, waiting for confirmation that I'd made it in time. Two second later, the little window popped up telling me my open note to my stalker would indeed appear in the morning edition.

I let out a sigh so big it ruffled my hair, then closed my eyes and fell back into my chair with a moan of relief.

"What was that?"

My eyes popped open to find Cal suddenly at my side, his gaze on my screen.

"Uh . . . my column. I forgot to send it in earlier. Just made it under the wire. Lucky, huh? Well, that's it for today. Ready to go?" I gave him my best attempt at a breezy smile.

His eyes narrowed. Unfortunately for me, Cal was no dummy.

I ignored him, instead grabbing my purse, flipping off my desk light, and heading for the elevator.

Only I didn't get far.

"Bender!"

I must have been a little on the jumpy side, because at the sound of Felix's voice booming from his office, I think I peed my pants a little.

"Yeah?" I squeaked out, my heart leaping into my throat. Please tell me the blonde did her job . . .

"Your column," he said, his eyebrows hunkering down in an angry slash.

I licked my lips. "What about it?"

"It's late."

I did a mental sigh of relief so loud, I swear even Aunt Sue could have heard it. "Right. Sorry. I just sent it in. Must have slipped my mind earlier." I smacked my forehead in a super-graceful move as if to illustrate the point.

Felix nodded. "Good." Then disappeared back into his office.

And I made a beeline for the elevators before anything else could go wrong.

At Cal's place we found a note from the aunts saying Sue had over-boiled the macaroni and they'd gone to pick up hoagies for dinner. Cal mumbled something about getting some paperwork done and headed off to his bedroom. Which was fine with me. After the nerve-wracking day I'd had, I could use a little me time anyway.

I plopped down on the sofa and booted up my laptop, checking my email. I half-hoped, half-feared another note from my stalker, but my inbox was conspicuously empty. As in no messages at all. Not a one. Marco was right, news of my involvement with the police was spreading faster than a summer wildfire, and my informants had all gone mum.

This sucked.

I prayed my article tomorrow did its job. Otherwise, I was likely to be stuck covering the baby bump beat with Cam for any kernel of a story.

Trying not to dwell on that unpleasant thought, I pulled up a blank screen and began typing my exclusive story on the fall of a child star turned murderer and the final hours of character actor Jake Mullins. I was halfway through Alexis's emotional confession—just to the part when she dissed her husband's acting abilities—when an IM popped up in the corner of my screen.

Hey, babe.

I sucked in a deep breath.

Hi, Black.

How you doin?

Got an hour? But I finally settled on, *meh.*

Meh? I take it that means not good.

This story, I explained. *It's . . . complicated.*

There was a pause. Then, *I'm worried about you.*

I felt my throat suddenly clog with emotion. Here I had blown Black off not once, but twice, and not only was he not mad, not even mentioning my standing him up, but he was genuinely worried about me.

I'm okay.

You sure?

I nodded at the empty living room. *Yep.*

I've missed you.

I've missed you, too, I typed, honestly meaning it. Okay, so I knew Black was a fantasy. And our whole relationship consisted of a few words on a screen. But I *had* missed him. I'd missed having someone who cared enough to ask if I was okay. I'd missed having someone I felt comfortable talking to. Really talking. Honestly. Maybe it was because of the anonymity, the fact that I'd never really expected to meet Black in person, but I felt I could be honest with him in a way I couldn't with anyone else in my life. I didn't really know why. And I didn't want to analyze it. All I knew was, he felt good. And I'd missed it.

Hey . . . Knock knock, he typed.

I couldn't help the corner of my mouth tilting up.

Who's there?

Madame.

Madame who?

Madame foot's caught in the door.

I laughed out loud.

Good one.

Thanks. Talk tomorrow?

Definitely. And this time, I really meant it.

'Night, Bender. Be good.

'Night, Black.

And then his little "online now" icon disappeared. I left the IM window open, rereading our conversation again to hold on to that comforting feeling just a little longer. And I found myself chuckling out loud a second time over his corny joke.

"What's that?"

I spun around to find Cal standing behind the sofa, looking over my shoulder, squinting at the conversation on my laptop screen.

I quickly flipped the top down.

"Nothing."

He raised an eyebrow. "Didn't look like nothing. You chatting with someone?"

"No!" Which in hindsight might have come out a decibel or two higher than convincing.

His other eyebrow lifted.

"Someone special?" Cal teased.

I rolled my eyes. "It's no one. Just a friend."

"Uh huh." He sat down on the sofa beside me, giving me an expectant look. He clearly wasn't going to let this one go.

"He's . . . a pen pal."

"So, it is a man."

"Sorta."

"Sorta?"

"No, he's a screen. I mean, he's not real. Well, I guess he's real in that there is someone typing, but he could be anyone, you know? Some loser in his mother's basement, some creep in prison, who knows?"

"So, your pen pal is a felon?"

"No! Look, I don't know who he is. He's just . . . nice."

He tilted his head to the side, his expression softening, going serious. "You going to meet this nice guy?"

I shook my head in the negative. "No, it's not like that. Look, he's just someone who . . . gets me. Not many people do, you know?"

He leaned in. The scent of fresh soap still clung to him. "Maybe that's what you'd like to think."

I pulled my eyebrows together. "What's that supposed to mean?"

He smiled. "It means if you'd quit being such a hardass, you'd see there are lots of people who care about you. Who care about your well-being." He reached out a hand and gently tucked a strand of my hair behind my ear. "Who get you," he said quietly.

I swallowed. Hard. My body felt frozen, my skin tingling, blood rushing to my head as I tried to read the look in his dark eyes. It was soft. Almost tender, if I thought Mr. Tough Guy did tender. His face was inches from mine, so close I could feel his breath on my lips. My tongue darted out to lick them, and I followed his eyes to my mouth.

Oh, God. He was going to kiss me.

What's worse—I *really* wanted him to.

Maybe it was because I still had a warm fuzzy feeling running through me from talking to Black. Or maybe it was the emotional toll of the day. Or maybe it was just the fact that I hadn't gotten *it* in long enough that I was beginning to forget what *it* was even all about.

But I found my mouth drifting toward his.

He leaned in a fraction closer, and his lips brushed over mine. I was surprised at how soft they were, that anything about him was this soft. They tasted like toothpaste, minty and clean. His goatee grazed against my cheek, sending shivers down my spine as I closed my eyes, drinking in the moment. I think I sighed into his mouth as his tongue touched my lips, gently parting them.

"Hello? We're back!"

I jumped off the sofa like a jack-in-the-box, immediately putting two feet of distance between Cal and me as the aunts bustled through the front door.

"In here," I said. I licked my lips, tasting Cal there, and felt my cheeks burn a bright candy-apple red.

Aunt Sue and Aunt Millie bustled into the room, dropping an armload of items onto the coffee table: a bag of sandwiches, a two-liter bottle of Coke, and a purple Tupperware container with Hello Kitty painted on the side.

"What's this?" I asked, pulling back the lid on the container.

"Hattie."

"Hattie? Hattie Carmichael!?" I took one giant step back from the Tupperware.

Aunt Sue nodded. "We picked her up from the crematorium on the way home."

I wrinkled my nose. "And brought her home in Tupperware? Don't they usually give you an urn for that?"

"They wanted to charge us two hundred dollars for an urn," Millie piped up. "Can you believe the nerve? I mean, we're just going to spread her ashes tomorrow anyway. Who pays two hundred dollars for an urn they're only gonna use for one day?"

I was at a loss to answer that question.

"So, Millie offered to go down the street to the dollar store and pick up a pretty ceramic jar or something," Aunt Sue said.

I looked down at the plastic container. "That's not a ceramic jar."

Millie shrugged. "I think my eyesight might be slipping a little."

Understatement alert.

But Aunt Sue waved her off. "No matter. This works. In fact, it's better. Spill resistant lid." She flipped the Tupperware upside down and shook it. "See?"

I looked from one wrinkled face to the other. Then to Cal for help. He just grinned, holding up his hands in a surrender motion as if to say, "Hey, they're your aunts."

"So, you are coming with us to spread the ashes tomorrow, right?" Aunt Sue asked.

I nodded. "Right." It was the least I could do. Especially considering Mrs. Carmichael was now residing in a leftovers receptacle.

"Good. We'll leave at eight. The gates open at nine."

"Gates?" I asked, grabbing onto the word. Suddenly I had a bad feeling about this.

Aunt Sue blinked innocently at me. "Yes. They don't open until nine in the fall."

"What doesn't open until nine?"

"Disneyland."

Mental forehead smack.

"Disneyland? Wait—you're spreading Mrs. Carmichael's ashes at Disneyland?"

The aunts nodded in unison.

"It's what Hattie wanted," Aunt Sue spoke up. "She was the first Mickey Mouse, you know. Her fondest memories are of the Magic Kingdom."

"It is the happiest place on earth," Millie added solemnly.

I shook my head. "Yeah, I'm pretty sure it's not legal to spread human remains there."

"No one will ever notice," Aunt Millie assured me.

I had a hard time believing that.

"I don't think this is a good idea." I looked to Cal to back me up.

Thankfully, he nodded in agreement this time. "She's right. They have security cameras all over that place."

Aunt Millie waved me off. "No one's going to bother a couple of old women."

"Dropping ashes from a Hello Kitty container?!"

"Oh, we got that covered," Aunt Sue assured me.

I hated to even ask. "Covered?"

She nodded. "We're going to transfer her into one of those souvenir soda bottles as soon as we get in the park. No one will bother us carrying around a soda pop. Then we'll just kinda tip the cup over a little and, voila, she's in her favorite place."

I felt faint.

"Where exactly are you going to do this?"

"On It's a Small World," Aunt Sue replied. "Hattie loved that ride. Hattie was the first Mickey Mouse, you know."

Yes. I knew.

"I don't think this is a good idea," I said for the third time in as many minutes.

But I got two pairs of bony arms crossed over two pairs of saggy boobs and two matching glares. "This is what Hattie wanted," Aunt Sue told me. "She was taken from this world too soon. The least we can do is honor her last wish. You'd honor my last wish, wouldn't you?"

I bit my lip. "Yes?" Only it came out more of a question.

"Then it's settled. We leave at eight."

I opened mouth to protest . . . but realized it was futile. With or without me, these two were going to deposit Hattie Carmichael on It's a Small World tomorrow. Unless I wanted to spend the afternoon bailing them out of jail, I'd better make sure they did it stealth-like.

"Oh, this is going to be so fun!" Aunt Sue said, clapping her hands. "I love Disneyland. You know, Hattie Carmichael was the very first Mickey Mouse."

Lord help me.

The next morning I awoke to the sight of fuzzy Elvis staring down at me. Again. What I wouldn't have given to be back in my own room.

I stumbled out of bed, rubbing my eyes, making my way on autopilot through the house toward the scent of coffee. Cal was already at the kitchen table, sipping his cup, reading the paper. Aunt Sue was frying bacon. Or, more accurately, burning bacon.

I wrinkled my nose. "I think it's done."

"What?" she asked, over the sizzling sounds.

"I think the bacon's done!"

"What did you say?"

"It's burnt!" I yelled.

Aunt Sue looked down at the blacked strips in her pan. "Oh. So it is. Oh well, I guess we'll just have eggs," she said, shrugging her shoulders as she reached into the refrigerator.

Just in case, I popped a couple pieces of sourdough into the toaster.

"By the way," Aunt Sue said, cracking eggs into a bowl, "your cell's been going off all morning." She gestured to my purse sitting on the counter.

I popped it open and looked at my phone readout.

Four calls. All from Felix. I bit my lip. Apparently he'd read my column.

I was just contemplating putting the phone on mute, when Cal slammed his coffee cup down on the kitchen table behind me.

"What the hell is this?" he asked.

I spun around to find Cal—a very pissed off Cal—holding up today's *Informer*.

I guess Felix wasn't the only one doing some early morning reading.

"Um . . . my column."

"Obviously. Are you out of your mind?"

Aunt Sue angled around him to read it, then did a subdued little, "Oh, my," her big, round eyes going my way.

I crossed my arms over my chest in a defensive posture.

"What the hell were you thinking?" Cal asked.

"What? I should just sit back and let this creep systematically destroy everything around me? I can't go home, I'm being babysat twenty-four seven, my neighbor's dead, and someone's trying to blow me up! Everywhere I go this guy is threatening me. I'm sick of it!"

"The police—" he started.

But I cut him off. "The police aren't doing jack. You saw them test the scene yesterday—they came up with nothing. I'm tired of chasing leads to nowhere. I'm calling this guy out in the open."

"And if he doesn't turn himself in?"

I sighed. "I'm not stupid. There's no way he's turning himself in."

Cal narrowed his eyes. "Then what exactly do you

expect to accomplish with this bluff?" He threw the paper down on the table.

"Don't you watch any cop shows?"

He didn't answer, just glared.

"If he doesn't want to see his name in the paper as a murderer, he's got to shut me up before I turn in my column for tomorrow."

Something shifted behind Cal's eyes. "Shut you up."

I nodded.

"You mean—"

"I mean he's going to come after me, and that's when I'll catch him red-handed."

A muscle twitched in Cal's jaw. "No."

"What do you mean, 'no'?"

"No way am I letting you use yourself as bait."

"This isn't about you *letting* me do anything. It's about me taking my life back."

"Over my dead body."

"Don't tempt me," I countered.

Cal threw his hands up in the air. "This is dangerous, reckless, and about the stupidest thing I've ever heard."

"Are you calling me stupid?" I thrust my chin up, hands on hips.

He ground his teeth together. "And just how, exactly, are you planning on catching this guy before he actually silences you?"

I bit my lip. "That's kinda where you come in."

"Me." A statement, not a question.

"Yeah. You're the trained bodyguard. With you watching my back, we're sure to get the jump on him before he does on me. Right?"

"No," he said again, shaking his head.

"You have to. You're being paid to keep me safe," I pointed out.

"But not if you're going to throw yourself into harm's way!"

"Fine." I squared my jaw. "I'll do it myself."

He stared at me, his nostrils flaring, his eyes flashing. "Like hell you will."

I planted my feet shoulder width apart, matching him glare for glare. We stood like that in a totally silent standoff for a full minute.

Finally Cal broke the staring contest, threw the rest of his coffee down the drain, and slammed his empty cup on the counter.

"Fine. Let's go to Disneyland."

Chapter Eighteen

When I was a kid, Disneyland was just one theme park, and it was all about the kiddies. Lots of rides, no security gates, characters roaming throughout the park being mobbed by children of all ages.

Now, Disneyland has become a virtual city that's as much for the adult members of your party as the little ones.

Downtown Disney spans a full mile of shops and restaurants, sporting such grown-up fare as the House of Blues, ESPN Zone, and Tortilla Joe's, where the margaritas are to die for. (You know, if I was ever touching tequila again.) Past the movie theater, shopping mall, and street performers sit the two Disney theme parks—the California Adventure and the original Disneyland. While Disneyland is all balloons and lollipops in the shape of mouse heads, California Adventure is the big kid version, featuring a winery, a "beers of the world" stand, and roller coasters that launch you upside down at near NASA speeds.

I looked longingly at the twelve-foot-tall "California" sign across the walkway as the aunts grabbed me by the arm and propelled my toward the security gates on the kiddie side. Cal grumbled a step behind me, still put out that he had to leave his gun in the Hummer.

I watched a perky college kid search Aunt Sue's huge beach tote and held my breath, hoping he mistook the Hello Kitty container for a sandwich and not our neighbor's ashes. Luckily, he'd been trained to look for weapons and drugs, not dead people, and gave us a cheery, "Enjoy your day at the Magic Kingdom!" and waved us through.

I gave a mental sigh of relief.

Aunt Sue gave me a coconspiratorial wink.

Cal gave an eye roll.

Millie gave us a, "Let's go on the pirates ride first!"

I put a hand on her arm. "Uh uh. No way. We're here to do one thing. We're going to do that, and then we're going home."

She pouted. "But I love the Pirates of the Caribbean."

"And we did pay full admission," Aunt Sue complained. "We should get our money's worth."

I clenched my jaw. "Fine. One ride."

The two suddenly ten-year-old octogenarians clapped their hands with glee and led the way through the mass of tourists toward New Orleans Square.

Cal remained a silent shadow behind us.

Ever since this morning, he hadn't said one word to me. Okay, maybe that was an exaggeration. He'd said. "Get in," when he'd held the Hummer's door open for me. That was it. Clearly, this whole bait plan didn't put him in the best mood.

I'll be honest, it wasn't doing a whole lot for my nerves either. I'd looked over my shoulder a dozen times on the escalator ride down from the main parking structure. On the tram ride into the park, I'd done at least three double takes at the guy in the Panama hat and sunglasses seated opposite us before ascertaining that he was, in fact, just an innocent tourist and not some ominous stalker.

Even though I'd set up this whole thing, it was still a scary thought that I could, in theory, be staring straight at my stalker and not even know it. He knew what I looked like, but I had no idea who he was. Or even if he was a he for that matter.

I now knew how those ducks in a barrel felt at the county fair.

I kept my head down, staying close to the aunts, infinitely glad for the hulking bulk of Cal behind me, even if he was giving me the silent treatment.

We wound past the Jungle Cruise and Tarzan's Treehouse, narrowly avoiding collisions with at least three strollers, and jumped into line for the Pirates of the Caribbean.

Two minutes into it, my phone buzzed from my pocket.

"Your pants are vibrating," Aunt Millie pointed out.

"I know."

"You gonna answer it?"

Considering I was pretty sure it was Felix calling? "Nope."

She shrugged, as if to say the younger generation's logic escaped her.

Aunt Sue opened up her tote bag. "This ride is going to be so fun! You're going to love this," she said to the contents.

"Please tell me you're not talking to Mrs. C.," I said.

She blinked at me. "Well, of course I am. This is her trip."

I tried not to roll my eyes.

"Did you just roll your eyes at me, young lady?"

Okay, I didn't try all that hard.

"Let's just get this over with," I mumbled as the line crept forward.

Fifteen minutes later we were being hustled into a soggy boat by a guy dressed like he'd just escaped from some 1980s version of *Pirates of Penzance*. The aunts took the front seat ('cause Millie complained she couldn't see a darn thing from the back) and Cal and I scrunched into the middle, while a family of four was seated in the seats behind us.

We floated past the bayou, the fake star-studded sky, crickets chirping, and the old guy playing his banjo on the porch of his swamp-side home. I fidgeted nervously in my seat, every diner at the Blue Bayou a potential threat ready to strike.

"I'm scared," I heard the little girl behind me say, ducking under her dad's arm.

Join the club, kid.

Only it wasn't an animatronic version of Johnny Depp I was freaked about.

I tried to settle into the ride as we slid down under the ground, past shipwrecks and ominous skeleton heads talking about ancient sea curses. Down here, it was just my boat mates and me, so unless the little kid behind me was some mini stalker, I reasoned that I was pretty safe. I sat back and tried to enjoy the ride. Though I would never admit it to Aunt Sue, it was actually one of my favorites, too. It was cool down here, the scenes were flashy, and it even had kind of a catchy tune. I almost started singing along when we got to the piles of gold and pirates singing, "yo ho," on top of their barrels of rum.

Almost.

That is until I heard a sound that made my heart stop. A Tupperware lid burping open.

I leaned forward in my seat. "What are you doing?" I whispered to Aunt Sue.

She turned around and gave me the big innocent cow eyes. "Nothing."

"I heard you pop the top on Mrs. C."

Again with the innocent act, complete with eyelash fluttering this time.

"I thought we had a plan," I hissed. "Remember the soda cup? Small World?"

Millie leaned in, joining in our whispered conversation. "Hattie loved this ride. I think she'd like a little of her to be here, too."

"Do not, I repeat, *do not*, dump Mrs. Carmichael into the Pirates of the Caribbean waters!"

"Relax," Aunt Millie told me. Which was so impossible at this point that it was almost laughable. "It's dark. Who's gonna see us?"

Cal had been silently listening to the exchange until now, but he leaned forward, poking Millie in the shoulder. Then pointed up to a skeleton head mounted on the ceiling with red, glowing eyes.

"Security cameras," he explained.

Aunt Sue guiltily clutched her tote bag closed.

"This whole place is wired. You're being watched by at least two security guards at all times on this ride."

I looked up at the glowing eyes. "How can you tell?"

"Trust me. I know security. You're being watched." He pointed to a particularly shiny jewel in a pile of pirate booty. "There's another one."

I squinted at it, half thinking he might be bluffing.

Not that I was going to call him out. If it kept the aunts from tossing Mrs. C.'s remains overboard, I was all for it.

We made it through the rest of the ride without incident (unless you counted the kid in back of me whimpering as we passed through the burned-out pirate town—which, I didn't) and exited back into the blinding sunshine of day.

"Not to put a damper on anyone's plans," I said, navigating the streets of New Orleans Square back to the main thoroughfare, "but if Pirates has security cameras, doesn't it stand to reason that Small World will, too?"

"One step ahead of you, peanut," Aunt Sue responded. "We already checked."

I narrowed my eyes at her. "How did you check?"

"Hidden Mickeys dot org," Millie piped up.

"Hidden what?"

"Hidden Mickeys. See, Walt Disney had a bunch of likenesses of Mickey Mouse hidden all over the park, and it's a game people play to try to find them all."

I gave her a blank stare.

"Anyway," she said, waving me off, "this website is the foremost authority on all things Disneyland. We checked. There are no security cameras, lasers, or any other sort of devices inside the Small World ride."

"Apparently singing dolls don't make people frisky the way pirates do," Aunt Sue said, elbowing me in the ribs and waggling her painted on eyebrows up and down.

"There is a rumor," Aunt Millie went on, "that there's some sort of guard tower hidden in the ride, and employees can watch you from up there, but it's unsubstantiated. And besides, it's gotta be a real pain to climb down from it. I'm thinking no one's gonna bother for a couple of old broads dumping their Coke into the water, right?"

For all our sakes, I hoped so.

"Great. Fine. Dandy. Let's go ride Small World then."

"You think I could get a pair of those mouse ears while we're here?" Aunt Sue asked, watching a little girl in pink ones walk past. "I want my name embroidered on the back in gold."

"I'm hungry," Aunt Millie said, eyeing the Bengal Barbecue down the walkway.

I looked from her three-inch bifocals to the restaurant. "How can you even see that? It's like fifty yards away?"

She gave me a blank stare.

"No, no stops. We're on a mission," I said, shaking my head.

"But I'm hungry," she moaned. "My doctor says I have to be very careful about keeping my blood sugar levels even."

I crossed my arms over my chest.

"And Sue has to take her heart medication. She can't do that on an empty stomach." Millie's magnified eyes blinked innocently up at me.

I threw my hands up. "Fine! We'll go eat."

"Oh," Aunt Sue piped up, "and after we eat, can we get mouse ears? I'd love some with my name embroidered in gold."

I thought I heard Cal snicker behind me, but he had the good sense to put a poker face in place by the time I turned around.

Reluctantly, I led the gruesome twosome to the barbecue and ordered them both chicken on a stick and pineapple coolers. By the time they'd finished the last of their meals, the crowds were beginning to pick up—families in every shape and size wearing sneakers, cargo shorts, and pasty white legs that had yet to see the California sunshine walked past. Mixed in with packs of teenagers, honeymooning couples, and groups of overseas tourists that snapped photos of anything that stood still.

I didn't like it.

The more people who jammed the walkways, the smaller my chances of spotting my stalker before he spotted me. The crowd made me feel antsy, exposed. And I was more anxious than ever to get this done and get out of here. Preferably back to somewhere Cal could carry his gun again.

I could tell Cal felt the same way. During the meal he barely spoke a word, his body rigid as if ready to jump at the slightest provocation, his eyes relentlessly scanning the crowd. Which should have made me feel better, but the tenser he got, the tenser I got. And the more I just wanted to get the hell out of there.

"There," I said, pointing to a vendor's booth, as the aunts wiped their fingers on a paper napkin. "Soda bottles. Let's go." I jumped in line and purchased a large, plastic souvenir Buzz Lightyear soda bottle with a sparkly purple shoulder strap and handed it to Aunt Sue.

"Go put Mrs. C. in this," I told her.

Aunt Sue gave the bottle a once over. "I'm not sure Hattie was a *Toy Story* fan."

"Just do it!" I shouted, my nerves frazzled to their breaking point.

Luckily, Aunt Sue recognized a woman on the edge

when she saw one and scuttled off to the ladies' room to transfer our passenger. Ten minutes later she came out, the bottle slung over her shoulder and a grin of triumph on her face.

I glanced down at Buzz Lightyear. "She in there?"

Aunt Sue nodded and gave me a wink.

"Good. Let's get this over with," I said, leading the way toward the Small World castle.

"Oh, look!" Aunt Millie said as we exited Adventure Land, "The Enchanted Tiki Room. Can we—"

"Not on your life," I yelled, cutting her off.

She snapped her mouth shut. "Killjoy."

I ignored her, instead navigating around a line of kids waiting to have their picture taken with Cinder-ella, and skirted the Sleeping Beauty Castle, pressing through Fantasyland, which, at this time of day, was bumper to bumper strollers. I pushed my way through, only getting dinged in the heel twice.

We reached the Small World ride just as the big moon-face guy and cuckoo clock people with their drums and cymbals were chiming the hour. We hopped in line, winding our way through a maze of ropes and shrubbery trimmed to look like zoo animals until we reached our boats.

The last time I'd been here the ride had been shut down for refurbishment. When I'd asked why, I was told that they had to dig a deeper moat. When Walt Disney had first opened the ride, it was built to accommodate six average-sized men. Well, the size of your average American has almost doubled since then, and the weight of our fatter selves meant that the boats fre-quently bottomed out, getting stuck along the narrow canals. Every time this happened, the ride had to be shut down and the larger persons had to be escorted off the ride in a flurry of apologies and embarrassment. Consequently, the ride had been shut down to outfit it with deeper canals and new boats that were designed to hold guests of every size.

At the time, I'd been tickled to no end by the irony. Apparently, it isn't really a small world after all.

We all crammed into a boat, Millie and Aunt Sue in front again, and started into the tunnel of singing dolls, the strains of that infectious song hitting my ears even before we entered.

As in the pirate ride, the smell of recirculated water permeated the cool caverns. The corners of the rooms were dark, but dozens of colored lights shone down on the main displays. There were so many things going on at once—dolls and animals and dancing, creatures popping out from corners—it would take a dozen trips through the ride to see them all.

We were about three minutes into the journey through the world of children when the repetitive song began to get to me, and I started getting antsy again. I leaned forward and poked Aunt Sue in the back.

"Hey! Let's do it."

Aunt Sue gave an exaggerated over-both-shoulders look, then winked at me. "Operation Hattie Drop commence."

Oh, brother.

I bit my lip, scanning the rows of dolls for some sort of hidden watchtower as I heard Aunt Sue unscrew the top from her souvenir bottle.

"Shouldn't we say a few words first?" Millie asked.

I shot her a look. "You're serious?"

"She deserves to be laid to rest with dignity."

"We're in a moving ride, surrounded by the most annoying tune known to man, sung by a bunch of talking dolls, carrying a woman's ashes around in a Buzz Lightyear soda bottle. I'm pretty sure we passed dignity at least two harebrained schemes ago!"

Again, I could swear Cal was snickering beside me, but he quickly covered it with a cough as I whipped my "don't start with me, pal" gaze his way.

"Alright, alright, let's just do this," Aunt Sue said. "We're almost to Africa."

Aunt Sue leaned over the edge of the boat, slowly tipping the contents of her bottle into the water. Grainy white ashes mingled with the chlorinated water, swirling under the boat.

"The Lord is my Shepherd," Aunt Millie began to recite in a solemn tone. "I shall not want. He maketh me lie down in green pastures."

I bowed my head, at a loss for what else to do. Cal followed suit beside me. Though, that snicker kicked up again when Millie recited, "He leadeth me beside the still waters."

I guess in our case, flowing waters and tourist boats. But I kept my trap shut, my head bowed, trying my best to think dignified thoughts as Aunt Millie's parting words mingled with the strains of "It's a small world after all!"

Finally she closed with, "I shall dwell in the house of the Lord forever. Amen."

"Amen," we all repeated. Then I raised my head.

Just as the ride came to a screeching halt.

Oh. Shit.

We'd been caught.

I wildly whipped my head around, my gaze pinging

from Aunt Sue's empty Buzz Lightyear bottle to the singing dolls. I squinted through the darkness, trying to make out if any had glowing red eyes like the security skeleton.

Aunt Sue shoved the bottle back in her bag, clutching the tote closed. Millie sat up straight, clasping her hand in her lap. Cal tensed next to me, instinctively reaching for his missing gun.

We sat like that for a full thirty seconds, my heart hammering in my chest so hard I felt each bruising beat. I held my breath. What was the penalty for unlawful disposing of human remains in a theme park? A slap on the wrist? A fine? Surely not jail time, right?

Just when the patrons of the boats in front and behind us were starting to fidget in their seats, a voice came over the loudspeaker.

"We're sorry, folks, but there seems to have been a slight mechanical malfunction. We're going to have cast members escort you from your boats and to the nearest exit one at a time. Please remain seated until a cast member can assist you."

I let out a sigh of relief. Mechanical malfunction. Thank the gods. We hadn't been made. We'd just broken the ride.

Fleetingly I wondered if Mrs. Carmichael's sinking remains had anything to do with that malfunction, but I brushed it aside, telling myself maybe they hadn't made the canal quite deep enough still in some parts.

Five minutes later, a pair of women in cheery blue uniforms appeared, leading the people three boats ahead of us out of their seats and toward an exit behind one of the curtains. As soon as the people in the boat in front of us saw movement, they got up too, completely ignoring the instructions to wait for a cast member. Pretty soon, every boat had emptied out and the two women in blue were frantically trying to herd people in one straight line out the exit.

"Let's get the heck out of here," Aunt Millie said, still nervously glancing back to where we'd deposited Mrs. Carmichael.

I couldn't agree more.

Cal helped the aunts out of the boat. I followed a step behind, tripping on an animatronic dog and losing my balance. I pitched forward, but a hand grabbed my arm, stopping me from plowing headfirst into a little doll wearing a sombrero.

"Thanks," I said, turning to thank the kind tourist.

Only, when I looked up, instead of a Panama hat and camera, I came face-to-face with the muzzle of a gun.

Chapter Nineteen

"Stand up slowly. Don't make any sudden moves," a voice said. I couldn't have told you who it came from, though, as my entire being was focused on the gun barrel pointed right at my forehead.

I complied, slowly easing upright, hands up in a surrender motion. I squinted through the colorful lights, trying to make out the face behind the menacing weapon, but it was obscured by the shifting shadows. All I could tell was that the voice was female.

"What do you want?" I asked, even though the gun leveled at me was a pretty clear signal she didn't want to play Parcheesi.

"I want you," she said.

"You want me to what?"

"Shut up."

My gaze darted around for Cal. I caught his retreating back as he protectively put an arm around Aunt Sue, leading her out the exit. God bless him, he was still worried about her getting caught.

Unfortunately, that left me high and dry.

"Back up," she said, taking a step closer, the gun jutting into my chest. "Behind that tower."

I glanced behind me, a looming tower painted in

sparkles and glitter with a handful of dolls wearing fruit on their heads on top, still dancing and singing.

If I had to pick my least favorite place to die, this would probably be it. Could there be a worse fate than the strains of this stupid song being the last thing on earth that you ever hear?

However, considering I wasn't the one with the gun, I had little choice. I backed up, praying that one of the ladies in the cheery blue uniforms would see us.

No such luck. Between herding tourists, the colorful lights, the singing dolls, and the boats backing up one after another behind us, no one even glanced our way.

I walked slowly backward, deliberately veering to the left, where a stream of pink light shone down from overhead. As my captor followed me, the light played across her face.

I sucked in a breath. "You! You're the one who's been threatening me?"

Lani Cline chuckled. "Gee, what tipped you off, Sherlock?"

I narrowed my eyes at Jennifer Wood's co-star. Hey, you try being brilliant when you've got a gun pointed at your tatas.

"You killed Hattie Carmichael," I said, the gears in my head churning overtime.

"Who?" she asked.

"My neighbor."

"The old lady in your condo?"

I nodded, though I wasn't sure she could see me through the darkness.

"Look, I swear she was an accident," Lani said, in

her perky fake-teen voice. "All I meant to do was trash your place, scare you. But this nosy old hag comes barging in like she owns the place, yelling about the TV being too loud. I didn't have any choice. I had to shut her up."

"So you killed her," I said, my throat thick with emotion. So Mrs. C. hadn't been my favorite person in the world. In fact, she was kind of a pain in the butt. But to hear her talked about as if she were nothing more than an inconvenience grated on my nerves.

"I just meant to shut her up. That old thing had a set of lungs on her like you wouldn't believe. So, I grabbed a bookend and hit her on the head."

"But why?" I asked, taking a small step back, my butt coming up against a wall. I tried to feel around behind me for anything I could use as a weapon. Unfortunately, dolls are notoriously safe. I shifted to the left slightly, trying to get a good look around the tower for any sort of escape route. To my right, Lani stood holding the gun. To my left was a line of dolls glued to the floor. If I could distract Lani long enough, I might have a chance of jumping over them . . . "I mean, why threaten me in the first place?" I asked. "I never even wrote about you?"

Suddenly Lani's perky little face scrunched up into an ugly mass of anger. "That's the problem! Three years I've been on that moronic show, having to play second fiddle to some nitwit teenager. I'm a classically trained actress. I played Ophelia at Harvard!"

I squinted through the darkness, getting my first real close-up look at Lani. Unlike her character, I realized she was much older than I'd thought. Early to mid-twenties at least. And by the way her eyes were taking on a wide, feverish look, I could well imagine her playing the crazed Shakespeare heroine.

"I have a masters in fine art," she went on, "I studied under the finest acting coaches of our time. And what do I get in return? Does anyone recognize my talent? No! Instead, you print stories about that twit Jennifer flashing her boobs!"

"So, you threatened me to make the stories about Jennifer stop?" I asked. I shifted to the left again, closing the gap between me and escape. Just a few inches more. I just had to keep her talking and wait for my opening.

"Exactly. Why should some trashionista get all the press?" Lani smiled, a creepy expression that never quite reached her eyes. "And, to kill two birds with one stone, I framed Jennifer. The first step was making the phone call from her production company's offices. Of course, I had to disguise my voice, but I was sure you'd be able to trace the call. Then, when no one was looking, I snuck into the hair and makeup trailer and grabbed Jennifer's hairbrush, leaving strands of her long blonde locks all over your place when I trashed it. Total DNA dump." She frowned. "Didn't you find the hair?"

"DNA takes ten days to process," I said. Then took another tiny step to the left. "Even if the police found it, their lab won't have results back for another week at least."

She narrowed her eyes at me. "That's crap. It only takes a couple minutes on *CSI*."

"*CSI* is a TV show."

She gave me a blank stare, not getting my point.

"You were supposed to be freaked into quitting. You were supposed to stop printing those stupid stories about Jennifer." She frowned again. "Only you didn't stop."

"Oops, my bad," I said, shrugging my shoulders.

"Shut up!" She took a step toward me, waving the gun at me.

I'm no dummy. I shut up.

"When it became clear you were going to be a problem, I went with plan B."

I hated to ask. "Plan B?"

She nodded again, her sleek hair shimmering a twisted blue in the pastel lighting. "Up the stakes. That's what my acting coaches always say to do when a scene is lagging. I upped the stakes by framing Jennifer for not only threatening you, but your murder. If Jennifer was arrested, guess who'd be in line as the new star of *Pippi Mississippi*?"

Personally I had a hard time picturing the show going on without Jennifer. *Lani the Loon* just doesn't have the same ring to it. But it was clear this chick had passed sane thought at least one dead body ago.

"That's when you planted the bomb on my bike?" I prompted, glancing to my left. One more step, and I'd be close enough to leap over the line of dolls.

Lani shrugged. "It was easy enough to boost some items from the pyrotechnics division on the lot." She did a short laugh. "Besides, what kind of freak drives a pink motorcycle anyway?"

If she hadn't been holding a gun, I would have given her the finger. As it was, I just gritted my teeth in the dark.

"And now," she added, "it's time to finish this act."

She took a step closer, closing the precious gap I'd created between us. "As much as I've enjoyed ad-libbing with you, Tina, this scene needs to come to an end so our heroine can finally get what's coming to her."

Her eyes took on a cold, determined look, glazing over, void of any type of emotion. Her fingers tightened on the trigger.

And I swear it was all I could do not to pee my pants. I dragged in a deep breath, inhaling the scents of recirculated water and dusty displays. Unless I wanted to die among the children of the world, it was now or never.

I jumped to the left, diving over the three-foot-tall line of singing dolls, landing headfirst on the other side. I scraped my elbow on a fake burro, but I hardly even noticed, my entire being focused on the sound of Lani swearing behind me, tripping over the dolls, coming toward me, gun drawn.

I bolted upright. Considering she was between me and the exit now, the only choice I had was to run deeper into the ride. Which I did, dodging the displays of little arms swinging, bodies twirling, tiny animals riding bicycles, heading full bore toward the next room.

I made it just as I heard the sound of Lani's feet pounding after me. I ducked behind a display of mermaids floating in the South Seas.

"I know you're in here, Bender. You can't hide forever!" Lani threatened, toppling over a display of fish.

I gingerly felt the wall behind me for any sign of an exit behind the curtains in this room. Unfortunately, none.

Even more unfortunately, I tripped over a coral reef, alerting Lani to my location.

"Aha. I've got you," she shouted, jumping out from behind a conch shell.

Only this time I was ready for her. I grabbed a piece of plastic seaweed and swung at her head, smacking her right in the temple.

"Uhn." She went down, tumbling backward and knocking into a hula girl. I didn't wait to see if she got up, bolting for the next room.

I flew past North America, charging right into the children of the world room, cursing that song with every step. I was going to have to scrub my brain with bleach to ever get it out.

Assuming I survived.

I rounded the corner, and the end was finally in sight. I could see daylight at the end of the very long (how freaking long was this ride anyway?) tunnel. I pumped my legs for all I was worth, not even caring how many little people I knocked over on my dash for freedom.

One that was cut short when I heard the crack of a gunshot behind me.

"Make another move and you're a dead woman!"

I saw the gunshot hit the little dancing cowboy next to me right between the eyes. I liked my forehead hole free. So, I froze.

In a second, Lani was beside me, pressing the gun to my rib cage again.

"God, you're fast."

"Thanks," I mumbled. "Hey, how did you even get a gun in here? They check at security."

Lani laughed at me again, the same tinkling thing she did every week in the fake hallways of her fake high school with her fake best friend. "I'm on *Pippi Mississippi*. I'm a star. You think anyone's gonna frisk me?"

Suddenly I really, really hated that show.

"Now, time to take your final bow, Bender," she said, and I heard the gun cock at my side.

I closed my eyes, sucked in a breath. Thought of Aunt Sue and wondered who was going to remind her to turn off the oven? To wear a scarf in the winter? To tip the pizza delivery boy when she burned dinner every night?

And, oddly enough, I thought of Cal. How pissed he was going to be when he found my dead body. I didn't want Cal's last thoughts about me to be pissed ones.

I felt a tiny tear gather in the corner of my eye, slipping down my cheek as the gun pressed painfully into my ribs. I waited for that last loud bang to go off.

Only instead I heard the sound of motors whirling, gears turning. I looked down. The boats were starting to move in the moat again. The ride was back on.

"Shit," Lani mumbled, her gaze following mine as a boat full of tourists eased into the room.

Quickly she herded me behind a display tower, fumbling in the curtain until she found an exit door. She pushed it open, shoving me out in front of her.

The sudden onslaught of sunlight blinded me. I blinked, trying to make my eyes adjust, as Lani propelled me forward, gun still pressing into my ribs.

"Don't try anything funny," she said. And I wondered what cheesy movie she'd gotten that line from.

Only I knew better than to ask. She was one small step from the edge, and I didn't want to be the first person she pulled over with her. Instead, I scanned the crowds suddenly at our sides for help.

We were threading our way around the front of the Small World building, past the Matterhorn, into the thick of the Fantasyland crowd. Hundreds of people bounced against us on either side. Surely someone would notice the girl being held hostage with the gun.

Or not.

Have you ever noticed how self-contained most people are? Every single person in that place had blinders on, focused on making the most of their vacations, oblivious to the people around them. I sent pleading looks to the young families standing in line at the Tea Cups. I mouthed "help me" to the goth kids waiting for the Dumbo ride. I shot alarmed, eyebrows drawn together, desperate tilting of my head toward the chick with the gun looks to the older couple holding hands by the carousel.

Nada.

I hated people.

"There," Lani finally said behind me.

I looked up to where she was pointing. Sleeping Beauty's castle.

"We can have some privacy there," she said, pushing me forward.

I bit my lip, seeing my chance at freedom growing smaller and smaller the closer we got to the castle. Luckily, the square was jam-packed with bodies, and it was slow going. The daily show of King Arthur pulling the sword from the stone was going on in front of the carousel, a guy in a Merlin costume directing a ten-year-old kid and his dad to step up to the stone and try their luck.

A stroller knocked into me, a kid with a lollipop got pink goo on my leg, and a guy with nacho breath bumped into me and burped in my face. But no one saw the chick with the gun, shoving me just feet from certain death.

Well, almost no one.

"That's her!" someone shouted.

Instinctively, I spun around, expecting to see one of Lani's fans pointing her out.

Instead, I spied a bony little old lady in a pink tracksuit hanging off a lamppost, pointing toward me.

Aunt Sue.

I could have cried, I was so happy to see her. In fact, I'm not entirely sure my eyes didn't leak a little.

"Now what?" Lani hissed. Then she shoved me forward, knocking into a toddler who fell on his diapered butt and began to cry.

"Stop!" Aunt Sue shouted. "Stop that girl! She's a murderer! She has my niece hostage!"

Unfortunately, already being in a state of Disney-altered reality, the crowd thought Aunt Sue was just part of the show. They all turned toward me, expectant smiles on their faces, waiting to see what the "murderer" and the "hostage" did next.

"Go!" Lani urged. "Ignore them!"

What choice did I have? I went.

"Unhand my niece!" This time it was Aunt Millie's voice. "Or face the consequences."

"Oh yeah?" Lani asked, spinning us both around to

face her, showing the crowd her gun. "And what would those be, old lady?"

Aunt Millie jumped (with surprising agility for a senior citizen) up to the Merlin platform. She pushed the kid out of the way, grabbed King Arthur's sword with both hands, and pulled it from the stone with a loud grunt.

The crowd cheered.

Lani laughed that annoying faux-teen giggle again. "And just what do you expect to do with that?" She leveled the gun at Aunt Millie.

The crow did the appropriate scared "Ooooo"ing.

I would have rolled my eyes at the ridiculousness of the situation had the gun not been real and the person holding it not really insane.

"Aunt Millie!" I warned.

Too late.

The gun went off, a crack shattering through the air. I held my breath, expecting Millie to fall, an ugly red stain through her midsection. Instead, she twisted the sword, the bullet pinging off the flashing steel.

The crowd roared with approval.

Lani look stunned.

Millie look stunned.

I felt faint.

"En garde!" Millie shouted, jumping down from her perch, her bony ankles showing between her balled socks and her powder blue slacks.

Lani, like the rest of the crowd, was momentarily stunned by the sight, and that was all that Millie needed, swiftly bringing the sword down on the hand holding the gun. Lani's weapon clattered to the ground, and the tip of Millie's sword went to the girl's throat, the point making an uncomfortable indentation as Lani swallowed in fear.

The crowd went wild, cheering, clapping, screaming. I only caught a few people whispering to each other, "Is that how the story really goes?"

I saw Cal break through the crowd, a line of security officers behind him. They quickly descended on Lani, clasping her hands behind her back in a pair of cuffs.

Me? I collapsed into Cal the second he got within arm's reach, clinging for dear life to his solid, comforting chest, the adrenaline of the moment leaving me weak, relieved, and feeling like my limbs were made of jelly. His arms went around me, holding me tight.

"Jesus, don't you ever do that to me again, Bender," he mumbled into my hair.

I hung on tighter.

When I finally loosened my grip, I looked up into his face. His dark eyes were a mixture of concern, anger, fear, and something else that made my stomach lurch into my chest.

He licked his lips and leaned in close. For a moment, I thought he was going to kiss me. And I wanted him to, no doubts about it this time. In fact, I have never wanted anyone to kiss me so badly in all my life.

But at the last minute, he changed his mind, his eyes going guarded as he pulled away. An awkward vibe immediately filled the air between us.

Luckily, before anyone could comment on it, more security guards descended on us.

"What happened here?" one of them asked me.

I detached myself from Cal and sniffed, realizing

those damned tears were leaking out again. "Aunt Millie saved me."

Cal looked from Millie to the sword, still in her hands.

"You've got to be kidding?" he asked.

Millie lifted the sword above her head. "Gold medal for fencing, 1928 Olympics." Then she gave me a wink. "And I've still got it."

Chapter Twenty

Security ushered us all into a little building behind the Magic Kingdom, where we each told our version of the day's events (minus Mrs. Carmichael's part in it) to the concerned officers. An hour later, the guys from homicide arrived, and we related the events once again. No small task between the four of us. Turns out, as soon as Cal had realized I was missing, he'd gone back into the Small World ride to look for me. Unfortunately, by then Lani had chased me into another room and Cal had been forced to give up the search when the ride started moving again. He'd then immediately alerted security, having them check all the available security cameras in the park for any glimpse of me. Which he got just as Millie had charged at Lani with the sword.

In Aunt Sue and Aunt Millie's version, they'd been directed to wait outside when Cal went back in to find me. But, as anyone who's ever met an octogenarian knows, they never do what they're told. Instead, the aunts decided to go looking for me on their own, figuring maybe I'd been rushed outside in the crowd ahead of them. They'd gone to the center of Fantasyland, where Millie had hoisted Aunt Sue up onto a lamppost to get a better view of the crowd. They'd stood there scanning the heads that walked past, until she'd spotted mine.

And I was very glad she had.

After having to repeat every other question at top volume for Aunt Sue, and printing out a very large print version of her statement for Aunt Millie to read, we were finally cleared to go home by the officers. But before we could leave, a Disney rep came out apologizing profusely for our ordeal and asking us each to sign a set of documents saying we wouldn't sue them for having allowed Lani into the park armed. When they sweetened the deal with annual passes for us all, we happily agreed.

But by the time we finally left the security office, the sun was setting, the air was cooling off, and even the aunts were finished with Disney magic for the day. We threaded our way back to Cal's Hummer, dropped Millie off at her retirement village, then headed to Palm Grove for the first time in days.

It was finally safe for me to go home.

Not, mind you, that the condo really resembled a cozy home at the moment. As we stepped through the front door, the scent of industrial cleansers burned our nostrils, a large, bleached spot on the living room rug a reminder of what had happened here. I made a mental note to get the carpets replaced ASAP. Our belongings were still in a state of disarray from the break-in, there was nothing to eat that hadn't spoiled in the fridge, and the place was like an oven from being sans air conditioner all day. But, still, it was good to finally be home.

Aunt Sue made a beeline for the kitchen and began immediately dialing for pizza. Which left me awkwardly standing in the doorway alone as Cal checked the place out.

"So . . . are you coming in?" I asked, suddenly fidgeting with my hands, though I wasn't really sure why. Cal's job was over. I was safe, the killer was behind bars. Really, there was no reason for him to stick around.

Cal's eyes stopped sweeping and locked squarely onto mine. "Do you want me to?"

Oh, boy. That was a loaded question. One I wasn't really sure I had a loaded answer to. I shrugged my shoulders. "I guess I don't really *need* protection anymore."

"That isn't what I asked."

I bit my lip. I know. "Well, I mean, if you're hungry, Aunt Sue's ordering pizza. So, if you want to . . ."

But he cut me off. "Do you want me to come in? It's a simple question, Tina."

But it wasn't. And we both knew it. I could feel his eyes intent on me, doing that looking-right-through-you thing.

I shifted onto my heels. I knew if I said "yes," I wasn't just agreeing to an evening of pizza and chit chat. And while part of me, the part that had melted into Cal's arms that afternoon, had melted into his kiss the night before, melted every time his dark eyes bore into mine the way they were doing right now, really, really wanted to shout "yes" at the top of my lungs . . . somehow I couldn't make my mouth form the word. What if Cal didn't really want the kind of pizza I was offering? Or, worse yet, what if he said he did, then changed his mind in the morning? I've been around Hollywood long enough to know that guys like Cal didn't end up with short, purple-haired, funky journalists like me. Guys like Cal ended up with supermodels, leggy blondes, stacked beach bunnies. So, as much as that little hopeful corner of my heart was rearing its ugly little head, my shoulders shrugged again, and I answered, "It doesn't matter to me."

Cal's face shut down, expression blank. "It doesn't." A flat statement, not a question.

I swallowed down a lump of some indefinable emotion. "I mean, it's just pizza, right?"

"It is." Again, not a question. He blew out a breath, shook his head. "Jesus, Bender, can't you let go for just a second? Just let the guard down and drop the tough chick attitude."

I cocked one hip. "In case you haven't noticed, I *am* a tough chick. I'm sorry if you find my personality so annoying."

"Right. You're so tough you don't need anyone. Don't need any friends, any man. Me."

I bit my lip. "I didn't say . . ."

But he didn't let me finish, his eyes going dark and unreadable behind his thick lashes as his voice rose. "Because I'm just a rent-a-goon to you, right? Just the hired muscle. Just some guy to use to your own advantage, just like everyone else in this town, then dismiss as easily as anything when you don't need him anymore."

"That's not fair!" I protested.

"No, you know what's not fair?" he asked, his fists clenching at his sides as he took a step toward me.

Instinctively I took one back.

"What's not fair is I really thought there was more to you, Bender. That beneath that armored shell of yours lay an actual caring human being."

I crossed my arms over my chest in a protective gesture, hating the way tears suddenly stung the back of my eyelids. "You don't know me," I countered.

"No. You're right. I don't. Turns out, I don't know you at all."

Those tears threatened to spill down my cheeks, but I defiantly held them back. I would not cry. I would not show him how much those words hurt. They didn't. He was right. Had he ever promised to be more than a bodyguard to me? No. He'd done his job. I was alive, the stalker was behind bars, awaiting a trial that would be providing me salacious headlines for months to come. What more did I expect? "Your job is done, what do you care?" I shouted back.

His nostrils flared. "You think this was all just a job to me?"

I bit my lip. "Wasn't it?" Again that nasty little hope flared up. Just a little. Just enough that I felt myself watching his lips anxiously as he replied.

He shook his head ever so slightly, his expression almost sad now. "God, Tina, if you don't know the answer to that . . ." He trailed off. Then ran a hand through his hair. "Clearly it was a job I never should have taken."

And just like that, the hope died a quick and painful death, shriveling into nothing.

"Well, it's over now. You can leave," I said, biting the inside of my cheek to keep those damned tears at bay.

Cal gave me one last look, then spun around and crossed the street.

I wanted to run after him, apologize, beg forgiveness even though I wasn't exactly sure what I'd done wrong. How that whole conversation had slipped away from me so quickly, I didn't know. But nothing about it had been what I'd wanted to say.

Only I didn't run after him. I stood with my arms wrapped around my middle as I watched Cal climb into his Hummer, slamming the door shut behind him so violently I was surprised it didn't fall off its hinges. Then he roared the beast to life and gunned the engine, his tires squealing as he raced out of the complex like he couldn't wait to be rid of me.

I took a deep breath. I counted to ten. I told those tears if they dared to fall down my cheeks they were dead meat.

"Tina?"

I sniffed hard. "Yeah?" I answered, my voice only marginally shaky.

Aunt Sue came up behind me. "I ordered a large pepperoni. Cal's not staying for dinner?"

Do not cry. Don't you dare cry! "No." I cleared my throat, swiping the back of my hand over my damp cheeks. "No, Cal's gone."

"Oh. That's too bad. Well, I hope you're hungry at least?"

I turned, pasted a smile on my face, and lied through my teeth. "Famished."

One pizza and three hours later, I'd tucked Aunt Sue into bed with a paperback Nora Roberts and slipped on a pair of sweats, snuggling into my own bed. But, as drained as I was, I wasn't quite ready to fall asleep yet.

There was one more person I had to talk to first.

I grabbed my laptop from my bag and booted it up, barely waiting until the welcome screen had cleared before opening an IM window and hoping he was still up.

He was.

My heart lurched as soon as I saw his little "online now" icon. I quickly typed.

Hey, Black.

Hey, Bender. I'd almost given up on you.

Sorry. Rough day.

There was a pause. Then, *Your column in the* Informer *this morning have anything to do with that?*

Yeah.

Tell me.

So, I did. Everything. From the ridiculousness of our makeshift funeral for Mrs. C. to the chase through the many lands of Small World and Millie's amazing Sword in the Stone rescue. Black interjected with a lot of *Wow*'s and *Are you okay*'s. The only thing I held back was the fight with Cal and the growing bruise it had left in my chest. Though, I guess I mentioned his name enough in my narrative that the first thing Black said when he responded was, *So, how do you feel about this Cal guy?*

I bit my lip. *I don't know,* I said, truthfully.

You like him?

I stared at the screen for a moment. Then typed, *Yes.* And for some reason my fingers added, *More than I should.*

There was a pause. A long one.

You still there? I typed.

We should meet.

I froze. Staring at the words. A mix of excitement

and fear washing over me. I had never intended to meet Black. He was my secret. My escape from real life. My fantasy.

But as I looked at that little blinking cursor, I realized he'd also become the closest thing to a best friend that I'd ever had. Cal was wrong. I wasn't all hard armor, and I did let my guard down. With Black. I'd confided in him, been comforted by him, was more honest with him that I probably was with anyone in my life.

So, as much as a protest was backing up in my throat, I felt my fingers typing, *When?*

Tomorrow. Noon.

I swallowed a dry gulp. That was soon.

Where?

Griffith Park.

How will I know you?

There's a bench. On the south side of the merry-go-round. Wait for me there.

This was so *You've Got Mail*. But I found myself nodding at the computer screen anyway. I took a deep breath. My stomach churned like I'd just eaten bad Mexican. And I typed the word, *Okay*.

No sooner did it show up on the screen than Black signed off, his little "online now" icon quickly disappearing as if afraid I might change my mind.

He was a very perceptive man.

I turned off my laptop, setting it on the floor as I snuggled into my empty bed. Only I didn't go to sleep. I was way too keyed up.

Tomorrow I was meeting Black.

* * *

I awoke early the next morning, a mix of fear and excitement still churning in my belly. I padded into the kitchen to find a note stuck to the coffeemaker from Aunt Sue. Apparently the entire complex was buzzing with the news about Lani's arrest, and Aunt Sue's presence was requested at the senior center for breakfast. I smiled, picturing Aunt Sue as the belle of the senior ball for the foreseeable future.

I made myself a cup of coffee and took it into the living room, dragging my laptop with me. I booted it up and began typing up all of my notes from the day before. But instead of formatting it into the killer story it was, true to my word, I emailed the whole thing to Allie. As much as it pained me to give the blonde my story, I actually had a feeling she'd do it justice.

Instead, I pulled up a screen and focused on my own column, typing out the headline:

**DISNEYLAND SECURITY NOT UP TO SNUFF WHEN
IT COMES TO CELEBRITIES**

Hey, I'd promised not to sue them over it. I hadn't said anything about keeping my mouth shut. Besides, I was still a little miffed at having that damned Small World theme *still* stuck in my head. Seriously, if the CIA needs a new torture technique, they need look no further than those singing dolls.

I finished typing up my column, emailed it to Felix, and jumped in the shower. Once I was clean and smelled like "Forest Rain" (or so my shampoo promised), I contemplated my closet, anxiety rumbling through my stomach as I tried to pick out the perfect "meeting Black for the first time" outfit. I tried on a sundress and heels, but, after a quick turn in the mirror, discarded them. Too girly.

I slipped on a tank top and a pair of khaki capris, but they felt a little too trendy. Again, not really me.

Honestly, I wasn't sure why I cared so much. I kept telling myself I was likely meeting some greasy-haired, goober-faced dork and was, in reality, in for an inevitable letdown.

Still, I tried on a third outfit, finally settling on jeans, my hot pink converse, and a purple T-shirt with a flaming pink skull on the front. Maybe not the trendiest or most feminine, but it was totally me.

I took a little extra time doing my hair, even gelling the ends, and put on some mascara and lip gloss before grabbing my Strawberry Shortcake purse and heading out the door.

While meeting Black was all I could think about, it was only ten. So, I took a cab to the *Informer*'s offices, figuring I'd put in an appearance with Felix first. Not something I was entirely looking forward to, considering the number of unanswered messages he'd left me yesterday, ranging from, "I saw the column. Call me back if you value your job," to the less subtle, "When I get my hands on you, Bender, I'm gonna . . ." trailing off into a variety of swear words that totaled at least six fifty.

Still, I made my way up to the second floor and bravely knocked on the glass door to Felix's office before pushing inside.

He was bent over his desk next to Allie, heads together, both staring at something on his computer screen. When I walked in, both immediately looked up, guilt marking their faces at being caught in such close proximity.

"Ah, so, um," Allie said, clearing her throat loudly, "I'll, uh, have final copy to you by noon." Then she quickly slunk out, head down even though it did little to hide the blush covering her cheeks.

Which left me alone with Felix.

I sucked in courage. "Hey," I said, giving a little wave.

"Bender. I was wondering when you'd show up."

"Sorry," I mumbled. "It's been a long couple of days."

"No kidding. Cal just filled me in."

"He was here already?" I asked, that bruised feeling hitting me again at the mention of his name.

Felix's eyebrows drew together. "Yeah. Just left. Why?"

I shook the feeling off, telling myself it didn't matter. The job was done. Cal was gone.

I cleared the lump of regret from my throat. "No reason. So, um, I got your messages yesterday."

He narrowed his eyes at me. "You know I oughtta fire you for that stunt you pulled."

I gulped. "Yeah, about that . . ."

But he didn't let me finish, instead plowing ahead. "But considering the story of the century Allie just showed me, I won't."

I shut my mouth with a click. "Oh. Good." Wow, saved by the blonde. Who'd a thunk it?

"I must say, I'm incredibly impressed. And surprised. Turns out you're one hell of an investigative reporter."

I couldn't help it. A big goofy grin spread across my face. "Really?"

"'Really?' Are you kidding? You've single-handedly solved two murders in the last week. Listen, how would you like a bump from gossip to real news? I could use someone as savvy as you on Hollywood's front lines." He paused. Then winced only a little as he added, "I could maybe even consider a small raise."

Wow. Felix talking raise was like the Grinch talking Christmas cookies. I took a moment to savor this rare occasion. However, as flattered as I was, I shook my head.

"Thanks. But no thanks."

Felix opened his mouth to protest, but it was my turn to plow ahead. "Hey, I'll admit I rocked this story." There went that goofy smile again. "But my love lies with gossip. My column is my baby. And I couldn't imagine seeing her in anyone else's hands. Besides, the celebs in this town trust me to rake 'em, break 'em, and make 'em. I can't let them down."

Felix shut his mouth, a rueful grin tugging the corner of his mouth. "Okay. You win, Bender. Gossip it is."

"Thanks. Oh, but I will take you up on that raise," I added.

Again the slight wince, but he covered it well. "Done. And in celebration of my star gossip columnist not only still being alive, but also getting us a story that's sure to boost circulation by at last 20 percent, I'm taking you to lunch."

Wow. Felix offering to shell out cash twice in a row? Had Hell frozen over? "Seriously? As in, you're buying?"

He nodded. "Absolutely." Then he crossed the newsroom, grabbed the Swear Pig from my desk, and turned it upside down, dumping a pile of quarters onto his desk. "There's got to be at least twenty bucks here. Where do you want to go?"

I couldn't help but laugh. "Tell you what, I have somewhere to be today. How about a rain check? Cool?" I asked.

Felix shrugged. "Suit yourself."

I turned to go.

"Hey, Bender?" Felix called.

I spun around. "Yeah?"

"Nice work."

I grinned. "Thanks, boss." And he'd better believe that I was going to cash in on that free lunch that I'd paid for.

But not today.

Today, I had other plans.

Griffith Park covers more than ten square miles at the east end of the Santa Monica Mountains. One of the largest parks in North America, it's home to such attractions as the Los Angeles Zoo, the Griffith Observatory and Planetarium, and the famed Hollywood sign.

The merry-go-round was located near the Los Feliz entrance, close to the zoo. I found it easily by following the squeals and shouts of happy children carrying over the vast expanse of lawn. I walked around the perimeter, finding an empty bench on the south side, and sat down.

I jangled my knees up and down. I tapped my fingers on the armrest. I whistled off key along with the organ music being pumped in time with the twirling horses.

I looked down at my watch. 12:01. He was late. Okay, one minute late. Which was hardly anything. I decided to cut him some slack and waited.

I blew out a big breath, trying to calm my tightly wound nerves. I tried to tell myself this was nothing, that it would more than likely be a singularly awkward encounter, and we'd both be relieved to go home and forget about each other.

But I knew that was bullshit.

Black had become my best friend. My confidant. As screwed up as my feelings toward Cal were, they were just as screwy toward Black. I mean, how could you fall for someone inside a computer? You couldn't. No more than you could fall for someone who was just doing his job, just looking out for you because he was being paid to, and then walked away as easily as anything when it was all over?

You couldn't.

And I wasn't.

I looked down at my watch. Black was still late.

I watched a kid fight with his sister over who got the gray mare. A couple of teenagers tried to share a horse, the girl falling off the back halfway through the ride, laughing. A guy selling ice cream from a little cart walked by, ringing a bell.

Twelve ten. Still no Black.

Well, hell. I'd been stood up.

Stood up by an internet loser.

Fabulous.

I was just about to take the walk of shame back to

the parking lot and call a cab home when I felt a shadow fall over me from behind. I paused, something akin to hope fluttering in my belly.

"Knock, knock."

My breath caught in my throat. Black.

My body suddenly froze, afraid to turn around and see the man attached to that voice. Instead, I made my own shaky voice answer, "Who's there?"

"Dewey."

"Dewey who?"

"Dewey get to meet now?"

Involuntarily, I let out a laugh, some of my built up tension escaping with it. I stood up and turned around to face him, hardly believing what my eyes were telling me.

And yet there he was. Finally real. So very real.

"Hi," Cal said.

"Hi." I shook my head, my brain not understanding what my heart was already singing at the top of its lungs. "You're ManInBlack72?" I asked.

He nodded. Slowly.

"But how?"

He took a deep breath. Shifted from one foot to the other. God, was he actually nervous?

"After we started chatting, I knew I wanted to meet you, but that you'd never agree. I knew from your profile that you worked at the *Informer*, so I went down to their offices to see you in person. I pretended I was there to see if they needed extra security in the building. Unfortunately, you were out, but Felix took my card. A few weeks later, he called me when you started getting threats."

"So, you knew who I was all along?" I asked.

He grinned. "I'd be pretty crappy at my job if I couldn't figure that out."

"And, it was you I was typing with all this time?"

Again, he slowly nodded his head. "Disappointed?" he asked, his voice low and gruff, as if the answer really meant something to him.

I bit my lip. And shook my head. "No," I managed to get out, before my throat clogged with emotion. "I would have been disappointed if it had been anyone else."

Cal's face broke into a grin, his eyes lighting up in a way that lit my insides right along with them. He stepped around the bench, and I flung myself at him, wrapping both arms and legs around his middle as he lifted me off the ground.

"I'm sorry," I said. "About last night. I never meant to—"

But he didn't let me finish. "Shut up, Bender," he whispered, then silenced me as his lips covered mine.

And then he kissed me. Long and hard and so all consuming that we were completely oblivious to everything around us until one of the teenagers on the carousel shouted at us to get a room.

"I just have one question," I said when we finally came up for air. "That night, with the margaritas. Did I . . . did we . . . I mean, I know I woke up in your bed, but did we . . ." I trailed off, hoping he got my point.

He did, a devilish grin spread across his face. He delayed his answer just long enough to make me worry before saying, "No. But that's something I plan on remedying in the very near future."

I couldn't keep back the ear-to-ear grin I felt spreading across my face. Coy I was not, and this was one time he was getting no argument from me.

"Well, come on, Cal," I said with a wink, grabbing him by the hand and leading him back toward his Hummer. "Let's go get a room."

Epilogue

HOT HOLLYWOOD HEADLINES

JENNIFER WOOD'S TWEEN SHOW CO-STAR, LANI CLINE, APPEARED IN COURT FOR THE FIRST TIME TODAY, PLEADING NOT GUILTY BY REASON OF MENTAL DEFECT OR DISEASE TO SECOND-DEGREE MURDER AND KIDNAPPING. THE ACTRESS IS CLAIMING THAT YEARS OF LISTENING TO THE PERKY PIPPI MISSISSIPPI ARE ENOUGH TO MAKE ANYONE SNAP. THE TRIAL IS SCHEDULED TO BEGIN EARLY NEXT MONTH AND, DESPITE REPEATED REQUESTS FROM MS. CLINE, THE JUDGE HAS RULED THAT NO CAMERAS WILL BE ALLOWED IN THE COURTROOM. IT LOOKS LIKE HER PERFORMANCE OF A LIFETIME WILL GO UNTELEVISED AFTER ALL.

GOLDEN GLOBE WINNER KATIE BRIGGS WAS SEEN LAST NIGHT AT MR. CHOW'S WITH A NEW MAN ON HER ARM. WHEN ASKED WHO THE TALL, DARK, AND CLASSICALLY HANDSOME STRANGER WAS, KATIE RESPONDED THAT HE WAS AN ACCOUNTANT SHE'D RECENTLY MET ON MATCH.COM. RUMORS ARE THAT KATIE JUST BOUGHT A NEW HOME IN BEVERLY HILLS (COMPLETE WITH A STATE-OF-THE-ART SECURITY SYSTEM) AND IS MOVING THE NEW MAN IN ASAP.

CAN A BABY BUMP BE FAR BEHIND FOR OUR FAVORITE DRAMA QUEEN?

EDWARD PINES, MOST NOTED FOR HIS BLOCK-BUSTER FILMS, WAS FOUND GUILTY IN AN L.A. COUNTY COURTROOM THIS WEEK OF POSSESSING PORNOGRAPHIC MATERIALS DEPICTING MINORS. HE'LL BE OFFICIALLY SENTENCED NEXT WEEK, BUT SUNSET STUDIOS HAS ALREADY PULLED ALL BACKING FROM HIS LATEST PROJECT. APPARENTLY, PINES'S CAREER HAS ALREADY RECEIVED A DEATH SENTENCE.

ANGSTY ROCKER BLAIN HALL CHECKED OUT OF THE SUNSET SHORES REHAB CLINIC YESTERDAY, SAYING HE WAS CURED OF HIS ADDICTION FOR GOOD. WHEN ASKED WHAT HIS PLANS ARE NOW, BLAIN SAID HE'S EAGER TO GET BACK IN THE STUDIO AND RECORD THE SONG HE WROTE IN REHAB TITLED, "I WAS A LONELY DRUID IN A WORLD OF SHAMAN TROLLS." HE SAID HE'S DEDICATING THE SONG TO HIS NEW GIRLFRIEND, CHERRY CHASE, WHOM HE FELL IN LOVE WITH WHILE FENDING OFF FALSE RUMORS OF THEIR SECRET LOVE CHILD TOGETHER.

LAST, BUT NOT LEAST, ALEXIS MULLINS, WIDOW AND ALLEGED MURDERER OF CHARACTER ACTOR JAKE MULLINS, ANNOUNCED FROM HER JAIL CELL THIS WEEK THAT SHE'LL BE PENNING A BOOK ABOUT ACTORS WHO HAVE DIED YOUNG. WHEN ASKED WHERE SHE GOT THE IDEA, THE FORMER CHILD STAR CLAIMED, "IT JUST CAME TO ME ONE DAY." SOURCES REPORT A MOVIE DEAL IS ALREADY IN THE WORKS.

I sat back, rereading my column one last time before emailing it to the boss. Feeling pretty darn proud of myself for getting it in early even, I clicked open my inbox to check for leads on tomorrow's column. Fifteen messages, ranging from what-was-she-thinking? outfits on Melrose to celebrity fights overheard at this week's hottest club. I scanned through each one, loving my network of loyal informants.

"Bender!"

I jumped up to find Felix's head popping out from his office.

"Yeah, boss?"

"Your column?"

"One step ahead of you. Just sent it in."

"Good. Cam just got a hot tip. Actor Trace Brody? His girlfriend's wearing a fat diamond on her left hand today."

I raised one eyebrow. "They get engaged last night?"

"That's what I want you to find out. Cam's down on Rodeo canvassing jewelry stores."

I grabbed my Strawberry Shortcake purse, notepad, and ballpoint. "I'm on it, chief," I promised.

"And, Bender," he called after me.

I spun around. "Yeah?"

"Don't come back until you've got a headline that's gonna make me drool, readers blush, and Trace's publicist cry."

I grinned.

God, I loved Hollywood.

The **HIGH HEELS** Series

by

Gemma Halliday

National Readers' Choice Award Winner
Double RITA Award finalist
Booksellers Best finalist
Daphne DuMaurier Award finalist

"The High Heels Series is amongst one of the best mystery series currently in publication. If you have not read these books, then you are really missing out on a fantastic experience, chock full of nail-biting adventure, plenty of hi-jinks, and hot, sizzling romance."
——Romance Reviews Today

Spying in High Heels
Killer in High Heels
Undercover in High Heels
Alibi in High Heels
Mayhem in High Heels

"A highly entertaining and enjoyable series."
——*Affaire de Coeur*

To order a book or to request a catalog call:
1-800-481-9191
Our books are also available at your local bookstore, or you can check out our Web site **www.dorchesterpub.com** where you can look up your favorite authors, read excerpts, or glance at our discussion forum to see what people have to say about your favorite books.

DEB STOVER

Blood . . . Rivers of it.

The visions are overwhelming. They come every time
Beth visits the scene of a murder. She lives the victim's
last moments, feels the pain, sees the perp. And it's
driving her mad.

*A flat tire . . . A deserted country road . . .
A man too hot to be true.*

Trading life as a Chicago homicide detective for
a job as a nomadic insurance inspector was supposed to keep her safe. Ty Malone is anything
but. What isn't he revealing about the missing
person's claim on his 'runaway' wife? What really
happened to beautiful Lorilee Brubaker-Malone?
And just how far will Ty take his seduction of the
one woman whose gift can uncover the terrifying
truth?

ISBN 13: 978-0-505-52606-9

To order a book or to request a catalog call:
1-800-481-9191
Our books are also available at your local bookstore, or you
can check out our Web site **www.dorchesterpub.com**
where you can look up your favorite authors, read excerpts,
glance at our discussion forum, and check out our digital
content. Many of our books are now available as e-books!

"Craig's latest will DELIGHT . . . fans of
JANET EVANOVICH and HARLEY JANE KOZAK."
—*Booklist* on *Gotcha!*

Award-winning Author

Christie Craig

"Christie Craig will crack you up!"
—*New York Times* Bestselling Author Kerrelyn Sparks

Of the Divorced, Desperate and Delicious club, Kathy Callahan is the last surviving member. Oh, her two friends haven't died or anything. They just gave up their vows of chastity. They went for hot sex with hot cops and got happy second marriages—something Kathy can never consider, given her past. Yet there's always her plumber, Stan Bradley. He seems honest, hardworking, and skilled with a tool.

But Kathy's best-laid plans have hit a clog. The guy snaking her drain isn't what he seems. He's handier with a pistol than a pipe wrench, and she's about to see more action than Jason Statham. The next forty-eight hours promise hot pursuit, hotter passion and a super perky pug, and at the end of this wild escapade, Kathy and her very own undercover lawman will be flush with happiness—assuming they both survive.

Divorced, Desperate and Deceived

ISBN 13: 978-0-505-52798-1

FALLEN ROGUE

WHAT YOU DON'T KNOW CAN KILL YOU

Harper Kane was well on her way to an Olympic gold medal in swimming. But now she'll never pass the doping test. Oh, it's not steroids. She doesn't know what exactly she was injected with—something so secret her brother died to protect it, something that's suddenly given her deadly psi abilities she can't quite control.

Special Agent Rome Lucian's instructions are clear: Find Kane and bring her in. She's a threat that needs to be terminated. What's not clear is exactly who's giving the instructions. Rome can't trust anything anymore, and his only ally is the woman he's been sent to kill, a woman who can cause massive devastation with only her mind.

It's sink or swim as the pair is caught in the murky waters of a dark conspiracy the depths of which they can't even begin to fathom.

Amy Rench

ISBN 13: 978-0-505-52812-4

INTERACT WITH DORCHESTER ONLINE!

Want to learn more about your favorite books and authors?
Want to talk with other readers that like to read the same books as you?
Want to see up-to-the-minute Dorchester news?

VISIT DORCHESTER AT:
DorchesterPub.com
Twitter.com/DorchesterPub
Facebook.com (Search Pages)

DISCUSS DORCHESTER'S NOVELS AT:
Dorchester Forums at DorchesterPub.com
GoodReads.com
LibraryThing.com
Myspace.com/books
Shelfari.com
WeRead.com

☐ **YES!**

Sign me up for the Love Spell Book Club and send my FREE BOOKS! If I choose to stay in the club, I will pay only $8.50* each month, a savings of $6.48!

NAME: _____

ADDRESS: _____

TELEPHONE: _____

EMAIL: _____

☐ I want to pay by credit card.

☐ **VISA**   ☐ **MasterCard**   ☐ **DISCOVER**

ACCOUNT #: _____

EXPIRATION DATE: _____

SIGNATURE: _____

Mail this page along with $2.00 shipping and handling to:
Love Spell Book Club
PO Box 6640
Wayne, PA 19087
Or fax (must include credit card information) to:
610-995-9274
You can also sign up online at **www.dorchesterpub.com**.
*Plus $2.00 for shipping. Offer open to residents of the U.S. and Canada only.
Canadian residents please call 1-800-481-9191 for pricing information.
If under 18, a parent or guardian must sign. Terms, prices and conditions subject to change. Subscription subject to acceptance. Dorchester Publishing reserves the right to reject any order or cancel any subscription.